LIFE, LIBERTY, AND THE PURSUIT OF IMMATURITY

MATTHEW HOFFMAN

Order this book online at www.trafford.com
or email orders@trafford.com

Most Trafford titles are also available at major online book retailers.

Printed in Victoria, BC, Canada.

ISBN: 978-1-4269-1934-3 (sc)
ISBN: 978-1-4269-1935-0 (dj)

Library of Congress Control Number: 2009938924

Our mission is to efficiently provide the world's finest, most comprehensive book publishing service, enabling every author to experience success. To find out how to publish your book, your way, and have it available worldwide, visit us online at www.trafford.com

Trafford rev. 11/11/2009

Trafford
PUBLISHING www.trafford.com

North America & international
toll-free: 1 888 232 4444 (USA & Canada)
phone: 250 383 6864 ♦ fax: 812 355 4082

*In memory of my father, Robert Julius Hoffman;
my beloved mother-in-law, Beverly Ann Lewandowski;
& the 1913 Congress*

CONTENTS

Preface: The Answer – page ix

1. A Note From The Author – page 1

2. The Evolution Of Western Immaturity – page 3

3. Prelude – page 6

4. Getting It All Figured Out – page 10

5. A Product Of The American Cycle – page 13

6. A Revelation – page 16

7. The Yearly Resort Vacation – page 18

8. Why Europe – page 22

9. Oktoberfest – page 25

10. Exactly Where And When – page 29

11. Who – page 32

12. Size Matters – page 35

13. The Invitation – page 38

14. The Three Scorpions – page 42

15. Working Out The Details – page 49

16. You Don't Know Jack – page 51

17. Getting Started – page 57

18. New York – page 59

19. The Guessing Game – page 62

20. Flight One: Iceland – page 65

21. Camera Games And The Layover – page 67

22. Flight Two: London Bound – page 69

23. The Sinkinal – page 72

24. Kensington Gardens – page 75

25. The Albert Memorial – page 79

26. Night One; London – page 83

27. Purses To Match The London Tower – page 87

28. Free Advice Across The Thames – page 91

29. Food Games With A Sunday Roast – page 94

30. History On The Queens Walk – page 96

31. Life On The Queens Walk – page 99

32. Big Ben, The Abby, & Buckingham Palace – page 103

33. The Race: Man vs. Machine – page 106

34. Paris Next Year – page 108

35. English Breakfast – page 112

36. Price List Comparisons – page 117

37. The Cheaper Pub – page 122

38. Monday Night Not On The Town – page 126

39. Goodbye London – page 129

vi

40. To Heathrow And Beyond – page 132

41. A Sour Taste Of Athens – page 136

42. A Ride Across Athens – page 139

43. Welcome To Piraeus, The Port Of Athens – page 142

44. The Delfini Hotel – page 145

45. Moutsopoulou Street – page 148

46. Greek Isles Or Bust – page 152

47. Highspeed-3 – page 155

48. Arrival On The Island Of Ios – page 159

49. My New Roomie – page 162

50. The Austrian Base – page 165

51. Ios Greece – Night 1 – page 170

52. The Village Square – page 174

53. Sweet Irish Rose – page 179

54. Moons Over My – Lopotas – page 183

55. Milopotas Beach – page 187

56. The Gambling Game – page 192

57. Two-Mar-Gar-Ita-Wake-Up – page 198

58. The U-Haul Story – page 201

59. More Drinks And More Tales – page 206

60. The Ios Special – page 213

61. The Confrontation – page 216

62. The Decision – page 221

63. Mount Charos – page 226

64. The Lead Scout – page 230

65. The Road To Our Last Night In Greece – page 236

66. Athens Anyone? – page 241

67. One Direction From Here – Home – page 249

68. Taking Off For Home – page 251

69. Almost Home – page 256

EXTRAS:

Original Itinerary Map used for the Invitation – page 261

Eurotrip 2009 Itinerary – page 262

Eurotrip09 Packing List – page 263

Three Police Stories – page 265

The Definition of Hoffman – page 269

PREFACE

THE ANSWER

I wasn't home ten hours from the trip before a co-worker asked me about Europe. Still exhausted, I was not prepared to answer. I didn't even have time to think about it. I was back to reality which included a whole lot of catching up. There were reports to generate, time cards to complete, and calls to return. Later in the day I was questioned again about my cubicle-free week. This time I was prepared. I quickly replied, "It was great."

That sums it up. What else could I say? Should I pick one little adventure, one short moment, or one enlightening fact to share with the class? I left work and went home. Again I was questioned, "How was Europe?"

"Great," I replied. My new description had somehow grown shorter.

Following a technique learned from a friend, I decided to write every interested party an email describing the details of my trip. This way I could tell the stories and narrate the sights to all. The details would never become lost over time or in repetition. So I sat down and began typing.

Three hours later I was on page twelve with nothing more than a rough outline. Over the weeks I kept delivering my verbal reply "Great" as I kept typing along. Three months later and I have an appropriate answer for you.

I hope you enjoy it.

Matt

1

A NOTE FROM THE AUTHOR

I woke up from a reoccurring dream as my heart was pounding with fear and adrenaline. In the dream my wife and I were sitting in the front seat of a sport utility vehicle or SUV. We were traveling on a last minute road-trip vacation. In real life I often embark upon this type of spontaneous adventure. I don't own a SUV and never have. When I think of them I am reminded of safety but also wasteful extravagance. SUVs and their qualities are often associated with the members of my generation. My kids sat quietly in the back seat of the dream SUV. They weren't fighting on this long ride as they often do in reality. We pulled to the edge of a high cliff and looked down into a wide river. It reminded me of the Susquehanna, a river which empties into the mouth of the Chesapeake Bay. A sign stood before us at the edge of the cliff. It instructed us to proceed with caution but strictly adhere to the painted line below. Before us stretched a thick line of white paint that was about one foot wide. The line went straight down the cliff and across the surface of the river. Then it continued straight up the rocky embankment on the other side. We proceeded carefully. As always, my wife was nervously instructing me to slow down. We were breaking every rule of gravity inside and outside of the SUV. The vehicle magically clung to the face of the cliff at a ninety degree angle. I concentrated on the line that supported my family and was too afraid to glance ahead. The white line before me felt like the center rail of an amusement park's antique car ride. Fearful and obedient, I kept the SUV strictly centered upon it.

We reached the bottom of the cliff and were now driving across the top of the water. I admired the fantastic technology that allowed our vehicle to drive firmly across the surface. I thought about stepping outside to see if I could walk on it. I reconsidered. I wasn't taking any chances or questioning the given technology. I continued to proceed with caution. We reached the ninety degree incline and began to move upward. I looked over at my wife. We both exchanged a precarious glance. Near the top we paused for a moment to wait for another SUV that was in line before us. It moved up over the top and went over the edge. It had disappeared from sight. With reservation I pressed down onto the gas pedal nearing the top. The last part of the incline angled inward. We were now essentially upside down. I felt like the SUV could detach at any moment and we would all plummet to our death. Like I was about to take a bungee jump I formed a mass of courage and pushed forward. The vehicle folded over the edge of the cliff and the front wheels dropped safely onto road. Relieved we pulled into a tollbooth line and waited to pay the fee. What was the price of walking *or driving* on water? My wife dug through her purse for some cash. As we sat a traveler approached a nearby customs agent. The two were standing next to the tollbooth entrance. The traveler was a simple man. He was thin and somewhere in his late forties. He was wearing a heavy metal t-shirt, jeans, and a mullet. Oddly the man was accompanied by a cheetah on a leash. He was being interrogated by the official. I anxiously waited to proceed safely across the border. I woke up.

2

THE EVOLUTION OF WESTERN
IMMATURITY

Right before World War I the elites of western culture had duped Americans into a new system of monetary control. It was the right place at the right time. America was sitting on one of the largest combined deposit of gold and oil. There was no better place to create a new bank that could control and regulate all the wealth of the working class. The elites wrestled for control of the assets throughout the world. Media, was the new agent of change. Combined with the new economic system in America it would culturally shape America and perhaps the rest of the world. The western elites were in financial control and the American people were along for the ride. There was no better time to be an American.

Advertised opportunity in the local paper motivated my grandfather and the Europeans of his generation to emigrate from Europe to America. The western elites needed to recruit a skilled work force. A mature educated German, William F. Hoffman was the prototype of the early American worker. Upon gaining American citizenship he enlisted in the U.S. Navy. He was commended for his service in World War I and gained a position as the assistant to a young Franklin D. Roosevelt. But before Frankie's days in the white house my grandfather was reassigned to naval recruitment. He performed his duty as a naval recruiter and introduced many recruits into the service of America. After Black Tuesday and the fall of the stock market the western elites held new consol-

idated power. The growing American government was forced
to make budget cuts which included the military. Along with
many other long standing and well paid officers my grandfather was forced to discharge. The military could reduce
costs by declaring fictitious physical disabilities. He did his
part as a faithful servant to the American system and his new
government rewarded him with an early retirement. After
reaching the pinnacle of his career he found himself unable
to function. The Great Depression was not a good time to be
a decommissioned soldier and a family man. Thousands of
disposed WWI veterans marched on Hoover's Washington to
protest their abandonment. My grandfather was not one of
them. He fell into depression and turned to alcoholism. The
former officer and military advisor found solace in bottle of
whiskey. He left his young wife and children to the streets of
Chicago. The Great Depression would forever haunt him and
the American immigrant generation.

My father and his brothers were adopted into the next generation of American working drones. Enlisting in the military
they followed the footsteps of my grandfather into American
servitude. They quickly grew to maturity serving in WWII.
While they spent their time on the beach at Normandy my
father raised himself on the streets of Chicago. Like many of
his classmates he lied about his age and signed up with the
U.S. Navy at age sixteen. He served his country on the U.S.
Coral Sea Air Craft Carrier and he considered it the best years
of his life. But the real service to his country began at the
end of the Korean War. The new American culture had determined his future. It was 1953 and like many people around
age twenty he got a job, he got married, and he produced children. He worked hard for every dime and spent every dime
he made. Americans worked to afford the current cultural
demands which included a suburban home, a car, and even a
television. He devoted nine hours of each day to the army of
the mundane. The rest of his time was spent managing the
duties of parent and homeowner. Other than ramblers considered beat he and his generation spent the remaining years
of life bound to the endless American cycle of work and debt.

He took family vacations. He owned a camper. He even had a dream. He dreamed of a traveling to a distant tourist town known as Branson, Missouri. He never went. After eighteen years of the Vietnam War a misnamed generation gave birth to another. The war scarred baby boomers delivered my generation directly into the American cycle of work and debt. We were a new unburdened generation raised unfettered by hardship and impaired only by the wounds of previous generations. Within the socials winds of divorce, disorders, commercialism and cold war, we learned how to have fun. We also learned how to spend ourselves deep into our cubicles. Why shouldn't we? The western elites were selling the country into world debt. America was being sold down the Yangtze River. We were just floating on tubes. In the prosperity of the eighties and nineties we could have everything the media offers. The big house, the big car, the big toys. Trampolines, pools, vacations. The Brady Bunch lifestyle has been realized. It was no longer the fictional existence of every kid that grew up in the sixties and seventies. We were in our twenties and thirties and were living the immature lifestyle of Bobby and Cindy Brady. Of course there was a downside. We gave birth to the next generation of extremely immature youth, the entitled generation. They expect free delivery of high tech toys and lavish vacations but expect someone else to pay for it. Like mounting credit card bills they are a problem that can wait. When the check comes there will not be a worse time to be an American. The work ethic of my father had been engrained into my back and the promises of television engrained into my soul. It's time to order another round. I stand barred within financial entrapment and still want another drink. I am the product of the improved American lifestyle. I am America today. Forty is the new twenty and the Federal Reserve is the new local brewery.

3

PRELUDE

A late night, and a moon lit country road, holds enough motivation to inspire an evening of reckless abandon. At twenty three years of age I was racing across the back roads of puberty and enjoying the off-road detours of my immature mind. My latest compact car, a Honda Prelude, had lost traction as the front wheels powered and spun loosely between the soft ruts of the cornfield. There was a herd of deer before us and they were spreading out in every direction to evade the headlights and the low front end of the car. It appeared as if there was no chance for Tarsia to catch a deer from the hood of the car tonight. The flat top of the old Japanese Prelude was perfect for both hood-surfing and for clipping the legs of potential grill fodder. But after many nights on the hunt we had not actually caught one. Tarsia, at twenty-six years of age was the late bloomer of the group and was always trying to make up for the years he had lost to sobriety and responsibility. He was a bit immature for his age, but consequently, he was the most fun and outrageous of my friends. Shyness had stunted his evolution. The pale Italian boasted ancestry from the island of Sicily. As I, he was a third generation European descendant. The former soccer goalie also took pride in his athleticism and balance. He enjoyed testing them on the hood of my car. Now he was living life far outside of the box. It was a lifestyle that often required downing a bottle of Wild Irish Rose Wine.

I gunned the gas pedal of the small Japanese car as Tarsia precariously balanced on the hood like a surfing primate with steel grip toes. Each time I saw him through the windshield it reminded me of a similar scene from the film Teen Wolf. As I veered left following the herd of evading deer I heard the familiar high pitch scream coming from the back windshield. It was the nasally voice of Jack who was gripping his long fingers tightly to the opening of my sunroof. His lanky body swung back and forth as the car bounced over the ruts of the cornfield. After consuming two sixteen ounce bottles of cheap vodka he had decided to join Tarsia on this evenings hunt. Jack was a thrill seeker and was outside hanging onto my car merely for the ride. Unlike Tarsia, he did not have plans to tackle any wildlife tonight. Always hungry and often broke we came up with the strangest ideas for obtaining food. In the prime of our lives the only goal was to turn every night into a misguided adventure.

The small car had very little clearance as it bounced wildly and pounded through the ruts of the cornfield. It always amazed me that Tarsia somehow managed to hang on. Only once had he been ejected from the hood of a car. Fortunately for everyone we were on a back road that night and not somewhere along Interstate 83. In fact, no one had ever been thrown from the Prelude as of yet. I purchased the car cheap from a friend named Georg who used it to travel the states with his band of Austrians. It came equipped with both a sunroof and a guardian angel. Just as we were catching up to a large doe the front wheels locked to the right and the steering pulled free from my grip. The car had dropped ten miles per hour in an instant yet Tarsia still managed to hang onto the hood. Jack had swung hard left and I could see his leg dangling behind the open window of the driver side. I stomped on the gas pedal and the little four cylinder engine pushed the front wheel over a large rut as I straightened the wheel and once again regained speed. Tarsia's near fall was enough to end the hunt. Our luck seemed precariously close to an end. We wanted to live for tomorrow night and for the next unordinary mission that awaited us.

The group of deer had disappeared into the nearby woods and was no longer in sight. They had won again. Now that the mission was over Tarsia and Jack were ready to return to the relative safety of the inside of my car. As I drove down the country road Tarsia looked back, turned around and then dove headfirst into the backseat. Once again he had successfully navigated his way into my open sunroof. Jack followed suit. He pulled his arms forward and propelled his body into the small opening on the roof of my car. He tucked his

head and shoulders as he crashed upon me and fell forward towards
the front passenger seat. I held tight to the steering wheel as his leg
snapped the rearview mirror and broke it free from the inside of the
windshield. I laughed and tossed the broken mirror that had landed
upon my lap. As we pulled back onto the road I could hear the sound
of the blasting rocks and debris chipping against the undercarriage of
the car. I then reached down and turned up the volume on the radio.
Ignoring the odd sounds of the car always made me feel much safer.
A couple more miles and we had returned back to the main road. I
straightened up the car and drove the short distance to my nearby
bachelor pad and the care free lifestyle we enjoyed. We all had to
work in the morning but at least our minds were still free of the six
by eight cubical confinements.

It was thirteen years later on a beautiful relaxing day and I
was sitting on a Jamaican beach telling my tales of youthful
debauchery to a couple of younger Canadian travelers. They
were in their early twenties and comfortable in their skin.
Like many of the new generation each girl was a slight bit
overweight. Both had a trendy name; a curse to those born
in the eighties. They were often named after obscure towns
or beauty products. Rebellion was projected in their fashion.
They were a new generation of youth. They display their wild
persona rather than live it. Via an unusually located piercing
or an expressive tattoo they intend to decorate themselves as
the wild child. Other than the occasion story of unfortunate
substance addiction they are usually plain. Like decorated
Easter eggs they look original, but on the inside they are all
just white and yellow. As they sat listening to my hood surfing tale I realized that these twenty-something rebels were all
bark and no bite. My friend Eddie sat smiling and gave them
a nod of reassurance when the two young ladies gave me a response laden with disbelief. Apparently these girls went right
from nursing school into the resort travel lifestyle. They must
have missed out on the adventures that accompanied many of
my reckless nights and impromptu vacations.
    Wearing a smirk and holding a frozen drink the nurse with

the tramp stamp asked, "Well Mr. Party, so why aren't you drinking now?"

"I just slammed seven of those little cups before walking out here." I answered.

Eddie again gave the girl a nod of reassurance. He smiled and said, "He always was the sprinter."

The tramp stamp smiled as she sipped her drink and sat back into her chair. She looked around for someone to bring her another frozen cocktail. I looked over at Eddie seated next to the lazy group of youths and said, "I'm bored. Next year I need a *real* vacation."

4

GETTING IT ALL FIGURED OUT

240 - Work
104 - Weekend Work
10 - Denoted Holidays
2 - Free

In contrast to the exciting American perception that is often displayed throughout television, movies, and print; most Americans live confined to the daily doldrums of the American reality. In actuality, the average American primarily works two hundred and forty days per year. A curse we inherited from our forefathers. Then we bustle through whatever days that are left. The other days known as weekends are one hundred and four yearly days of which we are condemned to paying the bills, cleaning the house, maintaining the cars and keeping up with just about everything we own. Our material possessions own our very souls. Occasionally we squeeze in a family weekend that is consumed with events that ultimately result in the loss of every dime we previously earned. Where did all that money go? I did work my primary two hundred and forty days of the year, didn't I?

Over the years we Americans have comfortably settled into this lifestyle and are even grateful to our generous leaders who have been kind enough to throw us around ten more bonus days we call holidays. These designated hallmark holidays socially dictate to the American public. They offer us specific instructions for how we should spend our time *and our money* in accordance with each particular holiday. On the fourth of July, we should buy fireworks. At Christmas, we should buy presents. Thanksgiving, a turkey, and of course President's, Labor and Memorial Day, we should buy a car. Add up all of the days dedicated to our jobs and our government and we are left with approximately two days. Two days for each American to be free. On these two days we are free to be sick, free to take "Paid Time Off" or free to actually get some rest.

The American system is set up for failure. It used to be called the American dream but those who achieved the dream never woke up. If you have realized the American dream what you've actually *not* realized is that you are now caught up in something else. You are caught up in the never ending circle of work, spending, and limited sleep. The very objective of this cycle is to lull us into a safe secure existence or in other words, keep us happily mundane.

The happily mundane oxymoron has never worked for me. I was not one to enjoy mundane. In fact, I despise mundane. I despise it so much that I bought a second house because I'm even bored of living in just one place all the damn time. On a limited budget it's hard to avoid being mundane. It started all the way back in public school. It started with the school announcements and then the pledge of allegiance. A fixed schedule continued for the next thirteen years of our planned mundane education. Pizza Monday, Spaghetti Tuesday, Taco Wednesday; even school lunch was mundane. Sometimes I begin to think I must be the crazy one. Everyone else must certainly enjoy everyday mundane living. If not, then why don't we all rise up, break out of our cubicles and demand the ten weeks of vacation that the Europeans enjoy. For crying out loud these boxes are only made of cardboard and cloth. My Ukrainian friend Sergey pointed out a correlation between American cubicles, American schools and American prisons. None had windows. The lack of windows may reduce heat costs but it also adds to the mundane environment of our American existence. Like veal waiting for slaughter we are conditioned to life within a fluorescent lit box.

I'd happily take a smaller salary and less useless crap in exchange for more freedom. Hold on, we do have freedom. It's called the family vacation. We save all year to have enough money and enough time off to partake of some grandiose event. I love taking my family on vacation, but those are usually the complete definition of mundane. Let's see, beach house on ocean, mountain cabin by a lake, Disney World. Have you ever been on one of these trips? I don't know about you but I've been to all of them just this year alone. Society dictates to parents and tells us how to raise our children. Kids need to be in camp, kids need to be in sports, kids need presents with their happy meal. It never ends. What about the adults? Why isn't society as kind to us? I never get a new watch with the number six meal.

To an adult the family vacation is a taste of freedom about as much as scotch tape is the solution to a cracked dike. To our kids these trips are not mundane. No wonder, they're still in the first ten years of life. Going to such places is still fresh, new, exciting and relaxing. Not to mention the fact that we, the parents, do all the work. We pack the kids, move the kids, pay for the kids, entertain the kids, and frankly, keep the kids alive until we joyously get home. Getting home is the best part. We finally get a good night of sleep. No more musical hotel beds or sweating in a tent. No more sand in my ass crack and no more fights in the back seat. So, knowing my self well, and knowing my position on every day American Life, each year I prioritize an escape to remove myself from the whole vicious American cycle.

5

A PRODUCT OF THE AMERICAN CYCLE

Most people never ever know they are caught in a machine I refer to as the American cycle. I was at least fortunate enough to recognize the pattern as I followed my family's path into my own six by eight cubical. I toil away to meet the demands of my lifestyle and family; demands that are determined by the advertisers of our modern American culture. In my twenties I had already watched my father conform to the cycle's every whim. He owned everything the American owned. He did everything the American did. And he worked as much as any American could work. It dictated the majority of his life and eventually killed him two years after his semi-retirement.

Coincidentally my father died with one quarter in his hand. He had taken a weekend break from his working retirement. At sixty seven a working retirement includes fifty hour weeks as a part time government contractor. He was always filling in for my generation that was taking as much vacation time as possible. Our extended family was having a weekend get-away at a nearby lake resort. He and my mother always tried to attend. It wasn't Branson Missouri, but it would do. My father, like many of the original television generation enjoyed relaxing in front of his twenty inch screen. During a commercial he walked to the nearby vending machine. He dropped in one quarter and died. Whenever I visit the lake I am always reminded of the other quarter. When I die I want my hand to be empty.

The American cycle is a curse that I, each of my siblings, and even the next generation have inherited from my father and from his father before him. It is a confinement that is disguised to the public and to all who fall victim. It is the transformation of immigrants into modern tools that were designed to maximize profit. It hides under a guise that we call work ethic. To me the cycle is a calculated formula that drives Americans to compliance. It steals our time, our families and our lives. It is the distraction that keeps us from anything that really matters.

America is a business and like any business the goal is to maximize profits. How does a country maximize profits? It makes the most out of the resources while minimizing expenses. The resources are the working efforts of the people and the expenses are the costs to manage the people. Control is the method which manages people and media is the tool of control. The best way to control people is to keep them motivated, working, and structured. Since the Roman Empire people have been successfully influenced by the church but today there is a better solution. Motivation can be suggested with advertising. Mass media tells us how to live, what to buy and who to believe.

No wonder religion is falling into the cracks; we have primetime reality shows. We have Hollywood and interest groups teaching our children. The Middle East and Islam don't hate America, they hate western culture. Why wouldn't they? American mass media has surpassed religion as the number one tool for control. That is why communist governments limit both religion and the internet. That is why religious governments lash at the West and foreign journalism. It's the same reason Americans are saturated with television, radio and the internet. We're digitally fed the control that non-western governments fear. In America and the West media is government sanctioned, doctor recommended and even mother approved.

Mass media has become the number one tool for controlling the world and America does it best. I've seen the power it wields. I've witnessed a group of young foreigners on the other side of the world cry over Michael Jackson's death. With that kind of power American media can do anything. Well, almost anything. It may not motivate me to strap on a bomb but it might justify taking a trip to Iraq. Media may not contain the intensity of religion but it subconsciously directs America and the West. Like rats following the pied piper we march under a hypnotic spell.

We live our mundane lives in accordance with the expectations of our government. We live drunk under the influence of mass media. What happened to life, liberty, and the pursuit of happiness? It was swept away while we were watching reruns of Hogan's Heros. Life is gone. Liberty is gone. And the pursuit of happiness remains strictly enforced by a set of designated U.S. guidelines. To free myself I seek out life. I pretend to have liberty. And I pursue immaturity. Immaturity can be excused as a physiological attribute. It is therefore still allowed under the U.S. health and human guidelines. It's the closest thing to happiness that I'm allowed to pursue. I could pursue stupidity but a large portion of Americas have already cornered that market.

6

A REVELATION

An escape from the American cycle may only last five to ten days, but for those days, I plan to be completely free and far from anything or anyone mundane. Some have graciously approved of my philosophy on American life while others have simply labeled me inertly immature. Either way, I don't care. I'm just glad that I realized the need for scheduled freedom early in my life while I was toiling away for the communist food chain appropriately named Store. Store Foods specializes in working employees into a life void of any other activities. The Store wants me to fill the salad bar trays and The Store wants me to restock the walls of milk. The Store wants me check out the herds of others that are caught in vicious nine to five mindless American cycle.

By hording up my Store given PTO or paid time off I started traveling on simple little ski and beach excursions. Young and finally outside of any restrictive parental environment; these escapes were true trips of discovery. These mini vacations eventually graduated and became more grandiose exploratory trips or perhaps what some would call highly immature trips. Spring Break, Mardi gras and eventually the full blown cross country experience were the early incarnations of the many future trips to come.

Wearing a white shirt and blue tie, the standard Store prison uniform, it was 1992 and I was performing my duties assigned by my overlord. He or she was usually a college dropout turned God. As I filled the bulk food bins, a friend and co-worker, Sperka, randomly suggested that we take his Dad's old Dodge Colt to see the United States. I had heard of this magical place, and I immediately agreed. Sperka was a neat freak who enjoyed good living and travel. At age twenty-two he was already ironing his shirts and slacks. His hair was always freshly cut and strictly managed by the most stringent hair gel. Standing just below six foot he is your average white bread American. He was another third generation American and stemmed from Polish origin. Like I, he worked at Store Foods to subsidize his college education. Between our shifts we planned and discussed all of the goals we had for our cross country adventure. At this time in my life the itinerary included consuming as much beer in as many U.S. cities as humanly possible. Just how much could we squeeze into just seventeen days? I was about to find out.

In just a few weeks our travel itinerary was born. Each adventure that presented itself from city to city became engrained into my personal philosophy on life. There is much to be learned from a summer snowball fight a top a mountain, swimming in a river heated by lava, or from waiting out a herd of buffalo. At twenty one I learned more about living from Chicago, Yellowstone, San Francisco, Phoenix and Memphis than I had learned in the previous fifteen years among the educationally mundane. Experiencing America first hand truly was filled with the eye opening experiences which led me towards one planned adventure after another. But now in my thirties, the inevitable curse of maturity had quietly snuck upon me. The spontaneous cross country explorations had shrunk into the yearly resort vacation.

7

THE YEARLY RESORT VACATION

The selection of the yearly resort vacation is likely a simple five day excursion to a nearby island; one that can provide unlimited alcoholic beverages and food. The primary goal of this type of trip is to lull me back into the confused state of mind that echoes, "OK. I'm all better now. I'm ready for three hundred and fifty one more days of the mindless servitude." Just last year I took one of these trips to Jamaica. With my two friends Ed and Eddie, we experienced good times that were had by all. Some memorable moments managed to sprout from this short escape from reality.

When planning such a trip, there are two equally important factors to consider. As much as the location, the selection of your fellow travelers is vital if you want to have an enjoyable traveling adventure. I always like to have a nice mix of the old and the new, the good and the bad, the introverted and the extraverted. If at all possible I love to mix persons with different backgrounds and or lifestyles as it can add some flavor to the trip. Variety is sure to create a less predictable, less mundane setting.

For a trip like Jamaica, a couple of laid back friends, Ed and Eddie were ideal for encouraging light hearted adventure. Both are compatible but very different. Eddie was a young, single, white, high profile, cocky, application developer. Ed was an old, married, black, low profile, modest, handyman. I looked forward to the many humorous situations that were bound to transpire. The three of us arrived in Jamaica, and I found that both handyman Ed and I enjoyed relaxing in the ocean on the nearby offshore water trampoline. On one quiet lazy day he, I and a young local Jamaican college student shared a float while relaxing under the island sun.

Ed was an astute member of the married club, as was I. We both had knowingly embarked on this trip not just to escape our every day jobs, but to escape the everyday duties that come along with being husbands and fathers. With the married factor in common, we had a lot in common. One thing that continued to bother Ed on this trip was the particular behavior of our non-married friend Eddie. Eddie had an obsessive desire to inform every traveler on the island that both Ed and I were members of the married club. The two of us floated on the raft lying near a local college student when Ed blurted out his disgruntled disapproval, "Why must Eddie always inform everyone that we are married? I know we're married. You know we're married. And every other fool on the island doesn't need to know that we're married!"

Immediately the young college boy lifted his head, looked at us with a raised eyebrow, and rolled off of the float. As the young man swam away and back towards shore I replied, "Perhaps you should have mentioned that we are NOT married to each other."

The Jamaica itinerary continued with many such moments. The three of us enjoyed poolside drinking games, and occasional banter with the locals. We were just being the three ugly Americans. I was approached by a member of the hotel staff as I lay swinging on a Jamaican hammock. The man walked over to me as if he was about to ask for my autograph. "Are you d' one mon?" he asked.

"One, what?" I replied.

"D one who ate d whole chicken lasd nyte?"

Proudly I responded, "Damn right! No Jamaican chicken can outrun me. If you pour jerk sauce on Usain Bolt, I'll eat that son of a bitch too!"

The man laughed and walked away. As he turned the corner Ed commented, "The average Jamaican family probably eats a whole chicken over the span of an entire month."

The best thing about these trips other than sheer relaxation is the little bits of culture you get from a foreign location. On my first trip to Jamaica I found that the rumors about Jamaica are true. Everyone does try to sell you weed. Sitting by the pool a man behind the hotel wall would constantly send puffs of smoke along with bird like whistles that were meant to attract potential customers. We affectionately named him the weed bird for the rest of our stay. I even had a woman carrying a baby pull a bag of weed from under her baby's bottom. "Weed Mon?" she asked.

"No thank you," I exclaimed.

"It is kind bud," she replied.

I waved her off. There's nothing kind coming from the ass end of any kid.

As much as Jamaica, Cancun and its local Mexican culture fulfill many of the respective stereotypes as well. Mexican etiquette and standards don't always live up to the expectations of Americans. One morning I awoke hung over, tired and hungry. I was traveling with my friend Adam and we were just south of Cancun near the ecological park called Xcaret. Other than one lone food vendor there was nothing to eat along the dirt path that led into the park. The vendor was a local man selling doughnuts from his small rolling food cart. Adam looked in through the window of the cart and watched as hundreds of ants crawled on a collection of fresh baked pastries. Adam decided to forgo breakfast and informed me of the free toppings that he discovered. Desperate to combat the acid in my stomach I took a second look. The pastries were fresh but covered by the collection of moving chocolate jimmies. Looking at the man I walked my fingers across the air. It was a hand gesture pertaining to the ants. The Mexican vendor smiled and pointed into the case. He nodded and casually replied, "YES! Bugs, is good."

I chose the one with the least amount of ants. I shook them off and made the most of my Mexican doughnut. Adam walked away and laughed at our amusing cultural exchange.

Overall, each non-American location I have visited, Jamaica, Cancun, Bahamas, Bermuda, Quebec, and many of the smaller Caribbean islands each have their individual cultural flares. Over the years I have been on many of these short excursions and continue to be entertained by the cultural differences. Combined with the chemistry of my fellow traveling characters I continue to enjoy these types of experiences. Even so, every few years I crave more than just the simple five day excursion. I desire to immerse myself and some select companions into a culture more foreign and further removed than the islands near the United States. In fact what I ultimately desire is to immerse myself into something far less mature. I want something that can produce the fun stories and adventures of the days before I slipped into the responsible roles of provider, husband, father, brother and son. I want to be surrounded by others who embrace the essence of youth, the fun of irresponsibly and the unexpected results of immaturity.

8

WHY EUROPE

The last two such immersions both led me to Europe. I have not yet had the gall to get into the more diverse cultures such as Asia or Africa. Consequently, thus far I have stuck to either the Latin or the more familiar European cultures. My first big European trip included stays with three friends. The first friend, the German Marco was living in Hamburg, Germany. I first met him when he was working as an au pair near my home in Columbia. He had originally become friends with my life long friend Mike while he was studying at the local community college. Mike had volunteered in the linguistics department and had met several European au pairs while assisting at the campus. Consequently today Mike is doing similar work at West Virginia University.

Marco was an enthusiast of beer and so was I. We hit it off as friends almost immediately as he joined me in many beer laden outings in the Baltimore and Washington area. He has a jovial laugh, a German accent, and trouble pronouncing the sound of the letter R. It was always fun going out with Marco and joking along as he would say phrases like, "Am I wite or am I wong?", "Get with a Hewo and not with that Zewo" or his famous saying, "Give me a BWEAK!"

I enjoyed my time in Germany with Marco as he showed me the ins and outs of "Hambuwg."

The second friend was the Austrian Georg who had moved

back to his home in Vienna. Like Marco he had been another employee of the American child care system that watched over the American ADHD brats while their parents slave away from eight to six. Foreign Au Pairs are great assistants to the U.S. government cubicle human control program. Georg is a character like no other. Where ever he goes, good times and mischief abound. Georg was famous throughout my circle of friends from the travel stories of Key West, Cancun and more. Goerg also organizes trips of escape for his Austrian entourage and our paths often cross. Georg is the original wild child, a true Jekyll and Hyde. He works by day as a manager of an Austrian information technology firm but by night he is a wild partying beast that lurks the moonlit streets of Vienna.

Finally, my third travel companion on my first trip to Europe was my friend Mike, the sudo-linguist. His superpowers enable him to order a beer in any language. My long time friend Mike was then living under the Peace Corps in Slovakia. Mike has always been the Laurel to my Hardy, the Costello to my Abbot. He and I have been through hell and back from grade school through our weddings. Mike is unpredictability in a bottle. He could be leaving for Europe one day and then back and married the next. His decision to join the Peace Corps was a perfect example of just that. Throughout the European trip we traveled together experiencing Holland, Germany, Austria, Hungary, the Slovak and Czech Republics. We welcomed each obstacle and partook of each adventure that fell before our path.

Five years later, I once again returned to the old country for my second European adventure. This time the plan was to meet up with Georg as well as several others in order to experience the German phenomena known as Oktoberfest. I had arrived in Austria and had spent some time with Georg and his family before taking the train to neighboring Munich, Germany. Georg warned me of the tourist trap that manifested in Munich under the guise of Oktoberfest. But stubbornly, I was still drawn to this particular historic location as I wanted to see the authentic festival. As I child, I would hear vague details of our Bavarian homeland from my orphaned

Grandmother who had previously escaped World War II Germany. My parents would take me on yearly trips to the local German Festhaus in Odenton Maryland and now I could finally witness the true Bavarian experience for myself. Oktoberfest had become so widely admired that it is now imitated every October throughout the United States. Sadly, most Americans still haven't figured out that the festival is actually in September. The festival ends on the first Sunday in October and hence the name. It was originally started as a wedding party and corresponding horse race for Prince Ludwig and Princess Therese back in 1810. I personally was so enamored with Oktoberfest that my middle school wood-shop project was a lamp built with a "Hoffbrau" beer can. The Hoffbrau House was the main beer hall of the German city of Munich. Mike once vomited there and had to pay a cleanup fee. A book I wrote in elementary school pertained to the German Oktoberfest as well. I had been enamored with the thought of this huge party even back in the second grade. And to think the real Oktoberfest of my childhood dreams stood only one mile from this very train station.

9

OKTOBERFEST

Georg and I arrived in Munich and walked the short distance to the festival itself. I could not wait to get inside and see this spectacle. Thousands and thousands of Germans literally sign in, grab a table, and drink beer for sixteen straight days. I thought to myself, "Is there a better way to continually celebrate the marriage of a dead prince from centuries ago?"

As we walked into the closest tent I'll never forget Georg's comment. In a deep Austrian accent he sounded like Arnold Schwarzenegger when he bluntly exclaimed, "I TOLD YOU SO."

I saw nothing more than tables of Japanese tourists taking photos of each other while holding their beer. Now I know why my grandmother had escaped. It had been taken over by the Japanese! We each drank one beer, turned around, and went directly back to the train station. I felt gravely disappointed but Georg confidently led me forth. Fortunately he did have a back up plan. He knew that in just a couple of short hours we would experience the real Oktoberfest in the German city of Stuttgart; he affectionately nicknamed Slutt-gart.

When the train arrived in Sluttgart we quickly walked over to an identical version of Oktoberfest and entered the Spaten tent that contained Georg's German posse. They were a boisterous group of Germans that Georg had met through work and college. They welcomed us with open arms and invited us to join them at the table. Surprisingly they didn't even have cameras as they celebrated and drank with one liter beers in hand. They gave me, the American, a hard time for arriving late. They alluded to the fact that my lateness was due to having difficulty while inserting my tampon. Drunken Germans are particularly good at the art of peer pressure. I ordered two liters of beer and deposited them down my throat faster than a frat boy south of the Mason-Dixon Line. With this manly feat I had earned the respect of the beer swilling bunch and the night could now continue boisterously festive.

The festival was more than anything I had ever imagined. It was nothing like my yearly childhood trips to the German Festhaus in Maryland. There were hundreds of picnic tables lined together in rows with countless Germans drinking from oversized mugs. The people would stand and sway as they sang songs with a German polka band. The band led the crowd from a stage located in the middle of the giant tent. The tent was large enough to house a circus and easily held a thousand people. Outside of the tent there were at least ten more like it; each one dedicated to a different brand of beer. These beer tents were setup within the center of what American's would consider a county fair. Carnival rides and booths surrounded the outside of the festival and were mixed with an endless number of food stands. There was also a train garden decorated with ceramic gnomes. It must be a German thing.

The patrons inside each tent were mostly men or boys. Only a few women were mixed into the bunch. Most of the women in the tent were working. They were carrying up to ten beers or more at a time. They worked as waitresses for their assigned section of the tent and sold whole roasted chickens and giant pretzels as well as beer. Apparently the German women weren't as interested in consuming beer for eight hours each day. The German men promptly arrive at noon, sign in on a paper log, and then sit at their designated family spot along the tables. The spaces along the tables are held by family reservation and have been so for decades. The head of the family eventually hands his family spot down to the next generation and so on. The missing women who choose not to attend leave openings for visitors such as me and Georg. The night went on in drunken revelry and only once did it come to an abrupt halt. Georg must have been in a mood to recycle when he decided to reach below the table and refill one of the empty beer glasses. Did I mention the fact that mischief tends to follow Georg wherever he goes; or perhaps vice versa. He casually brought up his fresh glass of piss and gently placed it onto the table. He then cautiously pushed the glass down until it rested in front of a rough looking skinhead German patron. The young man was standing and looking out towards the polka band and didn't see what Georg had done.

An obvious product of inbreeding, the pierced and tattooed young man clumsily lifted his new warm beer towards his lips. Just before it reached his mouth I blurted out "Nein trinken sie!" in my best German attempting to prevent this atrocity.

Georg nudged me, beckoning me to allow this alcoholic blasphemy to occur; but I would not. I started waving and using hand gestures to convince the man to put down the glass. The man looked at me with confusion and disdain as I reached over and removed the warm non-beverage from his grasp. "Es ist schlect! Es ist schlect!"

I yelled as I attempted to explain my actions while pouring Georg's homebrew into the rocks below.

The drunken young man and his unsavory bunch were about to jump over the table before Georg gave them the "Stupid American" speech. It wasn't long before we were all once again singing the festive "West Virginia Country Roads" song. I quietly thought to myself, "Stupid American my ass! You're the one singing our crappy songs about West Virginia, Alabama, and the Rocky Mountain High!"

At ten o'clock the evening was over. We followed our German host as he signed out on the festhaus log and then headed passed the carnival. Ten o'clock is apparently closing time on a weekday night. After all everyone had to get back by noon tomorrow in order to do this again.

Our plan was to follow the Germans back into town and stay the night in one of their homes. As Georg and I followed the group they opted to take the standard European transit procedure. This includes walking several miles, taking a train, taking a bus, and then walking several more miles. But it had started to rain and I had another plan, what we Americans call *the cab.* The Germans hailed a cab for me but refused to ride when the cab driver offered a price equal to twenty dollars. I offered to pay but the stubborn Germans refused. Over the years I've found that Germans tend to be frugal, stubborn and inflexible. This is the main reason why Austrians tend to publicly differentiate themselves from their German cousins. Georg worked as my interpreter and explained that the Germans would not ride in the taxi based on mere principle. They knew that standard transit was free and felt that twenty dollars was too much for a ride into town. I asked Georg to interpret this, "I'M AMERICAN, WE DON'T HAVE PRINCIPLES!"

I pulled out a twenty, crumpled it in my hand, dropped it on the ground, and walked away. One German quickly picked up the bill and reluctantly hailed a cab. I guess they got my point. At that moment I realized just how far I had come from being a German. Or maybe being an American meant that I had become more stubborn than a German?

Twenty minutes later we arrived back at the house. At one dollar per minute the ride was worth every cent. We entered the man's house and I was given a spot in an upstairs bedroom. It was a good place to work off the ten liters of beer I had recently consumed. A few hours later I could have been found vomiting over the side of his village balcony. Unfortunately the balcony was above the patio which belonged to the parents of our German host. And to me, this is Europe. I decided I was far overdue for a return. I was set on the prospect that my next trip would lie within some unknown place; but that unknown place would undoubtedly lie within Europe. This realm would surely help me find my long lost land of immaturity.

10

EXACTLY WHERE AND WHEN

Delving further into location selection I researched the places in Europe that I have always wanted to visit. I began the process to determine which two European countries I wanted to explore next. I had previously covered Central and Eastern Europe but not the outlying south, east and the coastlines. They were all still available for discovery. I was very interested in Italy and perhaps France, but I preferred to wait until my kids would be older and able to stay home alone. These places seem more suited for a romantic trip. I would rather save these locations for a trip with my wife if she hasn't disowned me by them. I know that my wife has a desire to see Italy and she also holds an odd distaste for the country of England. Perhaps this was due to Mel Gibson's compelling role in "The Patriot." Yes, France and Italy sound like a good combo trip to take with the wife. With this considered, Italy and France were out and England was definitely high on the list.

To the surprise of some I like to travel without my wife as much as I like traveling with her. I imagine many do not understand this or my personal desire to seek variety and avoid the generalized state of the mundane. But traveling with the wife and traveling without the wife offer entirely different vacations. She and I had recently traveled together to Jamaica just a few months back. We also enjoyed a kid free trip to

Orlando Florida a few months before that. A kid free trip to Orlando meant that we actually got to go on the water rides and not constantly worry about our kids drowning in the sea of people wearing Mickey Mouse goggles. As do many women, my wife prefers the comfort of her nest. She would prefer to spend her money on lifestyle improvements back home before spending one dime on any low budget excursions of discovery.

I thought more about my decision upon Europe which eventually came to include the second major destination, Greece. Even though my wife might also enjoy a trip to Greece I knew that I was thinking of a much different trip than the standard island cruise or Athenian dinner on the town. I was thinking about Ios. I had heard about the Greek island of Ios for about the last ten years. A traveling friend of mine who currently goes by the name Nico has gone to this island year after year and always returns with stories that rival my own. I had two connections to Nico. One, he was a mini-legend who once swam in the fishbowl better known as my college UMBC. The other connection stemmed back to Store Foods and my earlier travels. Traveling often with Store Foods friend, Sperka, I had met an Italian descended alcoholic named Tarsia. He coincidentally worked alongside of his infamous friend Nico. Back then Nico went by the name Jack. Neither the name Nico or Jack was his actual name. I imagine he must be wanted for national espionage or at least hunted by an ex-girlfriend's big brother.

I eventually became friends with Nico due to my continued travels and through partying in the same Washington and Baltimore circles. He is a very interesting character to say the least and I would come to know him very well. In fact, everyone knows Nico. I could randomly walk up to perfect strangers from Miami to Calcutta. I would find that not only did they know him but Nico once slept in that exact spot. Nico was my traveling hero. He would travel for years at a time and during those years the Greek island of Ios always fit into his itinerary. Via email, he would report back to me while I sat working away in my American cubicle. Trapped, I could only imagine the places and stories that were described in his emails. He would tell his tales of Asia, Africa, Europe and often Ios. Ios certainly didn't sound like a place that the wife would enjoy. Sleep all day, party all night, cheap beer and loud rambunctious parties. It sounded more like a place for pirates and not for my delicate flower. Yes, I think I'll add Ios to the itinerary.

Now all I needed was to figure out a traveling time frame and send out an email to discover who would partake of such an adventure. Already knowing that I wanted to be in London I looked towards early summer to avoid the infamous rainy London weather. I did a little more research and found out via Encyclopedia Nico that the island of Ios was best in late June. This is the time of year just before the Italians invade the island. It is also during the arrival of the Scandinavians. According to Nico, it was best to avoid the Italian season. The Scandinavians are much more pleasant as well as topless. At this point I had determined the where and the when; I just needed to find out who would be up for such a journey.

11

WHO

Determining ones travel companions for such an undertaking is a combination of luck and art. Luck, because you never know who is going to join any particular trip. Art, because you need to travel with the right mix of personalities or else you'll end up on an episode of "Survivor." There is also the fact that I was looking for a good balance of individuals who all contain "Grown up Immaturity." I define this as a person who is fun and perhaps a little off balance.

The immature grown up is hard to spot. He or she is like the proverbial millionaire next door. You could have been sitting a cube over for the last ten years and not even have recognized one. Like Jekyll and Hyde they are quiet co-workers, project managers, developers, human resource staff and all the calm friendly personalities you already know. They are the responsible husbands, wives, fathers, mothers, teachers, doctors, lawyers and bankers that you come in contact with every day. They can best be described as double agents who are professional by day and unpredictable by night. Over the years I have grown quite the collection of such characters and keep them handy in times such as this. Most of my friends probably contain a high level of "Grown up Immaturity." I knew that in order to accomplish this trip and the desired adventure, I needed to swim deep into my pool of characters.

There are other important factors to consider when planning this type of trip. These factors include group size and the gender of the group members. This consideration is equally important to the actual characters you invite. For example, women should never travel in packs of three. She-packs ultimately result in a pairing effect that leaves one dejected and depressed. She eventually ends up as a full blown psychotic. Women just don't travel well in odd numbers unless that number is one. Men on the other hand need a *minimum* of three travelers. The general consensus by men is that two men traveling alone might be construed as a homosexual couple. Even if you are a homosexual couple this is probably not the most desired persona when traveling in an unfamiliar foreign country. For men, three is the bare minimum. It gives the unpaired man his required cave time. The other two can grunt and point at whatever food or woman is in the nearby vicinity. When it comes to men, three is always better than two.

Over my many international trips I have never yet gone with the exact same group of individuals. I have traveled with an all male group, a mixed male-female group, and even once as the sole male on an all female trip. That last one was interesting. But in the reality of things, I've found that an all male, woman free trip is truly the best fit for me. Males have a natural understanding that standards and expectation are meant to be low. When traveling, standards are initially set low, everything is up from there. With little to no complaints; traveling with all men is more relaxed and simple. If I had a nickel for every time a woman said that she preferred to hang around men then I would have a shit load of nickels. Men generally agree with this theory as well. Henceforth this is the reason my trips often consist of nothing but men.

I witnessed the simplicity of men on my cross country road trip. I was just south of San Francisco and needed to stop for a car wash. The outside of our Dodge Colt was covered with vomit after my friend Sperka had a difficult ride across the San Mateo-Hayward Bridge. Sperka and I drove until we found what appeared to be an automatic car wash. As we pulled into the building there was no immediate spray of water or red spinning brush. This was a hand car wash and a team of young Mexican immigrants stepped out to earn their daily wage. I hid my face in embarrassment as Sperka put on the parking brake. We never intended to have someone hand wash Sperka's vomit from the car. But the men stepped up and began to clean. The first man realized what was now upon his wash mit and cried out, "NOOO, NOOO, VOMITOS!"

The other men began to laugh. The man took the vomit covered mit and threw it at the other men. The game was on. They didn't get angry and they didn't walk away. In the face of adversity these men laughed and even had fun while cleaning a stranger's regurgitated dinner.

12

SIZE MATTERS

The size of a group also impacts the trip. Large groups don't move well and workout best in one idle vacation destination. The largest group I traveled with was a group of eight men. We traveled to the soft beaches of Cancun. This was an excellent environment for such a large group. We could break off from one another as desired. We could just enjoy the surroundings individually or go off with whatever subgroup seemed fit. On this particular eight man adventure, each night was filled with stories that were all shared poolside on the next day.

When traveling with a large group, you increase the chance that perfect strangers will tell stories about someone in your party. For example, during the eight man Cancun trip I politely asked a family from Minnesota if they were enjoying their stay. The woman replied, "Everything has been great except for last night when some drunk was beating on our door. He was screaming oddly in a foreign language!"

My drink nearly came out my nose as I knew this had been my friend Mike. Just hours before Mike had told me of his night time door banging adventure. He had found himself drunk and lost on the wrong floor of the hotel. He began to lament about the passing of Pope John Paul II. Apparently in his intoxicated state he was religiously compelled to recite catholic prayers *in German* due to the passing of his beloved Polish Pope. Oddly, the next elected Pope turned out to be a German. Did I mention that Mike is an interesting character?

Mike was often the topic of stories such as this and henceforth Mike is always at the top of the vacation invitation list. Per my wife he is probably my best friend because he is also my most immature friend. I think she may be right considering the modern definition of immature as irresponsible, flighty and down right childish. Mike is always the ideal travel candidate on the road to immaturity. He is usually single, usually childless, usually jobless, and usually responsibility free. And how could I deny myself of Mike's friendly bantering that often earns a special title or nickname wherever he goes? On one particular trip to Cancun, the bartenders referred to Mike as "El Gordo Diablo" or fat devil on account of his manly sun burned gut. Mike has received more nicknames than perhaps anyone on Earth.

Traveling in large groups often seems to produce the real life humorous college pranks that you would normally only find in a classic 80's college movie. One year I developed the pictures on my disposable camera to find that I had spent the night with one of the local stray dogs of Key West. Apparently my friend Sperka had ushered the dog up into my bed after I had passed out. Consequently I and those in the immediate vicinity had unknowingly awoken covered in flea bites. The mangy brown Labrador still holds a place in my collection of unusual travel photos.

Classic movie scenes such as the comical "Walk in your friend during a lewd sex act" occur once in a while. Once again the setting for the next scene is Cancun. I walked into my room and found a fellow traveler in the middle of an act often associated with dog behavior. I went into temporary shock. My friend Eddie looked back with a smile and gave me a wink. I blurted out, "PEOPLE WORKING IN HERE!" as I stumbled back through the room entrance.

These trips are always full of spontaneous off the wall scenarios. I will never witness any of them from inside my modest American cubicle. Only on "You Tube" could I find something as twisted as a bald, overweight, hair covered friend jumping onto a stage for a best body competition. I know a character that goes by the name Kid Delicious who won some free drinks for that stunt.

Normally these scenarios only appear on television or in National Lampoon movies, but on these trips they are an every day occurrence. New stories are created, new nicknames are discovered, and new spontaneous moments erupt. They wipe clean the otherwise dull American existence that dictates to me for the other three hundred and fifty days of the year. Better yet they leave a trail of stories to share over the upcoming year that follows.

13

THE INVITATION

After writing a loose itinerary including destinations, time frame and approximate cost; I dug deep into my email address list to select the lucky participants that would have the opportunity for what I had titled "EUROTRIP 2009." It was early December and I wanted to weed out any undecided travelers and push the determined Eurotrip 2009 travelers into commitment via booking the flight. One of the best ways to ensure the commitment of a potential traveler is to have them pay for their plane tickets six months in advance. To hammer down their commitment have them cough up the flight money two weeks before Christmas. If a person can come up with a thousand dollars right before Christmas then they are most likely someone you want to have with you when traveling across the expensive continent of Europe.

This approach to trip booking has worked for me over the years. I often recruit fellow travelers and plan my trips right before the winter holidays. Only one time did someone pay for their flight and then bail out of the trip. That person was Mike. The new controlling factor or girlfriend in his life had determined that spending his money on a Key West bachelor party meant that he did not love her. Hello, red flag number one. Anyhow the best man in my wedding was the only one who bailed on my eight person bachelor party to Key West. I still give him a hard time about it, even today. He is divorced now but some things still never change.

I sent out the official Eurotrip 2009 invite. A day after sending the email I received replies from eight of the original twenty that had been invited. The first was good old life long friend Mike who was currently in the final stages of divorce. After ten years of personal and emotional confinement he was primed and ready for a trip of freedom and discovery. Ten years later he was still regretting the trip he missed to Key West. He was surely not going to miss out on this one. In the last two years of the divorce process he had acquired a new girlfriend. Explaining the trip to her would be his only setback. But he was a new independent man now and nothing could keep him from his destiny with travel. Mike stuck to his guns and followed through concerning the trip. He was a connoisseur of culture and languages that had been stymied by the years with his wife. Early in their marriage she had banished him to live in the cultureless hills of distant Carroll County, Maryland.

Another email dropped in from a friend named Bob. He had recently started working as a local police officer and had accrued enough time for his first vacation from his stint with the police force. He put in his vacation request at work and was excited about the trip. He knew all the ins and outs of Ios. He had been to the island to visit Nico in the past. Bob didn't want to miss this opportunity to get back to what he described as heaven on Earth. His biggest setback was a woman as well. He had been married to his wife for just over a year and he was weighing the effect of this trip upon his newlywed.

Another email dropped in from the Austrian party animal Georg. He informed me of his current plan to travel to Ios this year as well. He gave me some dates in order to coordinate our arrival on the island. He also wrote of the time he spent living in London and the fact that he had no desire to go back at this time. German Marco contacted me on a social site called Tagged and he expressed interest to meet for the London portion. Marco too was friends with Mike and also had two sisters living in London. He expressed the opportunity to visit four birds with one stone.

The next email came in from nearby neighbor Keith. He and I had enjoyed Thanksgiving together and I had discussed my intentions for European travel over our turkey dinner. In the end, he regretfully declined the trip. He realized that leaving his wife alone with four small kids was probably not a good idea. I would disagree. And still more email rolled in. Long term friend Tarsia replied with his interest of the London portion of the trip. He was retired from hood surfing but was interested in the hard pumping beats of the London music scene. He was considering crossing the pond to spend some time in the London music venues. Eventually he came to the realization that both the long flight and his girlfriends disapproval was too much to overcome.

Nico chimed in with confirmation of his June arrival time on the island of Ios and with the information of his upcoming return to the states. After finishing up the ski season in Switzerland he planned to come stateside before going back to his second home in Ios. The island of Ios runs a busy season similar to the beach resorts of the east coast United States. Nico planned to secure a summer job while he traveled and partied. He had used this technique to prolong his traveling adventures and often works as a bartender or surfing instructor.

Finally I received one more interested party who stated that he was ready to meet and work out the details of the trip. I was very intrigued by the positive response from my old high school and college buddy Kwab. I hadn't seen Kwab for many years and was shocked that he was not just willing to go, but ready to book as well. I might expect to receive a general inquiry from Kwab, but this reply was an unusual surprise. I liked the prospect of traveling with Kwab. There were a lot of unknown factors and a lot of mystery to him. Our history went from spending time along our high school football sideline to later pledging my college fraternity. He was a quiet cool sort of party animal that was always plotting his approach to the next woman that entered the room. He and I always had good chemistry. Comments and jokes would constantly bounce back and forth between one another. It was very similar to the chemistry I have with world traveling Nico. I replied to each person who responded to the invite and I setup a time to meet. Those who lived locally could easily meet to do the booking. Mike, Kwab and I showed up at my house on a December Friday, the week before Christmas. We booked our initial flights, shook hands, and went our separate ways. Mike's separate way is sometimes to my basement as he often spends time with my family when in between places. But considering his spontaneity, Mike's separate way could be some further location such as West Virginia or the even the Slovak Republic. Adding to the mystery that was Kwab, I didn't see him again until the day we left for the trip.

In later weeks additional emails trickled in from the other persons who were on the original invite. All others had reluctantly declined due to various financial or personal reasons, so it looked like it would be me, Kwab and Mike. I had hoped to hear back from one more person, my eldest foster son Elo. He had recently been home on military leave and had planned to meet up with me in London. I guess his leave time had been spent and I have not heard back from him to this day. As the weeks went on I looked forward to meeting up with my friends for the adventurous trip to come.

14

THE THREE SCORPIONS

The scorpion is the mascot of the high school that Mike, Kwab and I had attended. This trip would be the first in which the entourage contained three members of my old High School alameda. I found it interesting that this was my very first trip with all Oakland Mills graduates and it happened to fall EXACTLY twenty years after my high school graduation. I had recently been back in touch with Kwab due to the social networking site Facebook that was currently sweeping my graduating class as well as the world.

The first scorpion, Mike was practically my womb mate and was more like a brother than a long term friend. He was always easy to travel with, easy going, adventurous and always liked to seek out new information and experiences. He is obviously a good choice for a European travel partner as he can speak several of the European languages. He is also fascinated with European history and facts. It would be easy to motivate him for the trip.

Mike was born from European descendents and was very interested in the culture of his homeland Europe. His Polish descendents inhabited and overwhelmed the city of Baltimore after World War II. In fact, his parents still attend Polish festivals and occasionally attend a traditional Polish mass near the neighborhoods of Canton and Fells Point in downtown Baltimore. They even make a traditional Polish Easter meal complete with perogies, gwumpkies, and no less than three kinds of ham. I didn't even know there were three kinds of ham until my first Easter with the Myers family.

Mike additionally manages to fit the profile of every Polish joke ever written, and he always does it with flare. His unintentional uncoordinated motions and clumsy efforts all contribute to his persona. It wouldn't be too hard to imagine him having trouble changing a light bulb. As a clumsy teen Mike would often break things around the house and his father declared that he had the "Midas Touch." You see everything Mike touched, turned to shit. In addition to his natural slap stick fine motor coordination, Mike is an enormous monster of a baby face. Imagine the body of an athlete who performs tractor trailer pulls with his teeth. Then, attach the head of Chunk, the kid from the film "Goonies" and you've got a picture of Mike.

Everyone loves Mike the minute they meet him. He is a true gentle giant and comically a big chicken. It always amazes me that a man who can squeeze my hand until I roll on the ground in painful submission is also afraid of PG rated horror films. To this day he will not walk into any room that has "Silence of the Lambs" on the television screen. I remember my 150lb friend Gabe once telling me about the time he escorted Mike on a car ride down Route 40 to help him pick up a check. Apparently the outskirts of Baltimore City were too scary for Mike. When walking in the city it is amusing to see him sprint across intersections because of his fear that he will be hit by an unseen car. There is nothing quite like witnessing three hundred pounds of lightening speed pass a group of seniors as they stroll across Pratt Street.

I enjoy giving Mike a hard time and often play pranks associated with his fear. He once quit a rough job as a middle school teacher on the premise that he feared for his life. In turn I hired him to work with me on a night time computer help desk. He and I would fix caller problems while spending free time on the internet. Mike never had this much access to high speed internet before. He enjoyed spending his free time in chat rooms discussing his beloved football team, the Seattle Seahawks. I didn't have much interest in arguing with strangers on the internet but would listen in as Mike read back their responses. I jumped on this opportunity to play a prank on him. I peaked around my cubicle wall and saw the name of his particular chat room. It was SeahawkChat1 and he was logged in as BUDVAR1. After setting up the screen name STNKYGYMSHRTS I logged in to the same chat room. I simply typed in "Seahawks suck" and Mike immediately responded. In support of his favored team he proceeded to call STNKYGYMSHRTS a piece of shit. I typed back…

STNKYGYMSHRTS: Do you sometimes work alone?
BUDVAR1:   What are you talking about?
STNKYGYMSHRTS: I see you there in your green shirt.

Mike walked over to my cube and asked, "Can someone see me from a chat room?"
"No" I answered.

He went back to his computer.

BUDVAR1:   F You!
STNKYGYMSHRTS: And you drive a green Mazda Protégé too. You must really like the Seahawks with all the fancy green clothes and car.

Mike nervously called out to me, "Are you sure no one can see me?" I replied, "I don't think so."

BUDVAR1:   Where are you?
STNKYGYMSHRTS: Nearby. Say hello to your wife and son.

Mike called out, "HOLY SHIT! MATT, GET OVER HERE!"

I walked over unable to keep a straight face. I fell over laughing as Mike finally put two and two together. He called out to me one last time, "YOU ASSHOLE!"

Often and to his dislike I have compared Mike to a big version of the character George Costanza from "Seinfeld." He and Goerge have many similarities including neurotic fear, generalized anger and motivational spite. You don't want to piss Mike off. He won't beat you to a pulp but he might roll your bath towel in poison ivy. That particular incident cost me a roommate. I can only imagine the unknown acts of vengeance that I myself have been subject to over the years. I specialize at pissing off Mike. In fact I'm quite sure I'm doing it right now. But one of the simplest techniques is to refer to him as George Costanza. I like to remind him of his gigantic wallet stuffed full of useless receipts, his bizarre conflicts with people, and his stubborn refusal to do things based on pure spite.

Scorpion number two is extremely different than the first. Kwab is aggressive, confident, poised, and not born of European descent. Kwab was the first African American friend that befriended me. Before high school I really didn't know many African Americans. I grew up in a predominately white neighborhood that was built years before the surrounding ethnic melting pot known as Columbia. We were known for our wardrobes of flannel shirts and construction boots. Compared to Columbia, my neighborhood was a preserved redneck village in the middle of the racial utopia that had formed around it. Today the neighborhood has become racially integrated as did my family and most of the country. Now I have a black cousin in law, I married a woman of mixed race, and I raised two African American sons. When I was growing up there were only ten African Americans students over my first nine years of public school. Only one of them attended school with me from kindergarten through eighth grade. Ironically his name was Brian White. Kwab was no Brian White.

Kwab was a proud African American from a family with real African cultural flare. I remember walking into his father's apartment and being intrigued by the bright African decorative theme. It reminded me of the African themed amusement park, The Dark Continent in Tampa, Florida.

Kwab's full name is Kwabena. It means born on Tuesday in Akan, the local language of Ghana. Mathematically, I imagine the Kwabenas of the world represent one seventh of the population of Ghana. Kwab and I met and became friends through our high school football experience. He and I would stand along the sideline, quietly laughing as we made fun of the odd habits and behavior of our coaches. He and I knew the coaches were all full of shit and would insistently joke about it during practice.

Being a wide receiver Kwab was quite the opposite of lineman Mike. Not only physically, but personality as well. Kwab stood a thin five foot eight medium completion African American man. Back then he could probably outrun any lineman on the team. Kwab isn't scared of much, except maybe being tackled by a few of the football team starters. His confident, outgoing and aggressive personality doesn't shy away from the first opportunity to talk with an attractive woman. He was very flirtatious in High School and it carried on to college.

In college his football skills were obsolete but his female skills always came in very handy. I found that it was always a good idea to stand in near proximity to Kwab. He was quick to break the ice in any social situation that pertained to women. You never knew what spark might ignite when Kwab was in the vicinity. In college he would bring groups or pairs of women back to my off campus apartment to hang out and consume drinks before heading out for some sort of local dancing adventure. At nineteen years of age he would often bring back girls who were in the dating range of sixteen or seventeen years old. We would talk about the mature issues of the average teenager and play drinking games or pranks on others like my responsible roommate Joe.

It was fun to play pranks on Joe who was a bit older than me but a young man ahead of his time. Working ten hour days, and going to class at night, his hair continually thinned. One time we, or more likely I, played a little prank on Joe. He worked as a mature twenty two year old devoted employee at the local bank. He would go to bed early for work and in the winter had to get up before sunrise. One night when Kwab, the younger girls, and I were partying I snuck upstairs while Joe slept. I set his alarm clock back five hours. Instead of the assumed six a.m. shave, shower and breakfast he was now departing for work at two in the morning. Joe walked out the door and thanked me for the full egg, bacon and toast breakfast I had so kindly but strangely prepared for him. Moments later he arrived back home and silently gave me the middle finger. He removed his tie and marched up the steps to go back to bed. I can remember one of the young party girls saying, "Ooooh, I think we pissed off your Dad."

Joe was only two years older than me. Eventually I was forgiven and Joe still manages my finances to this day. Kwab and I had some fun times at Joe's expense.

Kwab was an excellent candidate to pledge my college fraternity and was an excellent candidate for this or for any sort of trip. He was familiar with the various complexities of my personality and I his. I knew that Kwab, like I, was a kind hearted smart ass that still had a few principles left. One time Kwab was being fraternally quizzed by the older brothers of the fraternity and the Pledge Kwab blurted out, "These asshole fraternity founders were a bunch of racists."

None of the brothers knew what to say. He was right. Kwab pledged for three semesters and was the longest running pledge that never got in. Not because of race but because he never bothered to read up on the history of the racist founders.

I saw similarities in Mike and Kwab especially pertaining to the topic of being stubborn. To this day Mike will not eat Heinz ketchup due to the fact that the Pittsburg Steelers *stole* a win against the Seattle Seahawks in Superbowl XL. Throughout the upcoming journey Kwab respectfully approved of Mike's refusal. To this day Mike refuses to ever pour one drop of Ketchup from a bottle labeled Heinz. I later found out that there was one more similarity between the two. Kwab, as Mike, had just come out of a long term relationship. Mike was at the end of his divorce and Kwab had also just ended his long term engagement. Just as Mike, Kwab was ready to travel relationship free and henceforth sent me his response to the email invitation for EUROTRIP 2009.

So here I was with two very different travel companions. Together, we were ready to embark upon a European adventure which held every aspect of mystery and discovery. We didn't know what we would see. We didn't know what we would do. And we didn't know how each of us would react in the chemistry of our scorpion trio. After booking the December flights, Kwab left early to go spend time with his nephew. After Kwab left, Mike and his neurotic imagination asked me, "What is Kwab like now? I mean, you haven't seen him for years. He could be a serial killer or something."

I laughed and told him not to worry. After all, Kwab primarily targets females and I'm quite sure he has no desire to wear Mike as a fat suit.

Finally, I can't forget to mention scorpion number three. He is quite the stud; but a little neurotic, highly unpredictable, and somewhat of a control freak. For the purposes of this chapter we'll call him, Powers... Studly... Powers. I should mention the fact that he is also mischievous. I still remember his favorite prank. Once again, a less than innocent roommate was the victim. I won't name names. It was a well known fact that this particular roommate had mastered the art of self-eroticization. One night, Studly slipped into his roommate's lair. He located the required accomplice needed for a particular prank. It was a bottle of Jergens lotion that was stored safely under his roommate's bed. Mr. Powers decided to spice up his roommate's love life using none other than Gulden's Spicy Brown Mustard. A couple of squeezes, a few shakes, and it was done. Around three in the morning, Mr. Powers awoke to the howls of a hairy palmed werewolf and the splashing of a furious shower. He smiled and went back to sleep. The next morning he found his roommate researching venereal diseases. Which one could make your dick burn and turn yellow?

15

WORKING OUT THE DETAILS

As the months passed, Kwab, Mike and I communicated by email and worked out the details of our trip. We had decided on a hostel in London, a top notch hotel on the Greek island of Ios, and a well located hotel along the port of Athens. We figured out the final details of our transportation including our boat ride to and from the island of Ios. The cream had risen to the top and just as I imagined, those who booked in December, were the only ones going to Europe come June. My policeman friend Bob had teetered for a while but eventually dropped out. He determined that money issues and his marriage were more important than his heavenly island of Ios. Other details fell in to place as well; such as our plan to meet up with George and Nico once we reached the island of Ios. Georg would already be on the island with a group of Austrian friends and Nico had plans to be back on the island by early June.

The first of these two traveling characters is Georg. He is an intelligent, confident, multi-lingual, fun-loving travel enthusiast. Many who meet him immediately comment upon his personality and his physical similarity to the American actor, Christian Slater. Take the mental picture of Christian Slater, then add the accent of Arnold Schwarzenegger and you have Georg. Georg and his positive traveling attitude had been my companion for several adventurous trips. Fortunately for

Georg and the rest of Europe, the working-public receive up to ten weeks of vacation. Therefore Goerg often has the time to meet me for many of my adventures.

Georg and his common law wife happen to have a very similar relationship to the one that my wife and I maintain. Interestingly enough, his wife and mine both consider them selves very mature. Well I guess anyone who spends enough time around Georg or I would. Mature or not his wife managed to stick by Goerg through thick and thin. And my wife remained married to me even after finding out that I was the guy who threw the local gold fish swallowing party. But more importantly she shares my philosophy of personal freedom which enables both of us to individually do whatever it is that we love to do.

Fortunately for both Georg and I, our wives understand our need to travel and they give us the opportunity to travel in our own unique style. Georg and I both share a strong desire to see new places, experience new culture, and travel family free. As with my wife and I, he and his wife, take separate vacations in addition to taking vacations together. Goerg had been cross-county in the United States, to Cancun, Key West, Cuba, and Turkey. Of course he has vacationed all over the continent of Europe as well. And just this past summer, he and I traveled with both our families. Together we took a two week adventure which highlighted Cape Cod, Massachusetts.

I always look forward to Georg's comical antics and unpredictable bursts of spontaneity. You never know what kind of stunt he is going to pull. One minute you're having an intelligent conversation about history and the next minute he's kissing the horse of a nearby police officer. More than once Georg has seen the inside of a jail cell.   Also, if Georg needs to get out of a sketchy situation back in Austria he will often pretend to be an American using his excellent American accent. But I think you get the point, George is never boring. This brings me to the other character we plan to meet on the island of Ios, Nico.

16

YOU DON'T KNOW JACK

Nico is a horse of another color or perhaps I should say a whore of another color. Nico has always had a strong affection for the ladies, even far more than Kwab. Nico is like a human magnet to every woman that enters a room. You can find him carefully surveying the scene and working the crowd. Usually this behavior of the average male horn ball is not surprising, but with Nico it's different. He takes the act of meeting women to a new level. Nico treats women with the utmost respect, yet he courts them as if he is playing a sport or working on a hobby. Some people collect stamps or matchbooks while Nico collects female interludes like Ron Jeremy collects venereal diseases. Eventually, I believe that someday one of his prize catches will be his last. I imagine strolling along the Baltimore Inner Harbor and passing an odd thirty-something woman wearing a freshly skinned Nico mask.

Mike neurotically commented that he was concerned and that Nico genuinely frightened him. Once again Mike had managed to use a serial killer reference while describing a friend. In truth Nico is just a harmless swooner of the ladies. He only wants to prove himself to the women of the world while he performs his self prescribed role as woman pleaser of planet Nico. Comically, with his tall slender physique and his styled dangling hair he reminds me of The Simpson's character "Side Show Bob." He often looks sharp in his Austin

Powers wardrobe and youthful from his various botox treatments. It is always entertaining to sit and listen to Nico talk about the subtle tastes of his favorite wine and then suddenly pop out the word, "DUDE!"

He attempts to emit the persona of a surfing snowboarder that follows a greater sense of purpose. I always look forward to the antics that seem to surround Nico as often as they manage to find Georg.

Unlike Georg, trouble seems to find Nico much more often than Nico finds the trouble. Nico bounces back and forth between the continents of the world and often ends up back in the United States. When in the states, Nico often spends his summer at the nearby party spot known as Dewey Beach. Dewey is the perfect setting for Nico as it attracts the twenty, thirty and forty something party animal. Here, older women referred to as cougars prowl the bars in search of younger men for a one night romp in the high cougar grass. Nico was their nemesis, the male cougar, otherwise known as the mougar. The mougar spends his time perched within the cougar's high grassland waiting for his opportunity to pounce upon an unsuspecting fawn. If the hunt proves fruitless, the mougar will offer shots to nearby cougars in hopes of sharing a piece of their Dewey kingdom together. The later scenario was more often the case and each Dewey season Nico has returned to Baltimore with his new cougar prize.

I remember a trip I once took that embodies the lifestyle of Dewey Beach. Bob, Tarsia and I were accompanied by an acquaintance named Paul as we headed into the jungles of Dewey. Paul was a friend of Nico that lived as a young professional in Washington D.C. He was a little rat like fellow with thick glasses and protruding front teeth. He had a terrible combination of qualities which included being a close talker with horrendous halitosis breath. Paul would approach and hit on every single female he spied through his pair of thick glasses. He practices the theory of percentages and argued that his high number of female approaches would ultimately guarantee his success. Watching Paul approach women was like the hunting scene in the film Jurassic Park II. As he rode into battle he drove the women away in flocks. It was never a good idea to stand too close to Paul. If you positioned yourself far enough up wind you might find a remaining pocket of nice women. To add to his charm, Paul also liked to lie to everyone. I would listen as he told each female target about his career as a lawyer; when in actuality I knew he was really a fact finding paralegal. He probably worked as a groveling aid to one of the many blood sucking lawyers around Washington D.C. Anyhow, he was Nico's friend and so together we embarked upon a short road trip to a weekend in Dewey Beach.

After a rigorous night in the bars, we headed off to the local wing joint for some late night drunken feeding. Before the others had finished their meal, I wisely headed back to claim a spot to sleep in the overcrowded apartment. I knew I was competing with perhaps twenty or more drunks for a comfortable place to sleep. The rest of the group partied on into the night as I relaxed and watched a movie alone on the one couch in the apartment. I was glad to have ended my night early and looked forward to sleeping on the semi-comfortable couch while those around me would have to sleep on a hard floor. These types of beach arrangement are first come, first served. I sat with a smile of accomplishment as the drunks rolled in one by one and found their spot on the floor. The women who were also staying at the beach apartment had the privilege of sleeping within the relative safety of the bedrooms. These of course had private cots behind their locking doors. On the other hand, all the men were destined for the open comfort of the combined living-dining room floor.

The apartment looked a typical third floor beach housing unit. It had a deck staircase that led to the only door which entered into the living room-dining room combo. Behind the living room was an open ended kitchen and a hallway. It led to some bedrooms and a full bath. The place had beige wall to wall carpet and the plain white walls were adorned with pictures of lighthouses and the beach. I got comfortable on the couch and relaxed. As the night went on, the party patrons strolled home. Tarsia came back first, then Paul, then Bob, and finally Nico. It was probably an hour or so before sunrise and each man grabbed his spot on the floor. Since I had a head start and the most comfortable resting place I was the first to fall asleep. As I dreamt I imagined cool flowing waterfalls such as the Dunn's River Falls in Jamaica until I was abruptly awoken. As I opened my eyes I realized that the sound of the waterfalls gentle flow was not coming from Jamaica but was actually coming from somewhere within the room.

I heard the undeniable sound of water being poured onto a carpet and opened my eyes to take a look. In the dim lit room I could see Paul still asleep, face down, but in an odd arched formation. He was up on his knees with his face pressed directly into the carpet. From his crotch I could see a thick flow of urine running directly through his jeans and onto the carpet below. It appeared as though everyone else in the room was in a deep drunken sleep as no one else had witnessed a thing. Once Paul finished his release he laid back down into his personal hot tub while still managing to remain in a drunken slumber. The sound of Paul's River Waterfall was enough to send me off to the bathroom. I now needed to produce a waterfall of my own. Rather than join Paul in urinating myself and the floor I quietly left the couch. I disappeared through the kitchen and into the nearby bathroom.

When I returned to the room I could hardly believe the scene before me. While I was in the bathroom, Paul had crawled up and taken my lone spot on the couch! "Son of a bitch!" I said to myself.

I was the rightful couch owner but considering the wet circumstances I decided not to reclaim my previous spot. Just then Nico arose from his nearby spot on the floor and stumbled drunkenly towards the backroom toilet. Defeated, I decided to curl up under the dining room table, a technique I patented to avoid being stepped on by drunks in the middle of the night. I learned this trick from my series of yearly Spring Break adventures. Additionally, Spring Break had taught me that man could not live on vodka alone as well as the fact that I should never try to climb through the small back window of a pick up truck. Drunk and stuck with your ass end hanging out of a pickup is not place you want to be, especially at Spring Break. As I got comfortable in my new sleeping hideaway, I felt safe under the table roof and surrounding chair legs. Moments later Nico entered back into the room. I watched from under the table as he staggered passed and dropped into the open section of the living room floor. I wanted to scream out as Nico had flopped down into the spreading puddle of urine that Paul had freshly delivered. It was too late. Nico was lying in it and he didn't seem to mind. Without a sound he fell right back to sleep and I saw no reason to wake him up. Wide awake after the urinary travesty, I woke Tarsia. I had to tell someone about what I had just witnessed. I wanted to leave now. It would be best to avoid the awkward morning that would soon follow. After hearing the story, I had no trouble convincing Tarsia. It was a good time for an early morning getaway.

Weeks later I ran into Nico and he informed me of the terrible deed for which he was ashamed. He had apologized to the owners of the house and gave them money to have the floor steam cleaned. He was now banished from the apartment. More so, he expressed concern for his personal health. After all he had never before wet himself in his sleep. Apparently he was harshly ostracized for the bed wetting accident and even Paul had delivered a few stern words of shame while driving on the long ride home. Needless to say, Nico was extremely appreciative when I filled him in on the actual events of the evening. At the very next opportunity I'm quite sure Nico repaid Paul in kind. To this day the ratty little character named Paul is still known as the infamous "Pisser Paul." For a long two weeks it must have been tough to be Nico, the Dewey Beach bed wetting mougar. Now his reputation could be redeemed.

In the weeks leading up to my new adventure, I received informative emails from the mougar to prepare me for the island of Ios. Nico planned to stay at a local hostel on the island while he searched for employment. He informed me that he would find us when we arrived. It sounded like an instruction from a secret agent. I never did hear back from my German friend Marco or my eldest foster son Elo. I would have loved to have caught up with Marco and seen London's "PicaWilly Square" with him. I had not seen him since my bachelor party ten years earlier when he went on a drunken angry rampage because I threw his cigarettes into the hotel pool. It would have been great to have Elo along as well. My eldest foster son was serving in the U.S. Army in Germany. I would have liked to have partied with him in London but at least I had just spent a month with him back home while he was on leave. I enjoy the laughs and strange reactions we get from the white-dad, black-son jokes we use in the local bars.

17

GETTING STARTED

Friday June 19th – Once all of the emailing and planning was complete, Kwab, Mike and I met up in Columbia. We were starting our adventure where we left off in 1989, but this time we were older, wiser, and yes, fatter. It seems like only yesterday that the three of us would have easily fit our luggage and accompanying abdominal carry-on into any compact Japanese automobile. For starters Kwab had packed a suitcase large enough to bring back a family of dwarf elephants; which coincidentally were once known to live on the islands of Greece. Additionally, the Japanese design has not kept up with the ever changing American lifestyle and physique.

I always bought small compact Japanese cars as my friend Tarsia always bought small compact Japanese cars. He has a thing about keeping his car spotless and in perfect condition but doesn't like driving cars that have over one hundred thousand miles. This works out well for me because I frankly don't give a shit. His reluctance to let anything go from cars to t-shirts puts me in prime position to purchase his used vehicles at a good price. I also get to see my future car each time he buys his new one and I try to weigh in on his purchase. In fact I already know that my next car will be a lovely silver high end Honda Accord.

So with a little creative packing, leg twisting, and gut sucking; the three of us managed to compress ourselves into my

Acura Integra for the estimated four hour drive to JFK airport in New York City. We were flying out of JFK because it happens to be the only location that has a direct flight from Greece back to the States. There is nothing worse than layovers when flying home so we would avoid them with this direct flight. After all, it would be an easy commute passed New York and to the long term parking at JFK. Why book a puddle jumper from BWI? We'll just drive! Mapquest estimates two hundred and twenty two miles or four hours and four minutes when traveling from Columbia, MD to JFK, New York.

18

NEW YORK

The three hour ride to northern New Jersey was a piece of cake. As we passed the exit for the Jersey Shores I thought of an upcoming family trip to visit friend Gloria and the needle laden beaches of Northern New Jersey. We stopped only once to fill up on our last bite of American fast food. The eclectic rest stop restaurant, Burger King, supplied me with a fish sandwich and fries, the American equivalent of England's fish and chips. Mike and Kwab had... drum roll please... hamburgers. We drove on and caught up on old times. We told the stories we knew about the island of Ios and discussed the fact that we really didn't know much about London. We were excited about the first beer we would consume from our departure gate and discussed how we would soon graduate to beer consumption within an authentic English Pub.

As we approached our exit, a flashing road information sign kindly informed us to tune into AM 1600. I obliged. I thought to myself, "Could this be a Howard Stern attempt to overtake the right wing control of the AM frequencies?" Unfortunately it was not. We could barely comprehend the scratchy voice that warned of major delays due to a vehicle fire on the Goethals Bridge. We had to think fast as the exit was coming upon us very rapidly. The voice on the GPS sounded off. It was more like the voice of the Lorelei luring us to our doom. She sang in her mesmerizing digital voice "Exit right in three hundred feet…exit right in three hundred feet."

My intuition kicked into overdrive and I appealed to Kwab to make a decision as he sat next to me holding the electric Lorelei in his hands. I was hoping Kwab would make the decision and lift the weight of indecision from my mind. Kwab pointed up the turnpike and said, "Keep going straight."

And so I did. And what a poor decision it was. It was far worse than if I had made the same choice. We took the Lorelei's detour towards the Holland Tunnel. We soon arrived a few exits north and were surprised to find a large backup before us. It looked far worse than the delays for the Goethals Bridge. The Lorelei didn't seem to know that today the Holland Tunnel would have two vehicle fires, a small riot and random livestock wandering about. Like the t-shirt says, you've just *got* to love New York.

We crept through the tunnel inhaling enough fumes to euthanize King Kong and then worked our way across 34th Street in midtown Manhattan. I could think of better things to do at rush hour. The familiar sight of the Empire State and surrounding buildings encompassed our car as I slowly clutched block by block across the Manhattan streets. We passed through Broadway, then across Park Avenue as we crept along. With plenty of time for my personal tour, I pointed out the timeshare hotel that my wife and I often visit. Although I loathed driving in New York City I was quite familiar with the streets of the city that she and I both enjoy, but for very different reasons. My wife loves the theatre and I enjoy the nightlife. She prefers to see a musical while I like to head deep into the New York club scene to experience the underground culture. To give you an idea of how I spend my time in New York; here is the actual thank you I emailed after my last birthday NYC weekend:

To those who made it this year, thanks for joining me for my NYC birthday fun. To the rest, I hope you make the 2009 version. The motto of this year's trip was "Doctor Recommended." Myers called me this morning to inform me that he is still not back to solid foods but yet no hangover for me. Doctor

(Bahrain) must have been right. The recommended two bottles of Grey Goose were fully consumed and all I had was a horrible feeling as the overdose of energy drinks had me wide awake yet tired as hell. On the brighter side, the greasy McDonalds hash browns took care of business as well as made Myers dry-heave on the care ride home. My afternoon of napping and football was "love" and I never even had a headache. I even think that the overdose of vitamin energy drinks knocked out what remained of my cold as I can now talk in my normal voice for the first time in over a week. The techno club was awesome with extra hot eye candy surrounding me for the fastest three hours of my life. The broccoli pizza at 3:30am was also awesome. The highlight for me was the Myers "Charlie Horse" which prompted Gamble to deliver a stern blow to Mike's leg. Myers will have a nice bruise and now walks with a limp. The hotel lobby races and hall wrestling were also very entertaining. The "Goose will be Loose" again. Additionally, Myers still heaves at the thought of mixed energy drinks called "No Fear" and "Ecto-Cooler." On the ride home, I had giddy tired laughs thinking about how Gamble actually thought he was drinking Ecto-Cooler; a beverage that hasn't been made in over twenty years since "Ghost Busters" first came out back in 1984. Mark's quote of the night was a heart-felt, "I still got it" while out on the club dance floor. And YES, Myers did break dance for the masses once again! In fact, there was no major dance injury report except for the round-house that he accidentally landed upon a small Filipino girl.

New York is a great weekend adventure that offers a very unique brand of freedom. Driving passed the time share I imagined that I would spend at least one similar night somewhere along the way on this trip. With my companions, Georg, Nico, Mike and Kwab, how could I go wrong? Continuing on, we managed to pass the time share hotel at least one more time as we searched for a non-blocked entrance to the Queens Midtown Tunnel. Overcoming each obstacle and some New York City traffic laws we continued to forge forward toward our airport destination. We finally reached the JFK long term parking location somewhere within three more additional hours. The next time I decide to go from Maryland to the JFK airport I will call out, "We're half way there!" when I'm stuck sitting in the Holland Tunnel.

19

THE GUESSING GAME

Almost six hours after departing from Maryland we arrived at our long term parking location outside of JFK airport. We didn't find the parking lot which had our reservation but we were running out of time and were ready to take any available parking. As I pulled myself out of the car I nearly fell to the ground. My legs were cramped from the last three hours of working the manual clutch on the car. I staggered from the car as if I had just finished a glute workout with Richard Simmons. Eventually I worked out the kinks and quickly jumped onto the shuttle bus before I handed the attendant my key. Realizing the fact that they would need my keys I quickly ran to the front of the bus, tossed my keys to the attendant, and informed him of our Sunday return in ten days.

The parking shuttle took almost twenty minutes crawling through the New York airport traffic but we made it to our departure terminal with forty minutes to spare. We sat down at the terminal bar and immediately ordered three beers and three shots. The shots were the airport bar special that came along at a discounted price when you order a beer. Considering the amount of stress circulating through JFK, I could understand why. Without hesitation Mike immediately began a session of his favorite game, "Guess the Accent." This involves lengthy conversations with strangers in order to determine their country of origin. While sober I find this game very annoying. Today's lucky contestant was the lovely eastern European waitress. The Eastern Europe accent category is Mike's personal favorite. As the waitress attempted to take our order Mike continued to pick through each country attempting to secure an early win at the game. Mike's friendly charm had won over the waitress and she was now getting into the act. After numerous misses the waitress said, "You are so close, but you have not yet got it right."

I'm not sure how I came up with the answer but I blurted out "Albania."

She nodded in approval and walked off to get our drinks. I thanked God that the game was over as Kwab laughed hesitantly. He did not know what I knew. I knew that this game would likely continue for the next ten days and for every single contestant that Mike could possibly find. I informed Kwab of the games that were to come and he simply rolled his eyes.

The waitress came back and we ordered another round. I volunteered to consume the bonus shots that came with our beers as I was in an odd place from the three hours of New York City driving. Kwab gave me the look that said, "What the hell are you doing?"

I took the shots, gave Kwab a look back, and said, "Killin' IT!"

We all had a laugh. We all recognized the phrase. It came from the random facebook postings of fellow high school graduate Chris Miller. He was a football teammate that was quickly becoming a local personal training hero that ran a fitness program in Columbia. When referring to the efforts of his physical trainees, his facebook posts often contained the catch phrase "Killin' IT!" All three of us knew of the many Chris Miller posts that often went something like, "Good workout today Sophie, you were Killin' IT!" or "Way to put down that cheese-steak Steve, you were Killin' IT!"

Each time I read one of these posts I envision the Captain Freedom workout from Stephen King's "The Running Man."

This short phrase became the motto of Eurotrip 2009. It successfully summed up the approach we took to each challenge along the way. When we were on a long walk, we were "Killin'

IT." Eating some new food, we were "Killin' IT." Heading up a steep incline; we were "Killin' IT." Or especially when we were handed an unordered shot of alcohol, you guessed it, we were "Killin' IT!" It turned out to be a very fitting motto.

The conversation turned from Killin' it to being killed. While discussing our expectations for the trip we moved to the topic of the 12/22/12 Mayan Calendar end date. Considering the Mayan prediction we all agreed that life is too short to miss out on any opportunity. This was one of the many underlying reasons each of us had decided to embark upon this vacation. We were ready to experience life at this moment and in this place. Our number one plan was to make the most of our time. After all, we couldn't count on Will Smith to be our hero and save the world in 2012. Suddenly our time ran out. Our flight was called and our 12/22/12 to Iceland was here.

We paid our bill and loaded onto the Icelandic Air 747 flight east. We entered our plane and became situated in row sixteen, seats DEF and buckled up. I informed Kwab of my intention not to sleep on the flight. I also gave him the rundown on Mike's ability to sleep anywhere and almost immediately. I swear Mike must inject himself with horse tranquilizer before boarding onto any moving conveyance. Before the plane could reach five thousand feet Mike looked ready to snore away. We were on our way to Reykjavik and very soon Mike and his snore would be; "Killin' IT!"

20

FLIGHT ONE: ICELAND

Saturday June 20ᵗʰ – Iceland has some interesting food traditions that I learned on my first Icelandic plane flight. They sometimes offer local delicacies such as pickled ram testicles, jellied sheep head or rotten shark but today we settled on what they called the beef sub. I was really tempted by the ram testicles. They sounded so good after reading the description of their preparation. They are pressed into blocks, boiled, and then cured in lactic acid. Too bad I'm lactose intolerant. Since we ran late and didn't have time to order food at JFK we all decided to take a stab at the mysterious Icelandic beef sub. It included stringy meat that was covered in an ugly brown sauce. It was draped within a stale brown roll. Other than the taste, texture and smell; the worst part was the fact that we had to pay extra to eat it. We found out that Iceland Air charges for all meals and suddenly the fifteen dollar airport nachos sounded like a good deal. Unbelievably, we had to fork over ten dollars for this Iceland food experiment. Normally experimental test subjects are paid for their services, but apparently not in Iceland. My curiosity with Iceland and my desire to visit was rapidly deteriorating.

As we dined we watched the sun set and then rise in a matter of one hour. Oddly, we witnessed it on the same side of the plane. Tired, confused, and nearly poisoned I was not about to question how that happens or even point it out to Mike and

Kwab. After the meal I attempted to flip through the channels of the airplane entertainment system. I viewed some interesting Icelandic tourism images and stopped when I came upon a documentary about Icelandic high energy music. Techno appears to be the favored music of the country. I was hoping to listen but Iceland air also charges an outrageous fee for headphones so I decided to visually take in what I could. To my surprise Mike pulled out a pair of headphones and offered me the right side of them. We plugged into the arm of the chair and were enjoying the high pulse sounds of Iceland. As with everyone Mike is no exception to the phrase, "Take the good with the bad." The three minutes of music was too good to be true. Mike's tree trunk leg had crushed the headphone plug into pieces. We were once again music free.

Trying to fit Mike into the coach seat of a 727 airliner is equal to fitting Dom Deluise into a jelly doughnut. Add myself and Kwab into a three person row and we look like a vase full of sausages. Whoever sits along the isle drapes over the side and blocks half of the isle. Today it was Mike. It was highly amusing to watch the flight attendant slam the drink cart into Mike and then ram the cart between the adjacent seat and Mike's left trunk. For the next three hours it was my main source of entertainment. I watched the bathroom bound travelers jolt Mike as they passed. He would briefly awaken with a bug eyed look of terror before dropping back into a snoring slumber. Kwab continued to read through an Obama campaign book as he squeezed against the side of the plane. In order to get my mind off of the tight squeeze and the beef sub I tried to do a little reading as well. I was quickly reminded of how motion sickness can quickly set in while reading on a plane so I just sat there staring. I was content to watch Mike snore away as the perturbed flight attendants continually smashed into his funny bone. As we landed I mentally summed up my thoughts on Iceland: go for the natural hot springs, go for the top notch trance music, but *never* go for the food. I'm glad I didn't waste a day eating Icelandic rotten shark and I felt fortunate that the three of us were just passing through town.

21

CAMERA GAMES AND THE LAYOVER

As the plane touched down in Iceland I began to feel the affects of the exhausting drive that I had chased with multiple shots of Grey Goose vodka. We pried ourselves from the tight row and headed towards the exit of the plane. The arctic summer air was cold and crisp as we stepped from the plane. I thought about the fact that today was an early summer morning in Iceland and it probably felt like a hot day to the locals. The chilly inhale of cool arctic air was enough for me to remove Iceland from any future travel plan. I can get my techno in D.C. I can get my hot springs in Arkansas. And I can get my rotten shark on any array of mid-east beaches. I had adamantly decided that I would leave this place to the inhabitants of the Planet Hoth and to the Ton-Ton's from "The Empire Strikes Back." Before the layover I had considered taking a vacation to Iceland. It appeared to be such a romantic place in all the travel advertisements I had seen. But in one cold moment all considerations vanished as I heard the voice of my wife echoing in my head. She was referring to our 2004 summer trip to San Francisco as her voice rang out, "Never take me on a cold vacation AGAIN!"

After we arrived at the Reykjavik airport we waited out a short one hour layover before boarding our flight to London. As we walked along the people-mover towards our departing gate we caught the distant scenery of the neighboring landscape of Iceland. It looked like the flat lands of Utah arranged with a few distant barren mountains. I think NASA may have filmed the moon landing here. At the very least NASA got their recipe for squeeze tube fish from the Icelandic natives. Kwab went to get a cup of coffee and stopped at a money machine. He wanted to secure some pounds for our arrival in England.

With exhaustion setting in, I headed directly for our departure gate and attempted to sleep for a bit on the airport bench. Apparently once I had drifted off Mike came along and took revealing pictures of me while I lay dormant. Over the last twenty years Mike has made it a habit to catch me in more than one embarrassing picture. I'll admit; I've done the same to him. This photo opportunity was his first attempt of the trip. Of course I enjoyed deleting the pictures from his digital camera upon discovery. I love digital cameras. I was looking at the pictures that Mike took of Iceland and let him know of my discovery. As I deleted the picture I delivered a loud sound effect, *"Dooooowt."*

This accentuated my reminder that camera games in the digital age would be much more difficult to play.

One my best immature qualities is my habit to use sound affects. Mike is even worse. The combined years of Looney Tunes that Mike and I have accumulated have provided us with an arsenal of sound effects. *"Dooooowt"* was one of my favorites. I used it from everything to pointing out an attractive woman to sneaking out of a room. Mike has an endless sea of sounds and distorted words that he uses for an array of situations. He has a high pitched laugh and wheeze that he uses when he finds something particularly funny. The word *"love"* is used often in reference to food and the sound *"schhhh-hwooohhhh"* is used while sprinting for any number of reasons. Kwab was new to this game and I had a feeling that he wasn't a big fan of sound affects. Between me and Mike, Kwab was in for a long sound effect filled trip.

22

FLIGHT TWO: LONDON BOUND

After our short layover we boarded the next plane for London and flopped down into our row. Kwab took the middle seat this time and strapped on his headphones. He began singing the words of his music as I laid my head against the window of the plane. Hopefully no more camera games were played as I slept for most of the flight. After the long drive to New York and the flight through Iceland I was in a state of pure exhaustion. We landed around eleven in the morning London time and proceeded directly to customs. Going through customs always makes me a bit nervous. Perhaps I should not have watched so many episodes of the show "Locked up Abroad." The episodes of this show often go through a progression. The foreigner is first busted at customs for smuggling something like raisins into a raisin free country. Secondly, he or she is then quickly swept off to a nearby prison where they are enrolled into a class to learn the local art of fecal finger painting.

Even though I had no reason to fear customs I did reflect upon the fact that I had received a D in high school art class. Instead of paying attention I would giggle in the back with friends Susy and Beth. I spent my time being a sm-Art ass. The devoted art teacher would ask me to describe Matisse paintings and I would answer, "Ma-tisse are in my mouf."

Again it didn't help when he responded that Matisse was

an artist of the Fauves (pronounced Fav-a) movement and I called out, "No. My Fav-a is the one who beat me."

Anyhow, I didn't like making clay ashtrays and I definitely had no desire to master the poopie-heart.

As we approached the counter, Kwab was the first one called to his corresponding customs officer. To my surprise Kwabena Abdul Hussein Davis went right through with very few questions and absolutely no problems. Then it was my turn. I stepped forward to my designated customs agent. He was a young man who obviously took his job very seriously. First he asked me why I was coming to London and I nervously replied, "Sightseeing."

He then asked me what it was that I planned to see. Simple question right? Still groggy I went blank and I replied, "All the stuff there is to see in London."

This was not a good answer and not any of the many answers he probably would have accepted. He then shot off a random array of twenty questions which basically included the results of my kindergarten report card and just how deeply I could handle a cavity search by Arsenio Hall. Once I finally passed through customs I looked down the isle to find Mike still tied up as well. Mike had a similar experience except by the end of his exam he got Arsenio's phone number tattooed on his lower back.

Just as I thought I was free and clear I was nearly gang tackled by a team of customs officers. They continued to question me and finally asked me about my trip to Jamaica. A woman agent grilled me, "When were you there, who did you meet, what was your purpose?"

I was dumbfounded as to why until they reached down to my suitcase and pulled on the name tag attached to my case. It happened to say Jamaica on the backside. A word of advice: never keep name tags from vacationing countries that have a reputation for specialized green grass. After giving the officers a thirty second marijuana free briefing on my past Jamaican trip they allowed me to move down the ramp and into the Heathrow tube station.

For those who don't know, London refers to their metro or

subway as the tube. This name refers to the tunnels that the tube travels through as well as referring to what we call railings. You hold onto the tubes or railings when you are inside of the tube car. Confused yet? Each line has a particular color and the internal tubes or rails are also that color. It would be quite simple to call each line by the corresponding color but using names such as the red line, the yellow line or the blue line, would be much too easy for London. Instead each line was named after something local such as the names Piccadilly, District and Circle. Never mind the fact that the lines like Bakerloo and Waterloo tend to get a little confusing for the outside traveler. Try to guess which of the following lines will take you downtown: Central, District, or Metropolitan. The correct answer is none.

Moving on we looked towards Mike and his linguistic skills to interpret the English of the attendant who stood nearby giving tube instructions to passing travelers. I am pretty sure Heathrow management intentionally hired the thickest British accent available and deliberately designated this man to greet Americans. After five minutes of interpretation we had hopefully understood that we needed to take the Piccadilly line to Earl's court. The attendant also noted that we should not take the Baron, the Queen, the Princes, the Duke or the King's court. We traveled along in the tube listening to the overhead recording announcement that has become famous to the tourists and locals of London alike. In a lovely English accent, the kind female pre-recorded voice announces "Please mind the gap" as the tube comes to each stop.

This is the polite way that the English say, "Hey dumb ass, don't fall in the hole when you get off the train."

At Earl's court we transferred with the assistance of several kind locals. We were now on the District line towards Edgeware road. It would take us to our stop, Bayswater. As we exited the train, I turned to Mike and said, "Hey dumb ass, don't fall in the hole when you get off the train."

23

THE SINKINAL

Bayswater is an area of central London off of the Northwest corner of Hyde Park. For London it is a fairly easy neighborhood to find. After finding our way out of the tube station we managed to come within one block of our hostel. We also managed to miss it and walked about ten more blocks before we came back. We proceeded to once again walk within one block of our hostel and nearly missed it twice. Fortunately with the help of another foreigner we joyously stumbled into the reception desk of The Hostel 63, our booked hotel. A young man working the desk informed us that even though we had a reservation, there were no available rooms for our reservation. I thought that was the reason we made a reservation, so that a room would be reserved. Fortunately they were kind enough to have booked us just down the street in the nearby penitentiary. I mean they booked us in a nearby hostel, which was just three more blocks away.

We rolled our suitcases a little further down the cobblestone road until we reached cell block 22. That is the West 22 Hotel. None of us had ever experienced a hostel in the days of our youth. We were curious to try one while we were here in London. After entering the building I suddenly realized that I had stayed in a hostel. I lived in one that was called Westland Gardens and I lived there for three of my college years. In fact, if you ever want the European hostel experience, Westland Gardens is right outside of UMBC. The paint selection and cracking asbestos walls looked almost identical. The architect who designed the inside of this place must have been banished from London and tossed directly onto the boat headed for row home construction in the new world. As we creaked up the three flights of stairs you could catch the pungent scent of feces as you passed each shared rest room. If you were lucky enough the scent would soon be overtaken by the body odor of the unwashed European traveler. We reached the top and entered room thirty three. We quickly picked our bunks and affectionately began to refer to the West 22 Hotel simply as "Jessup." Although none of us had actually been to Jessup, the nearby penitentiary back in Maryland, we agreed that this must be one step away. All the West 22 Hotel needed was a few final touches and it would surely match the comfort of Jessup State Pen.

The West 22 had the potential of Jessup but could have been better if it had air conditioning, orange jumpsuits, and a four hundred pound male masseuse named Cindy. For the record I never met a male masseuse named Cindy. The place was hot and stale. It smelled like the thick coats of lead paint that lined the walls and the only cooling system was a trash can which was propped to keep the window open. The mattresses were old and sagging, the bunks rickety and wobbly, and the comforters old and pungent. I'm pretty sure I had donated these same comforters to the local animal rescue twenty years ago. The centerpiece of the room was the single sink which has served generations of travelers as a wash basin and urinal. All this for a mere two hundred dollars a night; London is such a bargain. On a side note, such foul surroundings and the sink centerpiece did contribute to a few laughs.

The "Kwab Toothbrush Incident." occurred the following day when Kwab was preparing to brush his teeth. He gingerly had the non-brush end of his toothbrush hanging from his mouth when it slipped and landed into the "Sinkinal." Kwab let out a loud holler that writhed in distress and pain. I nearly rolled out of my bunk with laughter as the toothbrush almost appeared to be in slow motion as it landed with a clank and bounced into the sink. Exposure to this sink was far worse than anything imaginable. Even the many college pranks which often involved a toothbrush, a camera and odd locations did not seem quite as foul. Some of my former roommates have received a picture of their toothbrush posing in an odd location such as a toilet.

For those who never played toothbrush games I'll explain. It requires three things; a friend's toothbrush, a friend's camera, and a good degree of immaturity. You simply pose the toothbrush in a nice location for a photo shoot. You could pick the freezer or a mousetrap or even the toilet. Sometimes it's fun to use some cake icing to decorate the toothbrush with eyes and a smiling mouth. It gives the brush some character. Perhaps you should dress the toothbrush up as well. Tin foil works well as a toothbrush space suit for a Martian themed photo shoot that could be filmed in the sandy desert of a cat box. Once the toothbrush is dressed and situated you can use the toothbrush owner's camera to take one or two model shots. It's best if you have a disposal camera. You don't want to take a large number of shots. Too many shots might make the camera owner suspicious. Make sure you clean off any toothbrush decorations and put it back where you found it. Eventually the owner develops their film and they discover a lovely pictorial surprise.

I'm not sure what happened to Kwab's toothbrush after the swan dive in the "Sinkinal." Being new and in excellent condition I imagine a hostel traveler may have pulled it from its rightful spot within the hall trashcan. I have a feeling that some of the other travelers staying in the nearby rooms were quite capable of adopting a used toothbrush. I base this theory upon the man who was in charge of maintaining the hostel. His hygiene was worse than the average American household pet. Say what you want about Americans. We may be obnoxious, we may be fat, but at least we're clean. Exhausted from the long morning, we climbed into our bunks and were ready for some sleep. In case Cindy the masseuse came knocking we locked and barricaded the door and were all fast asleep in a chorus of snores.

24

KENSINGTON GARDENS

We woke a few hours later. It was around eight in the evening local time as we clamored out for some food and entertainment. We headed down to the local restaurant zone on Bayswater Road and picked a quaint open air pub called the Bayswater Inn. This was your typical English Pub adorned in brass and cherry wood. It would have been considered a classy bar in the states but was standard pub décor in England. We ordered a round of lagers rather than a round of ales. The lagers are served cold while the ales are served at room temperature. Hot and thirsty, the cold lager was the logical choice.

We sat down at a table and were hungry from the long day of travel. I ordered traditional fish and chips. They looked, smelled and tasted amazing! The large pieces of fried fish were breaded with a very light flavorful batter. Mike ordered the barbequed chicken special of the day. He had no complaints, but he rarely ever does. Kwab must have been feeling adventurous for his first English pub meal because he ordered up... drum roll please... a hamburger. With the arrival of our food Kwab requested matches from the bartender. He doesn't smoke but wanted to add to his eclectic but trendy matchbook collection. It was not meant to be. London was another great smoke free environment but not a good hunting ground for matchbook enthusiasts. We watched the people walk by in the living scene of main street London as we finished our first meal in a London pub. There appeared to be a large number of females compared to males and many of the people were dressed as young professionals or tourists. Cars whizzed by and were not afraid to use their horns. They stopped only for the flashing yellow light. These lights are set up all over London and allow time for the pedestrians to get back and forth across the high flow of cars, taxi's and delivery vehicles.

After taking in the scenery from the widow of our pub, I suggested taking a stroll though Hyde Park before heading back to Jessup. It was a good time to work up a sweat before showering and preparing for our first night out on the town. Feeling rested and full of pub food Kwab and Mike both agreed to join me. We headed three blocks south towards the northwest gate and entrance to Kensington Park. I had a good idea of the immensity of these parks but I was still overtaken by the sight of it. A vast opening of pathways, fields, trees, water and decorative statues stood as far as the eye could see. Kwab and Mike didn't have any idea of how much walking I had in mind. Both were currently in worse shape than me. I had been taking long runs in preparation of the trip. They were about as ready to cross this park as they were to swim the English Channel. I tried not to smirk when I thought about what was in store for them on our sightseeing hike tomorrow.

As we walked Kwab began to question how far across this immense park we were going to go. I only wanted a taste of the park and informed him that I didn't plan to walk too far. I didn't have this part of the trip scheduled on my itinerary. We were merely crossing the short north to south section of the park. This area runs along the east side of Kensington Palace, the palace where Princess Diana once lived. We were fortunate to have spectacular weather for London. It was such a relief from the previous forty days and nights of rain we had experienced back in Maryland. At home there had been a steady run of bad weather that was more European than American. Ironically we were now enjoying sunny clear skies here in London. The temperature was a perfect sixty-five degrees with a slight breeze and no humidity. We had come upon the summer solstice and it was still light outside even though it was nine in the evening. We strolled along the forty foot wide path. It was big enough to house the grandest processional of English royalty yet it was almost empty for Larry, Curly and me. We stopped to look at statues and took a long look at Kensington Palace. It occupied a large chunk of real estate off to our right. I found it odd that English royalty lived in a big house that was more or less inside of the park. Imagine Oprah Winfrey or Donald Trump living somewhere in Central Park where locals just strolled around their gates. This could never happen in the United States. Too many crazy stalkers would try hopping the fence every day.

We moved on passed the swan pond and stopped to take a look at the inhabitants. It turns out that Kwab has a particular fondness for swans and was close enough to get bit. He must have thought that these swans were tame enough for cameo pictures. I thought Kwab was going to start a friendly game of swan leapfrog. To my surprise there were hundreds of swans on the pond. I knew that swans stay in one location for life and live with one particular mate but I had no idea that they were such social creatures. My only knowledge of swans comes from a pair that floated around Columbia's Lake Elkhorn. Both were tagged with a collar which made each one look like it was tangled in a piece of trash. Eventually one of the two swans died and the Columbia Flier wrote an article about the life of a swan and how they mate for life. It included the sad details of a swan funeral. It was all very depressing. Thanks for that bit of joy Columbia Flier.

I was the only one carrying a camera so I got to be the lucky tourist who takes swan pictures for Kwab. He must be one of those people who takes their camera to the zoo and snaps pictures of the caged animals. I'm pretty sure I already have a few pictures of a swan, so why would I need another in 2009. Has the swan evolved that much in the last thirty years? As I pulled out my camera Kwab took note of the extremely large size of it. The first digital cameras were oversized much like the first cell phones. I tend to purchase cameras the same way I purchase sunglasses, cheap and easily replaceable. This particular camera that I had packed was my old, old digital camera, the predecessor to my two most recent cameras. Kwab took one look at the camera specifications and couldn't help but comment, "Damn, that thing's got two whole mega pixels."

Here I am wasting my mega pixels on his swans and he's complaining. I informed him that the next time he goes swan hunting he can be sure to pack his own camera for the impressive swan shots.

Knowing my habits well I had packed this particular piece of trash because I knew the camera was destined for destruction. I had foreseen it when I was packing for the trip. At that moment it was obvious to me there was no point in packing a new digital camera that would certainly end up smashed to bits. Over the years I've learned that following my intuition usually pays off. I don't claim to be a psychic but on one vacation I did display some impressive psychic ability. My traveling companions were amazed after I walked up to three complete strangers and correctly guessed the first names and the type of car each one drove. Considering the Jersey accent; Lisa, Heather and Donna obviously drove a Mustang, a Camaro and a Trans Am. Just as much as Jersey girls love muscle cars, it was obvious to me, that this camera would end up broken.

25

THE ALBERT MEMORIAL

Moving on we walked further into Hyde Park and finally came to the southern exit or entrance between the Albert Memorial and the Royal Albert Hall. The Albert Memorial is a breathtaking spire that rises above a statue of England's Prince Albert who died of typhoid in 1861. The memorial is over one hundred seventy five feet high and was built at the price of one hundred and twenty thousand pounds back in 1872. You don't want to know what that would cost in today's pound or U.S. dollars.

The element that is most interesting about this memorial is not Albert himself. He is just a man sitting upon a throne. The most interesting features are the four surrounding statues placed upon the four square columns at the corners of the memorial. Each one depicts the conquests of England that inspire a new perspective. England truly is the creator and sculptor of today's modern empire. It seems as though Americans, me included hold onto the false belief that America perpetuated the current western culture. In actuality England and Western Europe are the true architects of modern western culture and continue to be the model to this day. Contrary to what some Americans might think, Western culture does not refer to cowboys, Indians or to Hollywood. It spans far back before any American or Australian phenomenon. The "West" actually refers to the western half of Europe, not any place called Texas or California. When walking the four corners of this piece of 1872 art you can find evidence that defines the source of western culture.

When I looked at the four corners of the Albert Memorial it was quite evident that England is today's architect of western culture. The first corner depicts an elephant being ridden by an Asian woman and a handful of clinging Asian men. Each man is of different Asian origin and henceforth depicts the English domination over the entire continent of Asia. The next column held Africa. It was similar to the column of Asia as it obviously depicted the English domination over the regions of Africa. It was also built with the same majestic but eerie style although the woman was sitting upon a camel instead of an elephant. You could see different African origins in the faces of the sculpted men surrounding the camel. Column number three depicts the American conquest with a Native-American prize riding upon a buffalo. Finally, the European column had characters of various European origins gripping to a bull. Looking up at the memorial I got the feeling that I was staring at the alien trophy room from the movie "Predator 2." The memorial is vivid reminder of which country actually thrust its culture upon the world. The United States may have added some spice but the recipe for old world domination still comes directly from England.

After a short philosophical discussion about the big picture pertaining to the Albert Memorial we looked across the street to see the Royal Albert Hall. Mike is a huge enthusiast of English based music. He began to explain the many facts associated with the hall and the specific acts that had performed there. Prince Albert must have been a fun guy because he requested to have this Hall built as well as the construction of other recreational facilities for the use of the general public. Unfortunately he died just before it opened. If he had known that a flamboyant musician named Elton John would become the first singing knight he may have built a gladiator pit instead. Mike continued with his instructional lesson on the hall. The hall has held some big names over the years including: the Beatles, the Rolling Stones, Jimi Hendrix, Pink

Floyd, Led Zeppelin, the Who, CCR, ABBA, and James Taylor amongst others. Hopefully Prince Al was able to tune into a few of those shows from beyond the grave. We had walked for over an hour and were ready to find a spot for some refreshments. We decided to venture across the road to find food in the consulate district. Kwab had developed a habit of calling out "Hallo" using a poor version of an English accent. Each time he came across an attractive woman he bellowed the word "Hallo." As we walked Kwab called to some well dressed young ladies who were walking in front of us, "Hallo. Where y'all going?"

One of the young ladies answered back. She was headed to meet her friends. She noted that the place was not a good place for American tourists. As social leader of our motley group, Kwab continued to badger the woman until she gave him the name of the place. He suggested that we join them on their outing. She disagreed. I subtly reminded Kwab that the place was not good for American tourists. I looked towards Mike to see if there was any forthcoming reaction. I wanted to see if Mike's lesbian detector had gone off. He did not reply. Mike claims to have an astute ability to detect lesbians. After years of late night Cinemax his study of the subject far exceeds both Kwab and I combined. He is one of *those* guys and is purely fascinated by the phenomenon. Sarcastically I asked, "Why would they deny themselves of our overwhelmingly charming company?"

We moved across the street and came to The Spaghetti House. Italian food seemed like a safe bet as we were not in the mood for surprises. We agreed to test out the restaurant and walked in through the front door. We had a traditional Italian meal with traditional service. It was nice to have a waiter like back home in the states. The Bayswater Inn Pub did not have table service and we soon realized that English pubs do not have waiters or waitresses. Mike and I both ordered the Chicken Carbonara and Kwab ordered the... drum roll please... a hamburger. Just kidding, he had the hamburger ravioli. As it turned out The Spaghetti House is a small but popular Italian restaurant chain in London. After a

carafe of wine and some good pasta I suggested that we head
back to our hostel in order to shower and get ready for our
first night out in London. We crossed the street and took a
combination of tube lines back to Jessup. I am naturally a very
impatient person. I mentally noted the fact that it takes longer
to tube than it does to walk. The tubes seemingly run fairly
infrequent in the later hours of the evening. This makes the
taxis more attractive. Even so, the London tube was still better than any metro back in the states. The London transit system worked, but it was a far cry from the German, Austrian,
or Czech systems that I have experienced.

26

NIGHT ONE; LONDON

Once we arrived back at Jessup Mike and I grabbed our flip flop shower shoes and headed for the five foot shower room. Stooped over, we each grabbed a shower stall and used the dog-wash-like nozzles to take the most time efficient showers possible. People in Europe do not seem to enjoy their showers like we do in America. I base this opinion upon the body odor emanating from many Europeans and by the fact that most European showers are built to handle a dog no bigger than Benji. This fact continues to prove itself time and time again as I continue my travels through Europe. While traveling in the city of Prague I showered with nothing more than a hose while standing in a wash bucket. Interestingly, the shower bucket was located in a kitchen. Even more interesting is that I showered while the mother of the house cooked dinner and the kids ran around playing a game of tag. There was no room for shy Americans in Prague. This particular dog shower within the confines of Jessup was only slightly better.

I headed back down to our humble cell to catch up with Kwab. He had taken the first shift guarding our luggage and was preparing for his own shower adventure. Kwab had done a little exploring while Mike and I showered and managed to find the one "good shower" in Jessup. While I dressed myself in my finest duds I suggested that Mike do the same.

This was the capital city of London and it was Saturday night. Before heading outside to catch a ride downtown I suggested a few shots of Jagermeister. I wanted to take the edge off of what would surely be an exciting cab ride. To this day I have not been on a cab ride across a major city without praying for survival. I imagined that riding in a cab on the left hand side of the road wouldn't make me feel particularly safe. I've had too many wild cab rides on the right hand side of the road. Besides I did some research concerning the drink prices in London. I wisely packed a bottle of my favorite alcoholic liquor. I'm a big fan of Jagermeister and I remember reading reviews on the spirit when it first became popular back in the states. One review read, "Manly enough for the average man, but sweet and tasty enough for the average woman to drink." That description works for me. Red Bull has a similar allure.

We had originally planned to catch the tube before realizing that it was nearly midnight and would need to catch a cab. Unfortunately even on a Saturday night the tube doesn't run very late. A strategic move that I imagine helps boost the cab industry in London. We hopped into the first available cab and were on our way downtown to Leicester Square. Cabs in London are very unique and are a prominent symbol of the town as are the double decker buses. The cabs are also known as a hack. The black four door saloon cars are built by different car companies but all have the same distinguished design. They remind me of stretched out Volkswagen Bugs. After fifteen minutes of zipping along the circles of London we were stuck in a massive traffic jam. It engulfed the lights around Piccadilly Circus. We paid our driver, jumped out, and decided to simply walk through this famous area and into the hearts of Trafalgar and Leicester Squares. We took some pictures and followed the brightly lit streets. They led us into London's version of Times Square.

The walk through Leicester Square was a much nicer experience than my last walk through Times Square. Leicester square is closed to traffic. I just recently read that New York has taken the same approach for Times Square. That was likely an attempt to avoid the massive number of accidents between people and cars. The lights of Leicester Square were lit up with ads for movies and musicals. There were tens of theatres at every angle and in every alleyway. We looked towards the sound of a musical beat and followed it down to an area of clubs and bars. We enthusiastically walked up to the entrance of the first venue. The fast talking doorman offered a discounted cover for three such handsome young men. Hopefully this was not an alternative club. As we walked in I thought to myself, "If I see Sir Elton John being knighted I'm getting the hell out of here."

Most of the clubs were playing the electronic music favored by Elton's knights so who could tell which club might actually be "the round table."

We went in and ordered three lagers. They went down quickly in the hot club. The club had appeared large from the outside. We walked around to investigate the interior. It was actually no bigger than the average Baltimore City bar. The size and layout reminded me of the traditional layout of Looney's Pub in the downtown Baltimore neighborhood of Canton. The three of us grabbed a table and began people-watching while consuming more beer. Four pints later and the crowded room felt roomier. We couldn't talk or see beyond the loud bass thumping music and flash-lit dark environment. The scene became repetitive and we were ready to move to a better location. Already hand stamped we decided to go outside and roam around in the open square. The street had become crowded with patrons standing and mingling throughout the square. Looking around you could see droves of drunks walking from venue to venue. They were talking in groups or hanging out in front of the various fast-food joints. Here Kwab came across three drunken locals standing outside of the nearby Burger King and struck up a conversation.

I believe the conversation may have started with a game of Guess the Accent but they were obviously English. They informed Kwab that they were waiting for a cab to take them back to a college town just north of London. We were searching for "The It" place of London and they recommended something with a name like Octagon or Octopus. We never did find the particular club but it supposedly had eight levels of bars and dance floors. Continuing around the block we eventually ended up back to the same loud bar where we first began. Since we had already paid our entrance fee we considered going back into the bar. Entering a new venue at this time would run around twenty pounds or forty dollars. For obvious reasons we decided to stay put.

We moved upstairs to be close to the front window. It was a quieter and cooler area of the club. We sat down in the area set up as a lounge with couches and a coffee table. Earlier in the night I had noticed a young woman wearing an odd puffy dress. I thought that it surely must have something to do with the London fashion scene. Here she was upstairs, standing before us talking with several young men. Mike joined in the conversation and we soon found out that he was talking with a group of UMBC graduates traveling in London. I spoke up, "What are the odds?"

Apparently the puffy dress was something purchased at Arundel Mills Mall back in Maryland and had nothing to do with London fashion at all. We consumed a few more lagers, took in the scene and then decided to call it a night. It was somewhere around four o'clock in the morning locally and the long day had left us exhausted. We tumbled back through the square and then taxied back to Jessup. Our first full night of rest since arriving in London was well deserved. Throughout the night the sound of sinks faucets turning and room doors slamming filled the hostel. There is nothing quite like trying to sleep in a small room which contains three lager-filled snoring men. I popped a bed bug that was racing across my comforter and fell asleep.

27

PURSES TO MATCH THE LONDON TOWER

Sunday June 21st - I woke up feeling refreshed and ready to begin our big day of touring London. Even the stain from the smashed bed bug carcass was not going to slow me down. It was around noon and I headed out for some bottled water and beauty supplies that had been requested by Kwab. I found the needed water, washcloths and liquid soap at a nearby drug store and headed back to the hostel. Today was sightseeing day! I couldn't wait to get a jump on it. Mike and Kwab had finished dressing and we left Jessup to begin our journey. I was excited to finally get to experience the infamous city of London. Perhaps we would get locked away in the London Tower or ride the London Eye. There was so much to see and do. I had been watching London on the television and in the media for decades and would finally experience it for myself. The crew followed me towards the nearby tube station to get on our way. Before we got started, Kwab had to stop.

As we walked along the main street Queensway, Queenskwab veered off into a luggage shop to purchase his very first purse or "European Handbag." Since the beginning of our trip Kwab had become very jealous of Mike's lovely travel purse and was determined to get one of his own. I stood outside waiting on the sidewalk watching people bustle by while Kwab and Mike scanned over the collection of man purses. They were cleverly disguised as a small piece of

luggage but I wasn't fooled. Mike walked out and moved to
the shop next door to careen through a wall of poor humored
T-Shirts. They were covered with statements such as "I-Porn."
Apparently this was an attempt at humor referring to I-Pods.
It had a picture of an I-Pod with a suggestive sexual scene. I
just can't find the motivation to laugh at I-Pod humor. Mike
continually called to me from deep within the store, "Come
see this one. This one is you."

I stood quietly outside ignoring his requests. I couldn't
even imagine which one of those shirts was "me." It was like
walking with a teenage girlfriend on an Ocean City board-
walk. Finally Kwab reappeared and was ready to hike into
town. He was now in supermodel fashion. As we continued
down Queensway, Kwab noted his hunger and desire to have
an English breakfast. It was already noon when I informed
the diva that we should schedule it for tomorrow. I asked if
he was carrying any gum in his purse. He was. I wish our
High School football teammates could have been there to enjoy the scene.

We passed the Queensway Pub which had a chalkboard
sign advertising an English breakfast for less than eight pound.
With my current sightseeing ambitions, now was not the time
to eat, but I knew we would be back. It was time to go downtown! Now that Kwab was in full fashion and wearing his
new stylish green denim purse nothing could stop us. I led
the group as we headed into the tube station to catch our ride
to the London Tower. The Tower and the Tower Bridge lay on
the west end of central London. They are the furthest tourist points away from our Jessup location. As we moved along
passed various signs that noted "the west end" of London
Kwab began to sing the Pet Shop Boy song "West End Girls."
This song appeared to be stuck in his head. I continued to
hear him sing it at several points during our time in London.
I preferred this tune over the other songs stored on his MP3.
I often heard them as he sang along while plugged into his
headphones. I should have taken some video of Kwab singing lavish 80's tunes while wearing his purse with pride. I
looked back and caught a glimpse of the silent envy in Mike's

eye. He wanted a part of Kwab's music, accessories and style. Kwab looked so sheik with his new purse and hip songs. The three of us moved along on the Piccadilly train until we eventually arrived at the Tower Hill stop.

Tower Hill is where we would start our tour by first checking out the London Tower. This fortress and prison is one of London's biggest tourist attractions. But before we could get started again, we had to stop. Mike and Kwab required sustenance. They spotted a nearby hot dog truck and quickly began feeding upon hot dogs supplied by the street vendor. I momentary considered eating a foreign born hot dog. I too was starving but remembered a time in Cancun when my friend Sperka ate a Mexican hotdog. He subsequently vomited for two straight days. I'm sure the English dogs were more trustworthy than the Mexican dogs but I wasn't taking any chances. And besides, I was holding out for something better. I wanted something a little more authentic to London, and something without the word *dog* in the title. As they finished up I turned to take in the spectacular sight that thousands of surrounding tourists and I had come here to see. Mike and Kwab had just finished gulping their dogs and decided to join me in admiring the London Tower.

The London Tower is a fortress castle of ancient beauty. Looking down at the former moat, the bottom was now groomed with lush green grass. The grass was surely a better option than the smell of the old stagnant water that used to sit around the fortress walls. They used to keep the moat filled with water for protection and to keep it stocked with fish. The fish were used to feed the fortress occupants should they need to stay protected inside for any particular length of time. The fortress was originally constructed in 1078 by William the Conqueror. He built it to keep himself safe during tough times in England. I imagine that anyone with the word Conqueror in his title had made a few enemies. It also served as a nice place for King Henry VIII to execute mistresses and wives. Henry was a lady killer but was never bestowed with a menacing title like William the Conqueror. Henry must have been a much nicer fellow than William. As you walk along the tower you can read about the history of the tower and see the updates that were created by the many kings and queens over the centuries.

As we pushed our way through the tour groups we came to the south side of the tower. Here it opens into a promenade which houses food and beverage vendors. I particularly liked the high class vendors between the riverfront and the fortress. Here you could have raw oysters and wine while standing in the sun. This might come in handy if you would rather die from dysentery than a good old fashioned tower beheading. We chose not to stand in the two hour lines for the tour and moved across the Tower Bridge. The Tower Bridge is apparently full of significant importance as Mike blurted out random but unproven facts. Mike has always enjoyed theorizing the facts he remembers from A&E and the other cable channels that are cast upon his alter. The problem is that his partial memories were usually distorted by a bowl of Captain Crunch cereal. His brother John would always say to him, "Michael, food is your God, and the TV is your alter."

Mike takes distorted information and turns it into random facts. I've learned over the years not to repeat these "facts" as I have often ended up looking like a complete jack ass. Anyhow, it didn't matter to me if the section on the top of the bridge was also a prison. I just agreed and moved along. By the way; the tower on the bridge had never been used as a prison. The towers were used for watchmen to prepare the draw bridge at the arrival of an approaching boat.

28

FREE ADVICE ACROSS THE THAMES

Swimming through the mass of tourists on the bridge we crossed to the south side of the Thames River with curiosity and intrigue. Where do we go from here? We stopped for a moment to watch a group of local youths jumping skateboards from a ten foot staircase. They were fairly talented and were filming each other as they jumped. Sometimes they landed on the board and other times they did not.

We moved west across the street and followed a concrete path along a beautiful and quaint cathedral. I walked ahead as Mike and Kwab took pictures of some passing double-decker buses. The church was encompassed with a black iron rod fence. It was the same type fence that stood before every park, church or building in London. A middle eastern man seated nearby spoke up. He pointed out the trefoil which adorns every London church and nearly every thing including the British pound. The trefoils are added as an architectural design. Their intent is to show allegiance to the crown. The man also noted that it was meant to be a reminder to England and to the world. The trefoil was the symbol that stood for the dominance of the crown. Great Britain's reluctance to convert to the euro is evidence of this theory. The British pound also happens to be an ongoing tribute to the crown.

Mike and Kwab had caught up after taking some pictures. We followed the church fence around the building until we found the Queens Walk. This is a well designed modern walkway such as the one in front of Baltimore's inner harbor. The concrete path follows the south side of the Thames River. It was Sunday and the weather was amazing. London was alive and bound to have all kinds of sights to see along the crowded Queens walk. We moved onward to see what we could find.

We first entered into an open area on the Thames River which contained large steps for people to stop, rest, and enjoy the scenery. There were many people sitting and lying about. One man was wearing a sign that said "Free Advice. Not qualified for legal or medical." The true locals of London seemed very helpful and friendly thus far. The other ninety percent of London locals were tourists or immigrants. They were also very nice although not as helpful. Kwab walked up to the man and said his resounding, "Hallo." Kwab jumped all over the free advice scenario and took this opportunity to ask the guy a smart ass question. At first the question confused the man, but he soon managed a smart ass answer in return. I moved on and walked ahead at this point. I was not interested to hear Kwab banter with the strange man wearing a sign. I'm not sure how the conversation went. The average conversation between two men usually goes in one of three directions. I did not feel like hearing about sex, food, or feces.

Why is it that men seem to talk about sex, food or feces? Feces being the most prominent of the three. Gas also fits under the category of feces. On each of my all-male vacations feces was the most commonly discussed topic. Earlier Mike had mentioned that he recently and "supposedly" read an entire book dedicated to feces. It seemed as though he often refers to this book whenever I'm in the middle of a meal. Some sort of comment always seems to pop out like, "All that fiber will surely give you goat pellets." I imagine Mike's poop book is laid out like some sort of recipe manual for colon function. Perhaps it has a horoscope chapter which describes the most common turd associated with your sign. I'd hate to be the

Taurus in that scenario. Anyhow I just hope that Mike's poop book isn't a pop up or a scratch and sniff. Kwab caught up after he emerged from his conversation. Hopefully it went in a different direction than I presumed. Thus far, in my re-acquaintance with Kwab I noticed that he was far more interested in the topic of sex. Sex seemed to be on his mind more than the other two topics combined. As I walked I tried not to think about the sex pointers that the "Free Advice Guy" had probably given to Kwab. Kwab had been kind to give me sexual pointers along the trip although I'll probably never use any of them. I kept joking with him using fictitious sexual terms from the movie "Duece Bigelow." I asked him if he knew how to perform a *Filthy Ramirez*. Kwab is partially def in one ear. He didn't hear me or he tuned me out.

29

FOOD GAMES WITH A SUNDAY ROAST

As we walked along the decorative English pubs, Kwab and Mike stopped to take a photo of the sights across the Thames River. Often Kwab would run in and out of each pub to see if he could track down a matchbook for his collection. As Mike and I waited I looked around and noticed a pub sign announcing the "Traditional Sunday Roast." The description of an English traditional Sunday roast was entertaining my curiosity and my hunger just the same. Currently I was hot dog free, and starving. After Mike and Kwab read the meal description on the wall, they were starving too. Taking a break for the Sunday roast wasn't a hard sell. We headed into the pub. Mike and I first made an attempt to order the lamb roast but unfortunately they were all out of sheep. All they had were chickens. Hungry and already sitting at a table with a round of lagers, we ordered the chicken. Kwab ordered up the... drum roll please... a hamburger.

Kwab's burger came out with amazing speed and looked thick and juicy. He removed the lettuce. He didn't want to risk eating anything too healthy and I was all over it. Once Kwab gave me the go ahead, I devoured the poor scrap of lettuce in one gulp. You'd never know it by looking at me but I can't go long without some greens, veggies or non-meat type food. I took the liberty of ordering side salads for Mike and me. They were gone in less time than it took to prepare them.

After eating nothing but standard pub fare and the previous Icelandic food nightmare, the salads were a welcome site. In a foreign country you never know what you're going to get when ordering salad. In Germany, Austria and the Eastern European countries a salad is often some lunch meat and an olive.

The roasts came out after twenty minutes of a fat man's eternity and the food looked as if it was delivered directly from heaven. Mike and I tore into the roasts like a couple of mountain lions tearing into a ripe teen hiker. I looked up with a full mouth and managed to mumble to Kwab, "Killin' IT!" It was perhaps the best meal I have ever had in my life and I've had a few meals. No other meal could compare to the ten dollar meal that appeared and disappeared as quickly as it came. I looked up after scarfing down the roast and to my shock, Myers had won. His roast was gone first. As always I recognized this accomplishment and alluded to a future rematch.

Mike and I had always played games with food. It is probably an unhealthy habit, but fun just the same. Lunchmeat games, chicken soup flash dance, and other food sports invented by Mike have faded over the years. I was the champion of catching bologna in my mouth at over twenty seven feet but Mike was champion of almost every other game related to food. After eating the meal I expected him to bend over the table and suck up my leftover chicken skin with his hands behind his back. Mike would have had no problem swallowing it whole or donning it like a Hannibal Lecter skin mask. As we left I asked Kwab about his matchbook collection. Again he had walked out dejected and matchbook free. As we left the pub Kwab gave me the complete breakdown concerning the local smoking laws of London. He had been informed of them by the pub staff and continued to hear about them with each matchbook request. It was like being on a fraternity scavenger hunt trying to get a sorority nipple print in a jar of peanut butter.

30

HISTORY ON THE QUEENS WALK

Moving on, we had finished the meal and we were strolling down the Queens Walk. Many interesting sights were just around the bend and the first that appeared was an old ship docked along the Queens Walk. At first glance I thought the ship called "The Golden Hindle" was a fake pirate boat like the kind used in Caribbean tourist areas. I was expecting to see these types of boats when we reached the Greek Isles and was surprised to see one here. These types of pirate re-enactment ships market cheap rum punch and usually take vacationers on a lazy boat ride for thirty dollars per person. But I was wrong. This ship turned out to be the restored real deal.

The Golden Hindle was actually the boat that Sir Francis Drake used to captain and seek out new places of discovery. For his efforts he was knighted in the year 1581. He must have been eating from the street vendors of the London Tower because he eventually died of dysentery in 1596. But before his death he had a good run in battle as an English Admiral. He beat the Spaniards so badly that they named him Francis the Dragon. The accomplishments that propelled him to Admiral were his discoveries for mother England. He certainly deserved to be knighted for being the first known person to circle the entire globe. At least the King thought he was worthy of knighthood.

I thought about the positive benefits of discovering new

places. Floating around on a dingy in forty foot swells sounds like a job for someone else. I'd rather assign that duty to world sweetheart Kim Jong Il. The mere fact that early explorers crossed the Atlantic in oversized row boats and somehow survived is simply amazing. This guy went around the entire world on this tiny ship and I require a barf bag to get across the Thames River.

We continued passed another spectacular waterfront pub called The Anchor. Kwab went inside to search for his allusive London Pub matchbook. Again he was thwarted by the bartender who reminded him that you cannot smoke in London Pubs. Kwab was beginning to realize and resent this fact. The next attraction featured a covered dock which was built to house the China Clippers that once sailed in from the Orient. The building was an amazing piece of architecture which today would match the beauty of the clippers themselves. The covered dock appears pristine today but I do not believe the original dock looked anywhere near as nice. We came upon a tunnel underpass that leads under the overhead street and bridge. As we walked along the water and through the tunnel we passed the first of a number of street musicians. This particular group played classical music with strings and brass that echoed a nice reverb though out the underpass.

Next we passed Shakespeare's Globe Theater which continues to hold performances in the round as it did in the times of Shakespeare. I felt a burst of excitement as the lessons from middle school English class were finally paying off. I said to myself, "Here stands the original Globe Theater."

Mike sometimes likes to squash my enthusiasm. He kindly informed me, "The original Globe is in the town of Stratford On Avon."

I was successfully deflated. My mind drifted back to the middle school matching exams. I remembered matching William Shakespeare with Stratford on Avon. Upon further reflection I assumed he was right and quietly walked off. Mike's distorted A&E facts had won this time. After all I had always counted on Mike to be my personal living, breathing, walking memory.

Consequently when I arrived back home I did some research and found that this building was indeed the original Globe. It was and is located in London England along the banks of the Thames River. Although what I saw was not the actual original structure. I stood before the rebuilt version of the original structure as the original had burned down back in 1613. It is refreshing to know that I really did see the actual Globe Theater and that Stratford on Avon is simply the city where Shakespeare was born. Strike two on Mike's A&E fact check. I should never forget that although Mike has a better memory, my English grades were *always* better than his.

31

LIFE ON THE QUEENS WALK

We continued down the Queens Walk looking across the Thames. Along the gothic spires of English Parliament stands St. Peters Cathedral. Big Ben was also in the distance. I glanced over at the foot bridge that was built to cross the Thames River towards St. Peters Cathedral. It was fun to see the bridge that was digitally destroyed in the latest Harry Potter movie.

Thinking back to movie scenes set in London I suddenly realized one more benefit to touring London. I always found it interesting to watch action films that are depicted in familiar settings. Now I would be able to recognize all the London scenes in the countless number of movies filmed in London. I could cross this infamous London movie set off of my list. I'm sure I've seen St. Peters in many a movie and never even realized it. The dome of the cathedral looks so similar to that of the United States state capitals. I wondered how many James Bond movies I could now watch and say, "I've been there."

In fact I just watched the movie "The Golden Compass" and recognized their version of St. Peters in the background. I wonder if the Illuninati planned that cameo as well.

We stopped to take a few more pictures as we walked along the side of a historical battleship. Mike again went into his A&E information mode and I trudged on ahead of the group. Big gray boats do nothing for me. Mike caught up and force fed me additional information, "The HMS Belfast was Europe's largest and most effective cruiser from World War II."

I replied, "It was probably the boat that brought the prisoners to the top of the Tower Bridge." We continued to the next underpass and listened to the sounds of a new age style group playing brass and organ. They were playing a version of a song called Santorini by a musician named Yanni. I recognized the song immediately. Yanni is a short eclectic Greek who is also a new age music artist. I am a fan, and this, was a foreshadowing meant for me. In a few short days we would sail around the Greek island of Santorini.

As we popped out from the underpass we came upon England's National Theater. It is a modern looking building which had a display of oversized grass covered furniture displayed upon a faux lawn. Locals and tourists alike were sitting on the furniture that looked like a green version of the Big Comfy Couch. Just then a man riding a big wheel English bike zipped by and nearly ran over a kid and group of pigeons. These high-wheel bikes look extremely uncomfortable. Mounting one must be like taking a high jump onto the horn of a bull. I wonder what possess someone to say, "I've got to have one of those."

It makes about as much sense to me as the shiny blue gazing balls that some Americans display on their front lawns.

Moving on we walked through a collection of street artists and another musician. He was set up around an area of decorated trees. The musician was playing some Pink Floyd rifts on his solo electric guitar. The grove of trees looked as if they were straight out of a Dr. Suess book. In a display of art they were wrapped with red and white polka dots. Mike questioned this odd sight. I could only imagine who came up with this idea. They were most likely the result of a stoner who said, "Dude, what if, like, all the trees, had polka dots?" I imagine some rich stoner must have given him the funding.

Around the next bend was a low laying area along the walkway. It was designated specifically for graffiti and skateboards. As we walked by, one skater was doing daffies or whatever it is that skaters do. Tired of skaters we continued to walk and looked across the river at the spires of the house of parliament. We all took a few pictures. Gothic architecture must be one of the most difficult to create considering the detail involved in its construction. How does someone without modern equipment build the tall thin spires which reach high above the bulk of the structure? I'll let Mike figure that out.

We turned the corner and watched as numerous street performers entertained the watching audience. The first one along the promenade was very odd. He was a robot-mime dressed as a "Bobbi" or London police officer. It was wearing a white Tutu. He did his rythmatic robot gyrations for the perplexed audience. We decided that it was a good idea to avoid eye contact and we picked up our pace. More activities lined the Thames such as a giant blow up slide and a moon bounce. They were available to entertain the kiddies for a few pounds.

Next we came to the river front university where students and tourists had strewn themselves across the grassy quad area. I always find this to be an odd sight. In European cities people just grab a spot on a blanket and lay a few feet from one another. I guess it is par for the course in a city that tends to see a lot of rain. In America you only see people crammed together on blankets at the beach or on the 4th of July. On the side of the University quad was an amphitheater called the Underbelly. It looked like the underside of a cow with an utter and legs sticking out of the roof. It was an odd feature for downtown London. I thought it was more bizarre than the gnome gardens of Oktoberfest. But perhaps the Underbelly is a fitting temporary music venue for the adjacent college quad. The Underbelly doesn't match up well across from classy Big Ben. This brings us to the big topic of discussion amongst the locals of London, The London Eye.

Many of the locals do not like the four hundred and fifty foot high ferris-wheel structure called the London Eye. It is situated across the Thames River from Big Ben. I agree with some of the complaints. It does stand out a bit and doesn't exactly fit in, but I can see how it was approved for construction.

It is top notch as far as ferris-wheels go. It contains around one hundred enclosed capsules that rotate so slowly that you can hardly notice with the naked eye. It takes a solid hour for The Eye to circle from start to finish. I think it is a great way to see the entire city of London from the sky. It slowly rotates to give patrons a chance to see in every direction. It reaches heights higher than Big Ben and the other major points of interest. Unfortunately for me it was a gorgeous Sunday and the line was outrageously long. Not to mention the fact that Kwab and Mike both have a fear of heights. Neither were willing to wait with me so I skipped over the London Eye.

Concerning the hot topic of the London Eye I feel that The Eye fits in with the architectural layout along the River Thames. The architectural theme of central London holds a balance between old and new. The north side has the classic historical structures like Westminster Abby, Big Ben, St. Peters, Parliament and The Tower of London. While mirrored across the Thames River on the south shore is a selection of modern architecture buildings. These include the covered pier, the National Theatre, the University and the London Eye. Throw in the Ripley's Believe It or Not building called The Dungeon Fright House and you have Central London today. The old and new were separated by a river but joined by it just the same.

32

BIG BEN, THE ABBY, &
BUCKINGHAM PALACE

Moving north we crossed back over the Thames River leaving
the new and returning to the old. We looked up at Big Ben
and Westminster Abby as we walked. Standing in front of Big
Ben, Kwab ordered his first waffle with the works. The waffle
is a dessert topped with ice cream, whipped cream, and syrup.
I continued to refer to it as a chicken waffle in reference to the
movie Deuce Bigalow: European Gigolo. Kwab would have
fit the Eddie Griffin character named T.J. The chicken waffle
does exist but this was not one of them. As Kwab devoured
his chicken waffle Big Ben rang six times reflecting the current
London time. It's interesting to note that the Prime Meridian
or primary time zone runs directly through London. In other
words, every day starts and ends in London. We had now
walked more than half the distance back to Jessup. Moving
on we wandered near a statue of Oliver Cromwell. Mike gave
his A&E breakdown on this man who was hero of England,
yet demon to Ireland. Apparently, Cromwell had spent a
good part of his life dissolving parliament in Ireland. Then
he proceeded to slaughter Catholics in order to perpetuate his
Protestant faith. I assume this was the spark that lit the ongoing Irish religious feud that still carries on to this day. Kwab
and Mike took pictures for their scrapbooks. Looking at the
statue was enough Oliver Cromwell for me. Like a carrier pi-

geon I was homing in on Jessup. I continued east in order to swing by Buckingham Palace and visit the royalty that lives within.

Kwab asked for directions from a friendly local and we tracked back towards Westminster Abby. Apparently I should have zigged towards the Abby when I zagged toward Oliver Cromwell. I convinced Clark and Sacagawea (guess which purse wearer is Sacagawea) to follow me on a shortcut through the Abby. It was amazingly beautiful inside the Abby and we soon came across the Abby shops. They were obviously meant for men of the cloth and not for poorly clothed men such as ourselves. We passed by a shop that sells the latest in bishop wear. I commented on how well we would all look adorned with high hats. Little did I know that Kwab would take this seriously and purchase two hats in the near future? We cut around a gated entrance and into an open courtyard where some pre-teen boys were kicking around a football. I commented here as well, but it was tasteless as you might imagine. I'll just leave the priest comments up to your imagination. It looked as if we were going to be trapped in the courtyard with the boys but we managed to find a section of open fence to get back outside. We were now free from the Abby and back with the London scoundrels where we belonged.

We came to the main thoroughfare and crossed over into St. James Park where the park map was being examined by a few other confused tourists. Following suit we proceeded through the park towards Buckingham Palace. The first interesting scene was a father playing cricket in the park with his two sons. His wife watched from a nearby blanket. It reminded me of an English version of a Norman Rockwell painting. The father was pitching the ball and the oldest son was at bat. The younger of the two boys was playing catcher. As the father pitched the ball the boy continued to swing and miss. Walking passed I thought to myself, "The cricket big league is a long way off kid."

As we continued to walk I tried to convince Kwab and Mike to cross a pond bridge and go deeper into the park. I wanted to see Buckingham palace from a grand distance. I was out-

voted. After the long walk Kwab and Mike were more interested in the most direct route to the palace. I walked along
the straight path as Kwab and Mike stopped at a park vendor
to pick up some sort of vendor product. I was far ahead and
eventually waited near an unused bike rack. They soon approached and together we walked towards the circle before
Buckingham Palace. Mike explained to me, Kwab or perhaps
some stranger that the flags around the Palace were pinned
down because the Queen was currently home. This was yet
again another unproven A&E fact that Mike seemed to think
was accurate. I highly doubted his information but I really
had no idea. I did know that it was better to hold my forked
tongue than argue with Mike. It was only day two of our ten
day trip and I didn't want to hurt his feelings.

Mike's a bit sensitive for an oversized linebacker. When he
gets upset I mockingly ask, "Did I hurt your *babsen* feelings?"

I learned this tool of degradation from his older brothers.
When my wife is upset she claims that I am unsupportive, de-
grading and abusive. I affectionately refer to this with the
term "uda." Sadistically, I sometimes enjoy being *uda* to Mike
but for now I was holding back. We took our pictures of the
palace and decided to go directly to the nearest tube station.
We wanted to get back to Jessup before sunset.

We came to the circle which encompasses Wellington Arch
and I took a picture. Kwab felt that circling around the arch
would be faster than the direct walk through the arch. We
could see the tube station through the arch. With as little uda
as possible I pointed this out to Kwab and walked straight
across to the tube. A few steps passed the road and we arrived
at the Knightsbridge tube station. Coincidentally it was the
same tube we used the previous night. We were all beat from
ten miles of walking. Even so, I could not bare the thought of
being underground on such a beautiful day. Remembering
last night's tube ride and the wait for tube transfers I bid farewell to Kwab and Mike. I decided to jog across Hyde Park.

33

THE RACE: MAN VS. MACHINE

I jogged down the main path through Hyde Park along a long pond known as the Serpentine. It was a beautiful Sunday evening and the park was alive. I could not believe the immense population of park enthusiasts. I watched traditional roller skaters as well as in-line skaters utilize this popular area of the park. First I saw a group of men using a high jump bar to test their ability to jump with their in-line skates. I could think of better ways to pass my time, but it was fun to watch them. They managed three feet of clearance from the ground and raised the bar about another half foot. A dare devil attempting the three and a half foot jump failed; but he rose unscathed.

As I continued down the path I came across another group of skaters who were skate-dancing. This must be a European thing; such as with men carrying purses. It was odd, but interesting to watch. Some were roller-dancing while others cheered. A boom-box was lying on the curb and played music as the dancers were having a good time. One skate-dancer reminded me of an odd Mazda car commercial. In the commercial a girl moved around dancing inside of a Mazda while her friend drove the car. I can't imagine the commercial sold many cars. But comedian Dave Chapel did a great spoof to make fun of the odd commercial. I continued to zoom, zoom, zoom along.

I was determined to beat Mike and Kwab back to Jessup, not only for bragger rights, but to get the good shower. I imagined myself as John Henry, the legend who dug a train tunnel through the side of a mountain by hand. He completed his tunnel faster than his competition, the steam shovel. At the end of the story John Henry died, but hopefully I would not. I cruised to the top of the park passing a children's Peter Pan Park and then cut passed some beautiful park houses. They sat along Princess Diana Walk and looked like the inspiration for a Thomas Kinkade painting. I was in a section of park where Hyde Park meets Kensington Gardens. This area is dedicated to the late Princess Diana.

A cottage made of old carved stone blocks was the centerpiece of the Princess Diana Walk. The blocks were neatly arranged under the steep peak of the shingle rooftop. English Ivy grew on the sides of the home and a garden of bright colorful flowers surrounded the cottage. The gardens were separated by an old cobblestone path that led to the front door. Small sculptures and a stone bird bath accented the flowering gardens. I walked beyond the lovely home and exited the park onto Bayswater Road. The road followed east towards my Queensway neighborhood. As I walked the sidewalk I spied an interesting pub called The Swan. It had a large amount of outdoor seating. It reminded me of Oktoberfest and appeared very inviting. Perhaps John Henry would be alive today if he had taken a beer break.

34

PARIS NEXT YEAR

I arrived at Jessup tired from walking, touring and jogging. The good shower was empty and ready for the taking. I climbed the three flights of steps to our room and attempted to open the door. It was still locked. Mike and Kwab had not yet returned. I trudged back down the stairs to get a spare key from the desk. Begrudgingly, I once again hauled myself back up to unlock the door. The lobby attendant insisted that I return the key immediately so again I repeated my stair exercises. I was exhausted but wanted to prepare for a night on the town. After a shower I took a short trip to the store to buy some water and came back to wait for Mike and Kwab. Another half hour passed and they had not returned. To kill time I moved to a spot in front of the hostel to enjoy the cool weather and people watch. I had time to reflect and it felt odd to be alone in a foreign country. It was the first time I had ever felt lonely in another country. A few moments later my travel companions returned. I questioned their delay and they blamed it on shopping. I imagine they had a difficult time finding tampons small enough to fit their manly purses. They went into Jessup, freshened up, and we headed out for dinner. I suggested the pub I had passed earlier called The Swan. It took a minute to convince them of the walk. It would not be *too* far.

We shuffled down Queensway to Bayswater road until we

reached my chosen pub, The Swan. All of the tables were occupied but there was a spot available with two eloquent looking middle aged women. Kwab asked if we could join them and they approved. Mike and Kwab sat down while I went into the pub for some lagers and menus. The inside was small and cramped. Service was slow. The lagers were cold and available for our drinking pleasure but the kitchen had just closed at nine. It was Sunday. Unfortunately this meant that the kitchen closed early and that we were not staying for dinner. I grabbed the lagers and carried them out to Mike and Kwab.

I brought the beers and sat down at the shared table. Kwab and Mike were sitting with an older Asian-American woman and her Latino-American traveling companion. We chatted about London and about traveling through Europe. They had been traveling for some time and really loved Paris. The Latino woman went into the details of her trip to Paris. She could not say enough about the wonderful food available in the city famous for exquisite cuisine. My eldest son Elo had similar comments pertaining to Paris. He spent most of his military leave in Paris, partially for the food. Kwab commented on his desire to see Paris as well. He attempted to persuade one of the ladies to take him along on her next trip. He was offering his boy toy services. She laughed skittishly and Kwab gave her the answer, "No, I'm serious. You, me, Paris, next year."

She awkwardly laughed again. Kwab threw another remark pertaining to the sincerity of his intentions. The ladies quickly finished their meals and said farewell. Perhaps Kwab really was the serial killer that Mike feared. Soon we finished our lagers and left The Swan to find some needed sustenance.

We were starving and decided that the main thoroughfare through Bayswater would be our best chance for some late night food. A man holding up an Indian buffet sign stood along the sidewalk. We each silently weighed the possibility. We walked further down Queensway. A Thai restaurant was in the near distance. We stopped in and decided to try it out. The hostess informed us of an unknown wait time and we left.

We were too hungry for any questionable delays. Thinking back to the Indian buffet we wandered to where Mike first spotted the man with the sign. We saw the buffet sign and trudged down a staircase that led under a hotel. It was the entrance to the buffet. The spread of colorful food was decimated at the end of the day but there was no wait time.

The hostess waved us in and quickly ushered us to a table. It was obvious that she wanted us to stay. I don't imagine that they receive much business buried under a back street hotel. She directed us away from the near empty pans of food. Her desperate effort to recruit us was taken into account. She happened to be an attractive Middle Eastern woman and this was a consideration as well. The group consensus was to stay, enjoy the view, and eat. Kwab and Mike watched her every move. She was pretty; but also pretty slow. When I say she was slow, I mean she was MVA or motor vehicle administration slow. We sat and waited a few moments before I had to prompt her for the mystical tools used in restaurants. These items include drinks, silverware, plates, and napkins. I was shocked when she ordered the dishwasher to go shopping for napkins. I am not kidding. Anyhow there was enough food on the buffet and enough limited silverware to get the job done. So we quickly dug into the Indian cuisine. I found the owner and cook. He agreed to bring out more food. I should have received a discount for working as the temporary manager.

I have some experience with Indian dining and their selection was fairly good. The quality of the food was much like an Indian buffet back in the states but there was not as much variety. I had broken into an Indian sweat as the spices were sufficiently doing their job. Mike and Kwab commented on my sweat induction. The Indian food had obviously set me on fire. Due to the lack of napkins I had to take several restroom breaks. I would stick my face under the cold air hand blower. The lack of paper products in Europe is truly a huge pain in the ass. I'm surprised each bathroom stall doesn't have a machine to blow dry their assholes. Even so I was enjoying the spicy flavor and burn of the Indian food and my shirt served as a cloth napkin.

Kwab and I sat and ate while Mike informed us of his lesbian theory pertaining to the two middle aged ladies at the Swan. Kwab rolled his eyes. Mike was quite sure the two were traveling lesbians. He pointed out his keen ability to spot them. Kwab and I both laughed and protested but Mike seemed confident in his abilities. He continued on about his eye for lesbians. He thinks that any two or even three women sitting, eating, or breathing in the same proximity happen to be lesbians. I'm quite sure that Mike's lesbian spotting abilities would eventually come in handy. After listening to the reasons behind his lesbian accusation we walked back to Jessup full from the meal and full from Mike's bullshit. I never wanted to watch A&E again.

35

ENGLISH BREAKFAST

Monday June 22ⁿᵈ – We all awoke a little slow and a little stiff but ready to find Kwab an English breakfast. We got moving, got dressed and hustled down Queensway road to seek out a pub with the traditional morning meal of England. Out of several choices the Bayswater Inn Pub had the award winning advertisement for the infamous meal. This was the pub from our first day in London. The one where I had ate fish and chips. We entered, sat down and requested three orders of the English breakfast from a stout female bartender. She was currently in the middle of a long coughing session and appeared perturbed at our very presence. We sat down at a corner table and waited for our meal.

The English breakfast is an interesting combo of eggs overeasy, odd tasting sausage, bacon, (which is more like ham), cooked mushrooms (or tomatoes), toast and baked beans. Yes. Baked beans. Apparently the English are very fond of their baked beans. They have made their way into what is known as the classic English breakfast. This meal was conceived during the Industrial Revolution as a form of high calorie meal for a working class that actually had to perform physical labor. The locals say that the English working class went from digging mines to answering phones. This eventually resulted in the British obesity crisis. So what is America's obesity excuse? Mine is beer. Anyhow, the meal was OK at best. It was perhaps the worst pub meal thus far. As Kwab and Mike ate I pointed out another fact. In addition to the below average breakfast we would soon be hacking up a lung. I expected the sick waitress was willing to share her illness with our plate of food. Surely the swine flu had managed to cough its way into our drinks and meals. Feeling uneasy Kwab had finished eating. Mike of course had already emptied his plate and had once again won first prize in the speed eating competition.

After breakfast we decided to finish any London gift shopping before heading off on my next adventure. Mike took a peak into the local lingerie shop, pronounced, Ling-eR-E. Mike had a fondness for lingerie and wanted to see if he could find a lovely gown to match his purse. Mike went to browse in the local underwear store while Kwab and I headed into the local touristy junk gift shop next door. It was filled with crappy t-shirts, toy buses and hooligan wear. I thought deeply about what to bring back to my family. In the end I decided that no one on Earth needs any of this touristy London crap. Plus I didn't feel like stepping on a toy bus that my son left abandoned on the kitchen floor. I was quite content to wait until Greece before making the purchases I would haul around the world. Determined not to purchase one simple tourist item as a gift; it was easy to avoid purchasing shirts that say, "Check out this double-decker bus" with an arrow pointing downward.

Mike had finished his underwear shopping and joined us in the junk store. He was currently laughing at the double-decker bus T-shirt. His junk shopping was completed the day before while I was racing across Hyde Park. Kwab was at the register working on his street haggling skills. He tried to out hustle the middle-eastern salesman as he negotiated the price of his selected items. Kwab planned to purchase glass trinkets, various soccer paraphernalia and two new English hats. He did look sophisticated in his English cap and matching purse. The local bishops of Westminster Abby would have been envious. After the shopping spree with the girls had ended we dropped the gifts back on cell block thirty three and headed uptown.

The weather was a bit chillier this afternoon. It was over-
cast but the skies were still free of any rain. Mike claims to
have felt rain drops but I think they were a part of a fantasy
world he invented in the lingerie store. Considering the long
walk from yesterday I had to sell the new hike of the day.
I planned to walk to the Marble Arch on Bond Street, walk
through Oxford Circus and then walk down Regent Street.
That sounded like a lot of walking to Mike and Kwab. I assured them it was all downhill; and it was. Kwab rolled his
eyes. We started parallel to the north edge of Kensington
Gardens and Hyde Park and passed by The Swan Pub from
last night. Continuing east along Bayswater we soon reached
London's Marble Arch. The arch was once the entrance to
Buckingham Palace but was moved to Bond Street when
Queen Victoria enlarged the palace in 1851. This move was
the royal equivalent of moving a vase from a living room to
the dining room. It must have taken a boat load of pissed
off horses to get the job done. Other than a huge mantel it
is just an adorned piece of Italian architecture that had been
dropped into the middle of a London intersection. After touring many great London landmarks, we were not impressed.
Mike didn't even have an A&E story about the arch. I was
expecting to hear a story pertaining to the arch and the lost
city of Atlantis.

We continued down Oxford Street and worked our way
into Oxford Circus. There were no lion tamers or rope walk-
ers here, but this area certainly was a circus. One English
definition of a circus is an open circular place where several streets intersect. These areas include the Piccadilly and
Oxford circus as well as many others. This circus was just
like walking along any busy street in New York City. Mike
had developed a little bit of demophobia, or fear of crowds,
as we swam through the thick mass of people. I on the other
hand enjoy using the skill required to navigate a path through
wild herds of city humans. We moved down the street for a
few more blocks until Kwab pulled the emergency brake. We
had come upon another Chicken Waffle stand. Kwab ordered
the works with caramel syrup and ice cream. It looked pretty

good but I was focused on the task at hand. Food was not on my agenda. I wanted to check out the sights of this uptown zone and then move towards Leicester and Trafalgar Squares. Looking forward to relaxation in the famous squares I motivated the group to push forward.

Kwab finished his waffle and immediately dipped into a high end London fashion store. Mike joined him. I don't know why but maybe they wanted to take a look at more handbags while I waited along side the busy street. I felt like I was a child shopping with my mother. It could have been any day in Laurel, Maryland as she dashed into Fashion Bug while I stood outside on the sidewalk of an outdoor mall. Today's prices must have been high. Mike and Kwab had finished shopping in just a few seconds and we continued through the district. We had reached Regent Street and turned right to begin the southwest trek towards central London. Mike again stressed his phobia to the surrounding street crowd so we turned left to take a back alley that paralleled Regent Street. Mike's phobias tend to make him irritable so I was happy to take the detour. As we continued down the alley we passed several pubs where business men were dining and smoking at the outside tables.

I was looking at some business men having lunch when I came to the stark realization that the people of London drink a lot of ale, wine, and liquor. It was tough to get a descent soda, or iced tea in this town. Water was from the tap and the barkeep gives you a look of discontent if you even breathe the word. I was amazed that these people would be going back to work in a few minutes. They were sitting here schlepping down a bottle of sauvignon. Besides wine I saw a few empty beer glasses as well. They must be ready to head back to the office. It's no wonder America managed to win the revolutionary war. I will admit that I like this custom. I prefer English office etiquette to the strict American conduct codes. I've noticed that Russians and Germans don't have a problem with alcohol in the workplace either. One time I watched a group of Russians kill an entire bottle of vodka during a lunch break. Where did America go wrong? We continued down the alley and eventually popped into the Piccadilly Circus area. It was close to where we were going. We wanted to be in or near Leicester Square before we stopped for food and drinks. Our plan was to sit, relax and enjoy a few ales or lagers.

36

PRICE LIST COMPARISONS

As we entered the square we glanced at a Mexican restaurant menu posted along the sidewalk. Even though the items on the menu sounded appealing I still voted to eat English Pub food. After all I'd probably only be in England once and Columbia Maryland has over thirty Mexican restaurants. I saw some pubs in a side alley that led towards Chinatown. Mike is a big fan of Korean barbeque and also wanted to turn up the alley. Kwab didn't have an opinion and followed along. As we passed the first pub I took note of the prices listed on their menu. They were reasonable for London. England is very expensive for the average American. The U.S. dollar is only worth nearly half of the English pound. Even though a five pound burger sounded like a good price it would actually cost somewhere around ten dollars.

At the end of the alleyway, and near the entrance to Chinatown, there was a large, uniquely designed pub. It had caught my eye. I was immediately drawn by the sheer size of it. Keeping in mind the prices at the last pub, I wanted to see if the prices were similar. If they were the same, I planned to eat in the grandiose pub. I went into a massive entranceway and looked at the menu while Mike and Kwab jetted to my left. The prices were a bit higher. I saw no point in paying more money for the same food. A pub with the same menu and lower prices was just down the alley. I stepped outside to cast my vote for the cheaper pub. Mike was standing next to a nearby entranceway. He informed me to wait a minute as Kwab was "looking" into something.

Kwab was standing inside of a deep entranceway and facing down a dark hallway. I looked over his head and saw something posted on the wall. An arrow and a word appeared above this entranceway next to the oversized pub. I stepped closer and within the doorway there was a handwritten sign that read, "Models." Kwab was naturally a human dowsing rod that located women. Mike stood filled with curiosity and anticipation. "What could this mean?" Michael asked.

Kwab answered, "Hell if I know, but it's probably the entrance to a Chinatown gentlemen's club. I do know that I'm going to find out."

And like Santa Clause he was gone with a twitch of his nose.

Kwab disappeared for what seemed like moments of eternity. Mike and I nervously waited and wondered what could have happened to him. The ten minutes of anticipation seemed endless. Was this literally a tourist trap like in the movie Hostel? Where did Kwab go? What was up there? Our curiosity was getting the best of us. Mike and I would not enter. We were not going to become the next victim of the evil plan that waited upstairs. Finally, and to our relief, Kwab reappeared. He was back in the doorway as instantaneously as he had disappeared. "Well, what was up there?" I asked.

Mike continued, "Is it a modeling agency? A nudie bar? What?"

Kwab left us with a mysterious answer. "Go find out," he casually replied.

He obviously didn't want to let us in on his little discovery. Should we go up the dark stairway and see for ourselves?

Mike and I stood there for a moment just waiting for other to react. What was this little secret? I figured that if Kwab survived, then so should we. I gave Mike the classic line, "I'll go if you go."

Mike was hesitant but eventually agreed, "You first."

How could we possibly pass on such intrigue? Like Scooby

and Shaggy we cautiously crept up the turning stairway. It seemed like miles before we reached an old rustic door. It had a sign which read, "Ring bell for models." Ready to turn back, I mentioned, "We are not models."

The sign was meant for somebody else. We should probably turn back. But curiosity got the best of me. I pushed Mike forward inviting him, "Ring the bell."

Mike *knocked* on the door and I quickly stated, "The sign said ring the bell!"

As Mike reached for the bell the door swung open. A four foot tall elderly woman was standing in the doorway wearing a stern look and a food splattered smock. What was on that smock? It looked like marinara or perhaps human remains. While waving a wooden utensil she spoke in an eastern European accent, "Are you here to see the models?"

Mike and I looked at each other with a sheepish grin and answered, "Ah, yes."

She waived us in with the wooden spoon and then walked back into a nearby kitchen. I watched her as she stopped in front of a stove. She appeared to be working on her latest batch of goulash. For a moment I thought I saw the arm of another curious American tourist sticking out of the broth. It momentarily rose from the top of the bubbling brownish red liquid. Before I could back out of the room we were welcomed by a young woman. She was wearing a big smile and a pair of Mike's thong lingerie. She greeted us with a kind, "Heloooooowwww," and directed us into another small room.

She pointed at the wall above the bed and asked, "Take a look at the menu."

What could be on this menu I thought? Perhaps it included the price of Shepherd Pie? Either way I hope the old lady in the kitchen wasn't selling any of it.

As Mike began to play "Guess the Accent" I nervously scanned over a board. It was covered with handwritten prices pertaining to various sexual acts. I found it particularly interesting that the prices were similar to the food prices at the local pub. In fact I could skip lunch and save a few pounds using her services. This young lady was willing to urinate on me and save me money. What a deal. Pretty much every sexual choice was written on the board. And compared to the price of gas, food, and lodging the prices would be a bargain for some. I was married to a strict catholic wife and was not familiar with most of the handwritten items. Mike was a student of deviant sexual behavior and could fill me in later. But right now he was in the middle of a friendly conversation with our new friend. It was as if they had just strolled out of church and were discussing the bible verse of the day. Perhaps Leviticus 19, verse 29? I had questions about the menu options but was not about to ask for her version of the birds and bees. It was time to abandon ship. I didn't want anyone to urinate on me today. Mike had just finished a game of "Guess the Accent." It resulted in a Hungarian win. This seemed like a good time to kindly decline her services. I pushed Mike back passed momma and out through the front door. I don't think Mike appreciated my abrupt end to his polite conversation but talking was not priced on the menu. Therapy usually runs around one hundred dollars per hour. As we scuttled towards the exit, she offered a sincere invitation to return, "You come back?"

I didn't want to insult her so I waved back and exclaimed, "We'll think about it."

I quickly closed the door. Mike and I exchanged glances of approval concerning Kwab's little adventure. So far it had been the highlight of the day.

As we scrambled down the steps I thought about the acts listed on the menu. These various items were on the menu because somebody was choosing them. I flashed back to a bachelor party I once hosted for my friend Adam. He had two exotic dancers that put a leather mask over his face. It had nothing more than three small holes. Two were for his eyes and the other for air. I thought of the many drunken heads that had previously worn this mask and I cringed. Perhaps there was a leather mask option on this young ladies menu as well. The menu from our Icelandic flight didn't seem so bad in comparison. One item on the Hungarian Model menu read, "Licking - 10 Pounds." It flashed into my head and I was reminded of an old tootsie roll commercial. I envisioned an 80's advertisement that involved a wise owl testing the number of licks it takes to get to the center of a tootsie pop. As we fumbled down the long winding stairs I blurted out, "How many licks would it take to get to the center of a Hungarian model?"

With perfect timing, Mike responded as the old owl from the commercial, "One, Two, Three, CRUNCH! Thrrrrrrrrrrree! It takes thrrrree licks to get to the center of a Hungarian model."

When we reached the bottom and exited the doorway we were greeted with a rare smile from Kwab. "Well, what did you think?" he asked.

I replied, "I prefer the menu at the cheaper pub down the alley."

37

THE CHEAPER PUB

We walked back to the alleyway pub and ordered two lagers and a pale ale. The pale ale was slightly warmer than the lagers as England serves them warm. It was perfect on our first cool and cloudy day in London. We grabbed a table near the front of the pub and requested a menu from the lone woman tending bar. She informed us that the kitchen would not be open for another hour. That was just fine with us. Several drinks were definitely in our near future. At this point what we needed were drinks, foot rest and time to discuss our latest discovery. While we were three flights up reading the model menu Kwab had surveyed the street in Chinatown. He located many more doorways with model signs. I was surprised to hear this. Mini brothels were hand in hand along side of main street restaurants and the shops in tourist town. After growing up on movies like "Mary Poppins" I pictured London to be far more conservative and strict. I thought it would be like the state of Massachusetts in New England. In actuality London was closer to the liberal leanings of nearby Holland, France, and Germany.

We continued to have several rounds of drinks and Mike inevitably started a conversation with the barkeep. They compared travel locations and discussed commonalities within the neighboring European countries. She was an English native from a few hours north of London. Mike offered his suggestions as she expressed her ambition to visit or perhaps move to the west coast of the states. The woman appeared to be a mixed race of European and African and wore short spiked hair. She talked with a straight forward attitude and a masculine tone while sharing her desire for sun, tropic temperatures and palm trees. From her list of desires I don't think she had a very clear picture of Los Angeles or the west coast. She was definitely infected with a case of Scarlet Johanson Fever.

I suggested that she travel to Key West on the east coast. She was obviously a testosterone leaning member of the gay community. I described the lifestyle in Key West and described it as a welcoming place for a bartender that happens to enjoy the company of other women. She mentioned her appreciation of the author Hemmingway and we discussed the time he had spent in Key West. Meanwhile, Kwab was spending a bit of time in the basement testing out the plumbing. I imagine he was "Killin' IT!" Eventually he had arisen from the basement bathroom to join in the conversation.

Kwab came over and chimed into the chit chat with his continual quest for fire. "Do you have matches?" he asked.

The bartender started to pull out a lighter as Kwab rolled his eyes and motioned for her to stop. I explained that Kwab did not intend to start a fire but only wanted matches to add to his collection of matchbooks and human bones. The bartender gave a puzzled look of confusion and Kwab took over. Kwab's terrible affliction was about to rear it's ugly head. He has touch of what I call the "Billy D. Williams Syndrome." The introduction of alcohol may at any moment trigger an episode. There are several noticeable symptoms of his affliction. His voice drops to a smooth flowing octave and he starts throwing out suggestive comments like he's sitting at a piano with a bottle of Colt 45. The beer must have ignited a Billy D. Williams seizure because Kwab was now smiling inadvertently. He requested to have his picture taken with the barkeep and threw some suggestive comments in her direction. She caught them and threw back a comment of her own. She replied, "Not unless you've got TITS."

Mike went into some sort of dumfounded shock as apparently his lesbian identifying equipment had completely failed him. I answered back to the bartender, "We've got tits!" pointing at Mike and myself.

Mike was still in shock and asked me to repeat her words. I briefly filled him in with a complete description of each word and what they meant pertaining to the current situation. After the explanation to Mike I turned back to our bartender and stuck out my chest to exaggerate my rack. I also pointed out that I possess the subtle facial features of a beautiful woman. She concurred and informed me of a rise in temperature. She responded, "I need to go outside and smoke a fag."

I'm pretty sure this was not a sexual reference. She had just pulled out a hand rolled cigarette. Kwab asked her to roll one for him. She explained that it was a "rolly." A "rolly" is a term the English use for a homemade tobacco cigarette. He followed her outside for a talk and a smoke. Mike and I watched them from our window inside of the bar. I imagine Kwab was trying to convince our lesbian friend and her fag to spend some time with him at the Colt 45 piano.

By the time they had returned the kitchen had opened. It was passed time to soften the effects of the beer with some authentic English Pub fare. Reviewing the menu, Kwab suggested steak frites which is another English pub original meal. Mike and I had not heard of them before and were intrigued by Kwab's description. We followed suit with the recommendation of our bartender and requested two more orders of the frites. For variety, Mike selected the chicken frites. He knew that we would do a little taste trading like an old married couple. The meal came out shortly. It was pretty much over cooked chicken and steak. We had all imagined something more exciting like shish kabob, but these were just standard chicken and steak meals. Even so they were still very tasty along with of the next round of beers. As we ate I asked Kwab about his discovery of the Hungarian model. "How was your model experience?" I asked.

Kwab stated, "She didn't like my request."

I answered back with curiosity, "WHAT?"

Kwab continued, "Well, when I saw pissing listed on her menu I suggested that I piss on her; rather than vise versa."

"And what did she say?" I asked.

Kwab replied, "She pretty much threw me out." Only Kwab was capable of offending a prostitute.

After our meal I went over to our bartender to order our final round of drinks but this time I decided to be a bit more daring. I wanted to try a beer other than the pale ale. I wanted a little variety and thus picked the ale with the most unusual name. Our bartender gave me a short glass to taste the new beer. I immediately recognized the beer as extremely warm and sour. I asked if it was a cider and the bartender informed that it was not. I didn't pay attention to the fact that I just swallowed some swill. I declined the new beer and purchased another glass of the pale ale. After we finished our meals and the final round of beers we stumbled back and bid farewell to our bartender. We said our goodbye and before leaving I noticed a covered beer tap upon the bar that now displayed a sign. It was the beer that I had tasted in the short glass. Apparently it was now marked as *"closed for line cleaning."* I still thought nothing of it as we strolled out of the front door.

38

MONDAY NIGHT NOT ON THE TOWN

We continued out onto the streets of London and down to-wards Piccadilly Circus, Trafalgar and Leicester square. I hoped to see them in the daylight. Being the fast walker of the group I always found myself a bit ahead and decided to wait. It was eight o'clock in London and the sun was beginning to set between the buildings and over the square before us. We were taking a few pictures when I was disrupted by lower abdomen discomfort. I believe the steak frites or the rancid beer taste test had buried itself in my digestive system and was now making its presence known. Kwab and Mike were ready for more beer as they headed back towards the nearby Mexican sidewalk café. Normally this would have appealed to me as well but now I appealed for a change of plans. With a bit of convincing we hopped into the next cab and headed back to the commodes of Jessup. I was *"closed for line cleaning."*

After showering and taking a few shots of Jager my stomach had settled down. Alcohol works on so many levels. I felt like a civil war soldier about to have my leg sawed off before I forced down the first few shots. I was not going to be the party pooper. *(Pun intended.)* Mike and Kwab had purchased a few beers and were drinking them as we discussed the evening plan. The overall plan was to fly to Greece in the morning. With this in mind we agreed to stay local in the Queensway neighborhood and get to bed early. In other words get to bed by two in the morning. We had to be prepared for tomorrow's move to Piraeus. The itinerary included the following: a tube to Heathrow airport, a flight to Athens Greece and a train to the port town of Piraeus. Once we arrive in Piraeus we will need to use our travel skills to locate the Hellenes Ferry ticket window. Then secure our seats on the morning boat. Then check into the predetermined port hotel, the Delfini. This was our mission. Mike and Kwab both alluded to the fact that our trip felt like an episode from "The Amazing Race." It was a reality television game show with traveling contestants. Mike had always wanted to sign up and participate. Tomorrow would be our first test run for the show.

Our minds had moved to Greece but our butts still had one more night in England. Monday night is not a big night in our outlying neighborhood of central London. We were refreshed and a bit charged up. We headed into Bayswater and to the only local nightclub along the strip. All the pubs had closed up early and THE OASIS was the only place open after midnight. We went down a set of stairs to see what waited in our oasis below. As I walked into the basement night club I was reminded of many college bars I have visited over the years. We were greeted by the owner of the club. He was very happy to see us in his island themed establishment. There were not many patrons. The walls were painted with palm trees and the small bar was decorated like a tiki hut. Looking at the bar I could see that the Middle Eastern owner had hired an Eastern European woman to tend bar. I expected Mike to immediately start a game of "Guess the Accent" but to my surprise this game had already taken place. Perhaps it was yesterday while I was racing back to Jessup. That would explain their late arrival at Jessup and the reason they were familiar with this bar. They must have approached this young lady sometime before. Mike and Kwab apparently lost. As I suggested a round of "Guess the Accent" the bartender informed me that she had already won. She challenged me to a round and I blurted out, "It's not Lithuania?"

It was and she acknowledged my victory. She suspected

that I had been given some inside information from Mike; but I had not. My intuition continued to serve me well on this vacation. I simply guessed one of the countries Mike usually forgets. I've been around Mike a long time and I've seen him play *A LOT* of "Guess the Accent."

She was impressed with my guess and offered me a shot of vodka along side of the drink I had just ordered. I asked her to pick a drink that she enjoyed and she chose to make the recommended house drink. In the meantime the owner of the club sat across from us watching the bar. He came over to micromanage the amount of alcohol she poured into the drink. Apparently he designed the house drink and was concerned about using liquor. This was not a good way to keep paying customers around. The already empty club was about to get even emptier. The idea of watching this poor girl being micromanaged by her boss was very disenfranchising. Not to mention the fact that Kwab had taken over the deejay booth and Mike had begun to awkwardly dance on the empty basement floor. The atmosphere was as ugly as the bar scene in Star Wars except the creatures on the planet Tatooine were better looking. The only other patrons were the Middle Eastern son of the owner and a couple of African tourists. They sat watching Mike dance alone on the painted basement floor. As the evening had obviously peaked, we decided to call it a night.

Full of beer and Jagermeister we decided to stop and eat before going back to the hostel. I decided on a Lebanese version of a gyro. I had Greece on my mind. Mike and Kwab went directly for good old hamburgers. They walked to the nearby Burger King and purchased some food. As the restaurants were closing we finished up and headed back to Jessup for our final night in cell number thirty three of the West 22 Hostel. Tomorrow we would be paroled. As we fell to sleep we discussed the goals accomplished in London. We were satisfied with the England portion of our trip and were thinking of our rendezvous with Georg and Nico. Greece was going to be the wild and crazy party portion of our adventure.

39

GOODBYE LONDON

Tuesday June 23rd - Upon insistence of Kwab and Mike we awoke five hours before our departing flight to Athens. This gave us plenty of time to finish the ten minutes of packing, fifteen minutes of breakfast and the ten minute walk to the tube station. As we ate our pastry breakfast along Queensway I convinced our amazing race team to skip the first tube station. I wanted to roll our luggage across Kensington Gardens for one last farewell to the park. It was another beautiful day for a walk. Plus we could walk to a tube station that has transfer-free direct trains to Heathrow Airport. It would be less hassle and would save us about five dollars. I'd much rather kill the extra time on a walk around Kensington Palace than spending an extra hour in the airport.

The park was alive with patrons and commuters alike. The sky was clear and sunny with a slight breeze in the cool morning air. As we walked down the main path a kindergarten girl wearing a uniform rolled passed on her scooter. She was accompanied by her Jack Russell Terrier. Worry ridden calls to her dog reminded me of the drama filled screams of my daughter. Although this little girl had an adorable accent which made her screams almost tolerable. She yelled to the little dog that whipped passed us with reckless abandon. The dog weaved and dodged around the girl and her scooter as they moved down the path. After she passed I paused with my suitcase to wait for Mike and Kwab. The girl's mother and three year old sister walked by. Even small children were able to pass Kwab and his suitcase that was big enough to smuggle a king. Looking to our left I could see that Kwab's swans were more active this morning. They were looking for hand outs as the business men hurried by on their daily commute. We continued across the park following the many dog-walkers and bicycle-commuters.

As I took in the surrounding scene I couldn't help but reflect upon some comparisons between London and Washington D.C. London appears more civilized than any U.S. city I have visited. Kwab pointed out the inability to bear arms in England and the lack of privately owned guns. For the first time I actually pondered the possibility that a gun free society might be a safer one. An unarmed society has to put a lot of faith in government. I don't think that there is enough faith in all of America to trust our government with so much power. I know I'll never trust my government that much. But here English parliament or the English people had voted to remove guns from their society. Honestly, it appears to be working. I have never felt safer in a major city than I did in London. It was a very comforting feeling. But today, we were off to the thrill of the unknown. With a little help from the friendly London locals, we found our departing tube.

We caught the next train on the Piccadilly line directly to Heathrow. The train to the airport had plenty of room. Mike and I sat down in the back section of the car. Kwab went the other direction with his mega-suitcase and took a seat. He was greeted with a friendly "Hallo" from a nearby seated hooligan. From my vantage it appeared as though Kwab was enjoying the man's alcohol laced banter. Kwab smiled and chatted. He continued the conversation with this man named "Pinky." Pinky was a tired looking fifty year old that reminded me of a train hopper depicted in early American film. He looked thin and worn and had deep crow's feet around his eyes. His hair had receded beyond the middle of his spotted head. He wore a big smile and had a friendly demeanor. Kwab shared our itinerary with Pinky and it turns out that Pinky is a huge Ios enthusiast. He explained that he was a hardcore partier in his early days. This came as no surprise. A few more stops and our short interlude with Pinky came to an end. As he exited the train he yelled back to Kwab, "We won! And tell them that Pinky sent you."

I wondered exactly what Pinky meant by his exclamation. Perhaps he was referring to the results of the revolutionary war. Kwab filled me in. It turns out that his odd comment simply referred to a rugby match. The local British of Ios beat the local Aussies of Ios in the big rugby match of 1989. Kwab informed me of Pinky's morning state of intoxication which I had already surmised. Contrary to his suggestion Kwab did not plan to share his news of Pinky when we arrived in Ios. I reminded Kwab, "Pinky sent you."

40

TO HEATHROW AND BEYOND

We arrived at London's Heathrow airport with three hours to spare. They had not posted the gate for our flight so we picked up some snacks and sat down in the waiting area outside of security. There were nearby internet stations available at ten minutes per pound. Kwab immediately grabbed a station and logged in. He couldn't wait to get in touch with reality. I sat and hydrated myself with a couple of bottles of water while Mike finished eating the meal he had just purchased from the local airport shop. The enclosed sandwich, pickle, and chips did not look bad. Eventually my curiosity took hold and I left Mike to find what Kwab had discovered. He was reading the details of an article about a Washington D.C. metro crash. Some patrons had lost their lives in a recent crash on the metro's red line. I asked Kwab about his personal use of that particular line. We would soon be going home and he uses the metro to get to an office in downtown D.C. He had concerns about his sister and continued to read the article to see if it offered any details. No deceased had been named.

It wasn't long before I desired my own internet station. I wanted to know what was going on in the news. With a mooched coin I headed to a nearby internet station. After flipping through many useless emails I decided to give up on the outside world. I didn't want to delve back into reality and disrupt my illusion of freedom. I quickly handed the workstation to Mike before even typing the word "Facebook." Mike happily took over and jumped waist deep into his life in the states. I went back to check on our gate.

Once Kwab and Mike were finally unplugged we processed through security. Kwab was flagged for a bag check. Unfortunately there was a pilot in the security line who was also pulled out. The pilot had packed his case with just about every disallowed liquid imaginable. Apparently he was one of the privileged. He must have felt that rules do not apply to him. He continually argued with security. The female security attendant replied and reminded him of his responsibilities as a pilot. Even pilots are not immune to the regulations of security. Kwab looked over at me and rolled his eyes.

Ten minutes later the pilot was processed and the security search of Kwab's bag had begun. The security attendant was a soft spoken four foot tall middle aged woman. She looked down and to her surprise she was holding a strange box in her hand. It was labeled Magnum. By the look on her face I would surmise that it was the first time she held this particular brand of condom. I commented to Mike, "Maybe she thinks their bullets."

Mike snickered. The woman paused for a second to read the back of the box then put them back into the bag. Kwab was as prepared for sex as Tommy Lee. It was a good thing because this might be the security woman's lucky night. I looked over at Mike. He had a curious smile on his face. Perhaps he had plans to borrow one. You never know. A flight attendant might ask Mike to join the mile high club.

The security officer continued to dig through Kwab's bag and eventually found the culprit, a tube of toothpaste. Fortunately, it wasn't a tube of anal lube. After one last additional x-ray scan of his tube of Colgate, Kwab was allowed to continue through security. We settled down near our gate and waited for our flight. With the extra time Mike and Kwab could hit the shops once more. Now I realized the true reason we woke up so early; shopping. Mike came back with a new pair of headphones and sat down next to a middle aged woman from Greece. Moments later he had engaged her in

an inquisitive conversation. Two more hours of listening to
Mike and the woman had tied a Neuse to the rafters above
her chair.

Kwab used the two hours to read and finished his book on
the Obama campaign trail. I was a quarter of the way through
a book of my own. It was about traveling the small towns
of the United States, a gift from my friend Andrea. Kwab
mentioned that he left his other book at home. He was now
bookless and bored. While packing for the trip I had foreseen this moment. I was ready for anything and had packed
a few extra books in preparation for long flights. I pulled out
the selection available to Kwab. He chose a book about the
life of renowned psychic Sylvia Browne over a book about
Obama's Islamic roots. I had purchased the Browne book
in the Montego Bay airport when flying home from Jamaica
last spring. I had read about half way through her description of heaven before my wife commandeered the book. My
wife wonders why we don't travel more together. She figured
I wasn't going to heaven anyhow so what was the point of
reading about it. Kwab dug right in and became intrigued by
Browne. At least he was more interested than I. I jested, "Did
you know she can see into the great beyond?"

I hadn't picked up the book since packing it for the trip.
Finding out about heaven is still on my list of things to do but
that's why I was flying to Greece.

As Kwab and I sat reading I thought about the thirty five
years that I have never seen Mike pick up a book and actually
read. Not once did the pages of "Go Dog Go" trickle through
his fingers and yet I've spent an unlimited amount of my time
moving his small library of books. Mike has kept a huge collection of books at each of his living arrangements. They are
usually randomly stacked around his bedroom. I recently
moved them using trash bags. It was just weeks before the
trip. Every time I move the books I say to Mike, "Can't we just
take these to the dump?"

He always replies, "I need these books for my studies."

How would Mike's students survive without pornography
and his prized Dictionary of Feces?

Eventually we were called to board our plane and we clamored into our first Olympic Airline flight headed for Athens. I requested the window seat and climbed in first. I was tired from the early morning wake up and planned to get some sleep. As I sat down I noticed that the wing of the airline was a bit stained and appeared rusty and scuffed. Being accustomed to the pristine air vehicles of the United States this view was not very reassuring. I decided to close the window to try and get some sleep. As I reached to pull down the window the surrounding plastic frame popped off and fell to the ground. My confidence in this airline had dropped even further. I repaired the window and said a few "Our Father" prayers as we taxied towards the runway. I closed my eyes and hoped for the best. As the plane took off I bid farewell to the great English Empire. I was now officially getting my first taste of the once vast Greek Empire. Kwab leaned over and asked the stewardess for the airline frequent flier plan. She replied, "We're going out of business and the airline is being sold."

I looked at Kwab and nervously said, "Yyyep."

41

A SOUR TASTE OF ATHENS

I was beginning to drift off into sleep just before flight service began. I was looking forward to the sweet dreams of a fiery plane crash. But before I could doze off the flight attendant called to me, "Drink sir?"

As one can see from my manly physique I have never been one to turn down a drink. We were pleased to find that unlike Iceland Air, Olympic Air feeds their patrons free of cost. It didn't matter what mysterious foreign food was offered, it was worth a try. A full tray arrived including beef chunks with pasta. It was placed in front of me with a salad like container of common Greek food. This included wrapped grape leaf rolls. They could be best described as green moth cocoons. I dared Mike to fall asleep while I had one of these at my disposal. I thought of the film "Silence of the Lambs" and the cocoons that serial killer Buffalo Bill inserted into the throats of his victims. Once Mike drifted off to sleep I could gently insert one cocoon into his wide open snoring mouth. Two more for his nose as well.

There is an array of stuffed grape leaf recipes from Greece but this was the basic pickled leaf with rice filling. It was the perfect recipe for ending the incestuous snoring that would haunt the isles of Olympic Air flight 440. The other pickled items on my tray looked interesting to say the least. They were worth a taste but not worthy of consumption. Then there was

the airplane baklava. It wasn't fancy but even airplane baklava is good baklava. Mike and I finished our dessert while
Kwab passed over the cinnamon flavored wet cake. After the
meal I managed to nod off a bit. It was a relatively uneventful flight. Mike snored away until we started our descent into
Athens Greece. I fought for every minute of sleep.

As we exited the plane I could feel the hot humid air of
Athens Greece. It was familiar and very much like the summer weather of Washington D.C. and Baltimore. We forged
on and moved through customs and baggage claim with relative ease. I've noticed countries that lean toward a third world
status seem to have little restrictions. They don't care what
enters their country. The fact that the three of us skipped
merrily through the Athens airport and right into the train
station supports my theory. English customs required a cavity search but here I did not get checked by a Greek officer. In
fact I don't even think I saw a Greek officer. We stopped by a
money exchange station. The US dollar was now equal to two
thirds its value. This was far better than the two for one ratio
of pound to dollar.

With new Euros in hand we approached an extremely irritable woman who worked at the train station counter. I stepped
forward and requested one ticket to Piraeus. She glared at
me with subtle disdain. The young woman looked like she
should be working behind the register of a teenage fashion
store. She snatched my money and handed me a metro ticket
with a map. The map had instructions showing me where
to transfer for successful navigation on my way to Piraeus.
Kwab stepped up next with the same request. The woman
gave Kwab an even greater look of discernment. She was extremely perturbed. The fact that we were traveling together
but purchasing our tickets separately was obviously a problem for her. Kwab handed over his money and she snidely
commented, "Why don't you buy your tickets together?"

She was extremely irritated to accommodate our individu-
alized method of buying tickets. Considering we were the
only people in line I didn't feel guilty. We were forcing her
to do her job. Apparently poor work ethic is a universal phe-

nomenon. She's lucky she's not paid in tips. Perhaps she could use some time working with the Hungarian model for tips on customer service.

Mike purchased his ticket and barely received recognition from the woman. She obviously had a desire to gab with the coworker sitting behind her. Perhaps her little buddy should have been working in the next window. Mike and I moved to the escalator. Kwab followed; his rolling planet in tow. We jumped onto the train. It was waiting and available at the bottom platform. This was a nice ride. As the doors shut, I could feel the cool air conditioning in the modern metro train. The Walt Disney World shuttles had nothing on this ride. It was quite obvious that this metro train was built top notch in preparation for the 2004 Olympics. The city of Athens had spared no expense. The car was clean and the seats were comfortable and spacious. The plastic interior was bright and fresh, not like the dull worn metros of an old city. Thus far this train system appeared to be the prize of Athens and perhaps the prize of all metro's throughout Europe.

42

A RIDE ACROSS ATHENS

Athens had made a large number of improvements including the new airport, the new train system and cleaning up the city center. The tourist areas which surround the Acropolis had been updated and made visitor friendly. We were looking forward to seeing and enjoying the modern enhancements. But on this day we would experience pre-2004 Olympic Athens. The comfortable new train started to depart from the airport depot. We were headed for downtown Athens. We enjoyed the clean spacious train for a total of four stops before exiting and transferring to the blue line for Piraeus. The three of us exited the new train and walked onto the rusty platform. In order to reach our new metro line we followed a flow of riders into an old freight elevator. It contained the odor of a million Spartans. As we rose towards our departing platform we experienced a hint, or should I say whiff, of what was about to come. For thirty seconds I breathed through my mouth in order to avoid the horrific smell trapped within the elevator. I exchanged a glance of disgust with Mike and Kwab. Our elevator arrived at the platform as slow as the space shuttle docks onto the Mir space station. The doors opened and we harried out gasping for air. We were momentarily relieved inhaling the odorless breeze.

The elevator was the least of our problems. A short time later the Piraeus bound metro arrived. We lumbered onto a dilapidated metro car dragging our bags. Mike and I found an open spot to stand with our luggage. I held Kwab's oversized case as he squeezed forward into a section of seats. He sat down between me and an attractive but equally foul smelling Greek woman. I clung to my suitcase. It was stacked vicariously upon Kwab's Jupiter. Then the ride from hell began. Stop after stop; more and more Greeks poured onto the metro. If I moved in any direction my backpack would smack someone in the face. It was so crowded I began to wonder if the locals had climbed onto the top of the train. How many sardines could we fit into our rolling tin can? We were about to break the record.

I was cornered by an attack of foreign odor and trapped in the most unfortunate spot. A short, hairy, elderly man with extremely bad hygiene stood just below my nose. He was obviously living deodorant free. I recognized the scent immediately. He was wearing a fine batch of B.O. I was the lucky American of the day. The man had decided to lumber through the crowd and huddle up next to me. I should have felt honored yet my eyes began to water. It was as if his armpits were filled with freshly chopped onions. The stench was unbearable. It smelled like everyone on board had just completed a decathlon. This dilapidated metro had absolutely no air circulation and there was no air conditioning. There were no luxury features on this train which travels the entire length of downtown Athens. I tried every trick I knew to combat the odor. I tried breathing through my mouth. I tried imaging myself somewhere else. I tried clicking my heels. Nothing worked. I looked up at the metro map and thought, "Just fourteen more stops. So this is what Yanni's jockstrap smells like."

I'm not that big of a fan.

I looked from the window to seek a distraction in the passing neighborhoods. I saw graffiti, trash and the occasional mangy dog. I bet they smelled funky too. I looked over at Mike. He was looking outside as well. His face held the distinct expression of disbelief. It reminded me of an old commercial where a Native American sheds a single tear at the sight of litter along the road. I looked back towards Kwab. He sat low and protected from the undesirable view. He was only surrounded by the stink of his attractive woman. Compared to the old man under my nose she was a fresh rose drifting over a sea of lilac kisses. Stop after stop the view looked the same, the train smelled the same, and my situation remained the same. An overwhelming picture of filth and poverty overtook my vision. It felt like I was on a train from Cancun International airport headed straight for a third world hell.

How could this be Athens? Where were the magnificent marble structures? Where was the Acropolis? Supposedly it could be seen from anywhere in the city. I can guarantee it cannot be seen from the window of this downtown metro line. I went into Athens denial. Everything went blank. I drifted into a war like state of shock. The condition of my mind should only be experienced by those in battle. When I finally broke free of the mental haze, the train had stopped. A voice on a loud speaker made an announcement in Greek. I somehow became fluent because I comprehended the announcer's words clearly and precisely, "Exit the train now!"

43

WELCOME TO PIRAEUS,
THE PORT OF ATHENS

We unloaded from the metro car. Nothing smelled as sweet as the exhaust filled breezes of downtown Piraeus. I wafted the fresh sea air. It was mixed with gas fumes from the nearby port ships. As we walked onto the lower level platform I was welcomed by a warm humid breeze. The platform looked like the entrance to 1950's Disneyland. It had old tile walls and matching tile floor. The mixture of pastel and earth colors would have looked better in black and white. The Greek letters of the signs were posted in a form of *Blackadder Script*. We worked our way into an open market that was just beyond the metro station. Numerous vendors had set up tables and were selling their goods. Everything the Greek traveler could use was available. Sunglasses, lotion, towels, snacks, drinks and other items were spread across the tables. It looked like any market in a third world tourist trap. All of the vendors were sun baked, warn and unaware of the invention known as a razor. We stopped in a clearing amongst the tables and dropped our luggage. Kwab was thirsty and wanted to purchase a soda. I was too but I was more concerned with finding the hotel. I stood guarded. The vendors watched us like a crowd of beggars ready to tear us from our last coin.

Kwab walked over to purchase his drink while Mike and I protected the luggage. I heard an odd clicking sound approaching from behind. It became louder as I was stooped over my bag digging through some maps. I looked back and saw a raggedy gang of mongrel dogs moving across the tile of the market. Their claws made a clicking noise as their nails smacked against the tile. The noise increased with their pace. I considered their trot as I hastened my search for the Piraeus map. I was in no mood to be raped. The pack of wild dogs headed right for us. As they came within a few yards I sprang to my feet and turned around. I squeezed my butt in a defensive position. They stopped and looked up. Then with a dull glance they unenthusiastically trotted off. They didn't even stay for the faintest sniff. Looking around I realized that roaming dogs are very common in Greece and fortunately I was not their type.

I watched the pack trot off and spread about the market. For a moment I took a snapshot of their lives. A few of them had found a place to lay in the nearby shade. They were lying upon the cool tile floor. I noticed that most of the dogs were collared and licensed. I was surprised to realize this was the life of a Greek pet. They reminded me of the smelly man from the train. They certainly shared the same hair stylist. Their overall hygiene was very similar as well. I kept to myself and so did the dogs of Greece. I can only imagine what happens when the average child tourist wanders off and attempts to pet one of these beasts. Throughout Greece I continued to come across an endless number of wandering dogs, both human and canine. These dogs appeared to be a similar breed. It looks like they are half Australian Dingo and half Sandy from the musical "Annie." My pure bred dogs would not last ten minutes in the harsh conditions of Piraeus and neither would my wife.

I continued to reflect upon the dogs of Athens while Kwab drank his soda. They reminded me of a similar stray dog that followed me around the Caribbean island of Martinique. That dog was a begging professional. He made the average Canine American beggar look like an amateur. I once knew a Dalmatian named Duke who could drool all the way to the floor. Then he would suck it back up. Even Duke was no match for the old pros of Piraeus. Eventually Kwab finished his refreshing beverage and Mike sucked up *his* drool. We walked towards the port and spotted our next place of refuge, the Delfini Hotel. Surrounded by the lounging dogs of Piraeus we moved through the port with caution. We should have held hands like the characters in the Wizard of Oz. When would the cowardly lions of Piraeus attack?

44

THE DELFINI HOTEL

The Delfini Hotel sign was a fluorescent beacon of fortitude amongst the trash ridden alleyway of Piraeus. We headed for the entranceway and walked into a very clean and air conditioned lobby. The Delfini was a quaint place with modern flair in the middle of a dumpy port alley. It had clean tile floors, a marble desk and eloquent paintings yet my intuition warning light had lit. It was very nice, but something was not quite right. The lobby and the attendant were both well dressed. Both of which influenced a positive initial review. But as we worked our way through the hotel to our room we discovered that something was out of place. It was a condom machine. And it was oddly placed in the hallway just outside of the hotel banquet room. Upon discovery of the machine Kwab and Mike surmised that we must be staying at some sort of hooker hotel. Considering the cleanliness and modest price I had my doubts.

Perhaps the location of this condom machine was just another one of the many cultural differences of Greece. When the wedding reception has come to an end the new father-in-law can monitor his new son-in-law. He can be sure that Sonny purchases the appropriate Provo lactic. Perhaps the mother-in-law makes the first selection? Maybe this is a common Greek tradition. If not, then it certainly should be. Why should Greek condom dispensers be limited to seedy bars and truck stops? Bridal suites with condom machines would come in handy back in the states. If there had been more condom machines in Maryland perhaps many of my friends would still be happily single. We moved passed the banquet-condom floor and worked our way up a tight winding spiral staircase. We found our room located at the end of the hall on the third floor.

Our room could be best described as the Jessup Royale Suites. The room and attached bathroom were very clean. It even had a real shower. I noticed a small can next to the toilet marked "Paper." Apparently you can't flush toilet paper in Greece. The thought of a can filled with ass wiped paper was not very appealing but at least this was not a brothel. There was no can labeled "Condoms." The main room was furnished with a bunk bed such as the hostel back in London. But this bunk bed was new, sturdy and probably bug free. It was a very decorative and not just a simple metal frame. The bunk bed and the matching double bed had matching spreads. They were deep blue and the fabric was thin and course. It gave the room a look of modern European décor. These bed coverings were much nicer than the dog blankets of the Jessup Budget Inn back in London.

Kwab and I settled in while Mike took a look around the room. Mike exclaimed, "Where is the glory hole?"

Mike often makes reference to the "glory holes" of a "book store" in his college town. The store was famous for these holes. I usually avoid such book stores but Mike cannot resist the lure of the perverse. That particular hole-in-the-wall literally has holes in the wall. The holes are used by unidentified perverts for displaying their penis to fellow shoppers. Why anyone would do this is beyond me? I was just glad not to find a penis displayed here. But the hallway condom machine did have me a little concerned. I was relieved to find that our room was glory hole free.

Mike found the remote, turned on the TV and quickly scanned through the channels. He and Kwab were full of excitement at the sight before them. It wasn't long before he found the skin channel. It supported their hooker hotel theory.

By their excitement you'd have thought they had never seen "Skinamax" before. At least they've never seen Skinamax in a place with mythological hookers and a condom machine. They were happier than two boys who just discovered the peep hole in the girl's shower. I checked out the bathroom for peep holes. No peeps holes and no Hungarian model menu either. Surprisingly, I couldn't even find a hooker menu on the bedside table. They did have a menu for room service. According to that menu the place was pretty much hooker free. I don't think "Greek Club Sandwich" was the kinky term for ménage a trios. To Mike and Kwab's disappointment the brothel theory had been disproved and with only one night in Piraeus we decided to hit the town. After the planes, trains, and automobiles of a long, humid, foul-scented day; we were ready to find a beer.

45

MOUTSOPOULOU STREET

In preparation I had done some research before embarking upon the trip. I knew it would be difficult to find a nice spot for food and drinks in Piraeus. During my internet exploration I discovered the boat dock area of Moutsopoulou Street. I showed a map of the boat lined neighborhood to my companions. They in turn asked the Delfini door man for his entertainment recommendations. He too suggested Moutsopoulou Street. Thanks to the bellhop's reaffirmation Kwab and Mike were ready to follow me into the streets.

But before getting sloshed I thought it would be a good idea to know the location of our morning departure. I didn't want to seek out lost drunks at six in the morning; ten minutes before boarding time. If everyone knew the spot then I had nothing to worry about. I took us on a mission to check the docks and locate the Hellenes Ferry ticket booth. We walked over the main street to the docks. Near the entrance I could hear some dogs rustling around under a temporary office building. A long chain link fence surrounded the dock. I found an opening in the fence and followed it around to a small shed labeled Hellenes. It was right across from our hotel. I could see the glow of the Delfini sign across the street through the entwined vegetation that had attached itself to the fence. The building was a small blue shack with a section of sliding windows. It looked like a small portable shed that

Americans use to sell snowballs in the summer. We stood silent for a moment looking at the deserted shipyard. I could barely see twenty feet in front of me. The dock was dark and quiet at this time of night. It held a sense of foreboding dread as the tidewater slapped against the concrete pier. The dock breezes shook the chain link fence. Rippled pieces of trash that were caught in the fence sounded like the tail of a kite. Since the location of our departure had been confirmed we quickly exited the dock. We walked back onto the main road and grabbed the first cab off to Moutsopoulou Street.

Traffic in Piraeus is pure hell but local taxi service has a good reputation. The cab driver beeped and weaved up and down the steep traffic filled slopes. He eventually swerved and hung a right down a winding hillside road. This road led us to another street which was lined with outdoor bars and restaurants. This was Moutsopoulou Street. Each club had a large open air section in the front. The name of each club was posted on top of a large pavilion covering. Many motorcycles and scooters were parked in front of the sidewalk. The driver pulled over to let us out. The cost of the ride was a mere five Euros. A travel brochure stated that the cab prices in Athens were the best in Europe and so far it was right.

We hopped out of the cab and slid between the scooters to get to the curb. We hadn't taken thirty steps before Kwab instinctively pulled us into a club playing the sounds of Hip Hop. This was fine with me. I realized that he had been forced to endure techno music pretty much everywhere in London. He was not a big fan of techno. Mike and I are. But unfortunately for Kwab it ruled the music scene in Greece as well. We strolled down the main walkway through the center of the club.

The locals here didn't appear to be as rugged as the locals riding the metro. I had a feeling that each one of them did not arrive on the metro but probably by boat or motorcycle. We had just found the young high society crowd of Athens. They were the 90210 kids of Greece. Speed boats, sail boats and yachts were parked along the street. This appeared to be the party town of the upper-middle class. As we headed back towards the main bar I noticed that the patrons were sipping twelve ounce bottles of beer or bottled water. I wondered if they had a nice cold draft. We worked our way into the back then planted ourselves on three very comfortable bar stools.

It was dark and loud in the rear of the establishment. The bar was modern and the bartenders were young and trendy. A friendly bartender stepped up to take our order. We had just traveled through Hell and walked up to the gates of Heaven. To the right side of the bar held the one and only bar tap that was perched above. It was resting within a beam of glowing light. A green Heineken tap was frozen within a block of ice. We hastily ordered three drafts. They were large twenty ounce glasses and were covered with frost. The beers went down fast. Kwab was still finishing his first beer as Mike and I ordered two more. We sat and talked with the bartender who was very happy to have American's at his bar.

In this new country with different smoking laws Kwab had now found new hope. He said goodbye and went out into the clubs to add to his elusive matchbooks collection. Mike and I sat drinking and didn't bother to check on the price of each beer. We were in a pure state of glee and the beer price didn't really matter in this moment. Mike and I continued to drink cold drafts and munch down the nearby pretzel-nut mix while Kwab continued on his quest. Greece still allowed smoking in public bars and restaurants. Kwab felt that his matchbox search would go much better in Greece than it did in London. Unfortunately, he came back disappointed. He returned with only a generic pack of matches that did not have any special significance.

Kwab sat down and asked if we were ready to eat. Mike and I were always ready to eat. We turned to the American friendly bartender who informed us that the club only serves club sandwiches. This must be why Europeans are so thin. They don't market food at every waking moment and at every possible location as we do back in the states. Back home I'm never more than a few hundred yards or a phone call away from food. But since we were content and comfortable we agreed to order three Greek club sandwiches. I would have killed for a Double-T Diner Gyro Platter.

The club sandwich is pretty much equal in stature to a hamburger back in the states. When we think of hot dogs and hamburgers, they think of gyros and club sandwiches. Unfortunately when they think of club sandwiches they think of one slice of mystery meat, some cream style cheese and three thin slices of bread. While Americans think of thick bread, turkey, ham, real cheese and bacon. We were starved and nearly swallowed the mini clubs and chips in a matter of seconds. The sandwich and chips came with a side of barbeque sauce. Apparently the Greeks are big on barbeque sauce and use it to dip just about everything.

After another round of beers we asked for the check and decided to check out another venue. A heart stopping ninety five Euro bill slapped us in the face. We realized we were about to pay one hundred and fifty dollars for three lousy sandwiches and ten beers. That bill was enough to bring an end to the sub-par night in Piraeus. We chose to save our money and walk along the avenue. I saw people eating real meals and wondered how these post teens could afford giant platters of meat. A group of young couples were feasting upon a tray of food fit for Zeus himself. Perhaps club sandwiches and tap beer are a luxury in this town. We should have ordered meat platters and twelve ounce bottles like the surrounding patrons. When in Rome, live and learn.

We grabbed the next cab and headed back to the Delfini Hotel. We pulled up near the hotel and the cabbie requested twelve Euros. Kwab and Mike simultaneously let out a burst of discontent. After the huge bill we were not about to pay this outrageous cab fare. I informed the driver that the same ride to Moutsopoulou Street was only five Euros. "The traffic must have been worse," he exclaimed.

Actually it was not. He continued to argue. Apparently he was omnipotent but somehow ended up with a job driving a cab. I was tired of arguing along the busy road. We eventually decided to compromise. We paid the man ten euros; tip included. We all bid the criminal driver of Piraeus with a middle fingered farewell.

46

GREEK ISLES OR BUST

Wednesday June 24th – I believe I caught about an hour of sleep before the Sasquatch, aka Mike began to snore loudly into the early morning hours. Kwab and I remained awake catching up on old times as we watched some old American movies. Surprisingly they were being played on the local television station. Under the vibrations of Mike's snore I told Kwab the story of Mike's first college roommate Gamble. Gamble used to keep a jar of pennies in his bed with him at all times. He had adjusted his sleeping habits to overcome the snoring habits of Mike. While Gamble slept he trained himself to whip pennies from the top bunk into Mike's head whenever Mike reached peak snore volume. I witnessed this firsthand and apparently the technique worked as Gamble managed to get enough sleep to graduate. Mike in turn is apt to set off airport metal detectors. I can only imagine how many copper stools Mike has produced from Gamble's little game of "Mr. Mouth." Before this trip I had warned Kwab of Mike's snoring abilities and advised him to pack some ear plugs.

Additionally I informed Kwab that all beds must always be separated by open floor space or else he might wake up on the wrong end of the spoon position. I learned early in college that I should always take the floor over sharing a bed with Mike. I once awoke with the feeling of a sleeping bear nibbling on my ear and that bear haunts me to this day. There is also the possibility of waking up in someone's urine. It's best not to take any chances. On the night of Mike's twenty-first birthday he may have had a little accident while sharing his bed with a female friend. I might have put some snow onto the couple while they slept. Or… perhaps the bed was wet from the twenty one shots and twenty one beers that Mike had consumed. Would I give him a cover story to shield him from embarrassment? Or would I play a snow covered prank? You decide.

Kwab enjoyed the sleeping tales. He found humor in the fact that Mike's sleeping conscience had become acclimated to my voice. Like being under a hypnotic spell, Mike will immediately stop snoring at the sound of my command. Kwab gave it a try and Mike's sleeping brain completely ignored his request and kept snoring. We tested this together. Kwab would yell out, "Mike!" with no change in Mike's snore.

I would soon follow up with a simple but stern "Mike," and immediately his snoring ceased.

He would completely stop snoring for at least five minutes or more. Mike and I had spent many nights traveling in close quarters and amazingly his brain had trained itself to stop snoring. His brain also knew that if he didn't stop snoring he would receive a swift blow from a heavy handed pillow.

After Kwab started to drift off I began to think of our pending five hour boat ride. I decided to give up on any attempt to sleep. As the sun began to rise, I quietly showered and exited the room. I headed to the docks in order to secure our tickets out of Piraeus. I didn't even want to consider missing our ride to the islands of Greece. Waiting outside of the Hellenes ferry booth, I stood along side the random stray dogs of the dock. They seemed to congregate in a large pack behind a mobile news stand and were ready for any sort of hand out. I took watch as the ferries pulled in one by one. A team of boat workers prepared to load the growing number of people, cars, and trucks. The ticket window swung open. A few other foreigners were in line to pick up tickets. I helped a few of them as I obtained ours. I felt relieved to have our tickets in my hand and our boat within sight. Ready to go I headed back to the Delfini to grab Kwab and Mike and ensure our prompt departure.

To my unexpected and joyous surprise they were already packed. They were in the lobby and already checking out. We squeezed passed a group of traveling Scandinavians. They looked to be on their way to the islands as well. We headed out of the doorway and straight for the boats. There were at least ten ferries tied in along the docks. There were different boat companies and different boat sizes. Some of them were very colorful. We walked around until we found our particular ferry, the bright red Highspeed-3. We stopped a moment to take a picture of our ride. This was a speed ferry. It would take us at the fastest pace by ferry standards to the islands of Santorini and Ios. It turns out that the fastest pace from Athens on rough seas is approximately five hours. Just before we were boarded we stopped by some of the local vendors to buy some bread products that were similar to bagels.

As we began our ascent onto The Highspeed-3, some twenty-something girls were having difficulty. They could not haul their mini-planets up the steep loading steps and onto the ship. Rather than stand there and watch them struggle I decided to lend a hand. I believe their bags must have been full of curling irons and bowling balls. Along with their dead weight I pulled my suitcase as well. Before reaching the top I felt the slight twinge of a muscle snap somewhere in my lower back. We stumbled down the hall and into our row. Our seats were situated along the starboard isle. As I sat down I realized that I had definitely pulled something in my lower back. Mike gave me advice on the many healing techniques available for the average three hundred pound American. He spoke up, "Can I give you a hand with it?"

I replied, "Ah, no thanks. I think I got it."

I respectfully declined as I worked the knot out of my back. The last thing I wanted was some guy's hand rubbing my lower back. Mike's advice was starting to get under my skin. Looking out at the distant islands I quickly tuned out the health tips. I swallowed a few pain killers that I had just pulled from my bag. Travel "pains" were starting to set in.

47

HIGHSPEED-3

The modern ferry was quite nice and full of every convenience. In my imagination I had pictured a vessel similar to one from an Indian Jones film. I thought we would be sitting upon hard rusty benches out in the open air. But this modern day conveyance was more like the interior of a spacious airplane. Just across from our seats stood a full food and drink counter. It had already attracted a large line of people. People were shouting out their orders for "Fanta" and water as they reached the counter one after another. The rows of seats upon this ferry reclined. They had a foot rest and even a little pocket for storing magazines. I was comfortable in my seat with the freshly made bagel that managed to somehow taste stale.

The boat had pushed off and I could feel the sway of the waves moving the boat back and forth. Kwab came back with Mike and some drinks from the nearby counter. They both sat down to join me. Mike got situated and was fumbling with his headphones. Kwab began to read about the amazing afterlife that awaited him in Sylvia Browne's heaven. I picked up my book and tried to get reacquainted with it but the increasing waves reminded me of motion sickness. I soon decided that from this point on my goal was to stare at the horizon. I put my book down and looked out of the window. Motion sickness had become my Achilles heal.

I love travel, adventure and excursions but they don't always love me back. One time my wife and I went scuba diving in the Florida Keys. The water was so rough that the entire ship fell ill. There was a storybook family of four next to us on the boat. They were off on the perfect scuba diving vacation. My wife looked over at the family and a nearby teenage girl asked, "Why are they lying in a pool of vomit? Are they dead?"

Ten minutes later the captain picked up the loudspeaker to make his own announcement. He directed the crew, "Look towards the port side of the boat."

Another had fallen ill.

"Someone is having a Religious Experience." he joked.

It was my wife. It looked more like she was having an exorcism to me. All in all, around thirty people chummed over the side of that boat that day. The captain finally took us back to land. Would I have my religious experience today? As we cruised towards land I looked over at Mike and Kwab who were now falling in and out of consciousness. I never again took my gaze from the straight oceanic line outside of my window. As we trudged on hour after hour, wave after wave, passing island after island, I counted the islands like sheep until I finally nodded off.

I woke after an unknown length of time to the hollering of an extremely loud mouthed obnoxious woman. She had decided to scream out a drink order to her daughter across the ship. I didn't understand a word of it but from that moment on I could not get her annoying voice out of my head. Compounding nausea was growing in my stomach. If worse came to worse I knew exactly which way to direct my puke. Looking back towards the horizon I watched the different size islands come and go. I tried to make a game of determining if there was life upon them. Most appeared uninhabited which makes sense considering most of them were large waterless rock masses. They contained no food, no electricity and nothing to fulfill the other requirements of survival.

There are over fourteen hundred Greek islands of which only two hundred and twenty seven are inhabited. Many of the inhabited islands may only have one family or just a couple of structures. Some I viewed were completely void of life and had nothing more than a floating cloud which oddly hovered directly above. They resembled the island drawings of a primary school child or the secret hideaway of some super-criminal. The water was bright with a deep blue hue that changed color slightly as we crossed between islands. When we were out in the open sea, the Aegean was topped with wind blown white caps. They calmed when an island was on the starboard side of our ship. It was a great view except for the fact that it was making me nauseas. Heading into our fifth hour I hoped to see less of it and was relieved to hear the captain announce our near arrival to the island of Santorini.

The Greeks call the island Thira but it is referred to by the English speaker as Santorini. It is noted by many as one of the most beautiful places on Earth. I was anxious to see it in person. It is a crescent shaped island with a small offshore section. This section contains the exposed top of a volcano. Along the edge of the main island the red volcano cliffs or part of the volcano's caldera drop steeply from the town. The towns are set high above the crater looking down at the island which contains it. This lends to the spectacular view of this island and produces the infamous deep red volcanic sand beaches.

Many theorize that the Santorini volcano was the heart of the missing continent of Atlantis before the volcano last exploded sometime before the fall of Troy. The eruption registered as a six on the volcanic explosivity index. It is hailed as one of the greatest volcanic eruption on Earth within the last few thousand years. Only two other eruptions on Earth are known to have released more volcanic material into the atmosphere. As we drifted by the volcano I thought about our close proximity to it. My personal motto is to live for every day. You never know when it might all be over. We took pictures from the ship and watched as the exiting supply trucks lumbered up the zig-zagging caldera hillside. Our ferry departed as quickly as we had landed and we cruised passed the Cliffside villas leaving the island of Santorini behind.

The short ride over to Ios was long lived with anticipation. I could not wait to get settled in and catch up with my friends, Georg and Nico. They were already on the island sipping drinks and having night after night of fun filled adventures. I tried out my cell phone in order to arrange our hotel shuttle and to my surprise it worked. Good old AT&T has managed to stay networked even on the remote Greek islands. I was able to reach our hostess Stefania at our island accommodation, the Hotel Medditeranneo. After five hours on this floating conveyance I was ready to get off and experience the feeling of solid Greek rock under my foot.

The captain called for our stop and we hustled down below to prepare for the Greek version of the running of the bulls. We gathered together in the dark undercarriage of the ship enveloped within the smell of exhaust ridden air. There was very little light and the enclosed hull echoed with the sounds of the people talking and car doors slamming shut. Mike began to accuse the ferry cars of being involved in a plot to create the greatest mass asphyxiation in history. "They're trying to kill us!" he exclaimed.

I breathed through my shirt but was pretty confident that the majority of the fuel odor was coming from the ferry itself and not just the thirty or so cars ready to begin the island grand prix. I looked over at a guy sitting upon his little buzzing scooter with his helmet strapped tight. He was ready to pounce down the ramp and onto the island.

As the boat backed in, the large vehicle ramp slowly began to lower and the rays of the sun began to pour into the underbelly of the boat. Before the ramp was fully down and docked the mass of people were pushing out onto the plank. Many of them looked ready to jump onto the concrete dock a few feet before them. The crew jumped forth and immediately began to madly usher the people across the ramp and off of the boat. I imagine they wanted to unload in record time and get back to Athens. They wanted to make up time for the slow ride across the rough seas. We tumbled out with the others that were on foot as the vehicles started pouring out behind us. The Greek crew was screaming commands and pointing like drill instructors. We all looked like military recruits foolishly pushing our way out of The Highspeed-3 Boot Camp.

48

ARRIVAL ON THE ISLAND OF IOS

The Greek rock felt good under our feet as we were greeted by representatives of the many island hotels. They were waving at the travelers attempting to gather them and take them back into town. It was obvious that hotel space was available. The barkers needed to fill their vacancies. There were a lot of empty hotels this year as the tourism season had apparently started very slow. I combed the lines of hotel workers looking for the sign that represented our hotel. Confused by the barrage of signs I went down to one end of the advertisers. I looked back and saw Mike waving me in. Apparently he and Kwab had managed to find our friendly four foot Italian hostess Stefania.

The four foot Stefania had been holding a one foot Hotel Medditeranneo sign somewhere within the mass of advertisers. She had dark olive skin and had the look of a woman who spends a lot of time working in the sun. Her green eyes and short blond hair illuminated the look of a younger woman. In a thick Italian accent she asked, "Who is the blond haired friend waiting at the hotel pool?"

At first we denied knowing the fair haired stranger but eventually admitted that he was our friend Nico. She was obviously concerned that he might be a bum using the pool as a bathtub. Actually that description does fit Nico. But he was our friend and not NeeCooLiz the homeless pool vagrant.

She asked, "Where is your fourth person?" referring to our missing traveler Bob.

I informed her, "The filthy animal wading in your pool is his replacement."

We followed her away from the crowd as she waved us towards an old open air SUV. This ancient truck was right out of the movie, "Raiders of the Lost Arc." I'm pretty sure they must have filmed on this island and left the props to local business owners. The truck looked like an old Bronco II painted the color of a third world battleship. We tossed our luggage onto the roof as Stefania insisted and off we went. The car wound up along the cliffs of Ios towards the town of Choras. The town lies above the port beach of Yialos. I nervously watched as our luggage rolled across the top of the vehicle. It was precariously teetering near the edge of the rack. I pictured my bag flying from the loose metal rack and into a bottomless ravine below. She drove at a rate of speed too high for a road that hangs on the side of a cliff. She was interested about our friend Nico and looked back ready to ask a question. Nico is an odd bird and often the topic of conversation but I was hoping she would keep her eyes on the road. I pointed at the road ahead and spoke in my best pirate voice, "Dead men tell no tales."

Within a few minutes we arrived at our new island home. Stefania cranked the stick shift back into reverse and beeped at her coworker as she pulled into the lone parking space. She had prepared for our arrival and quickly introduced us to the owner of the hotel named Salvatore or Sal. Sal was her husband and partner. He was a short Italian man with a thick bouffant haircut. His hairy arms and sharp facial features reminded me of my Italian American friend Tarsia. As we shuffled through the reception area I looked over as we were greeted by a thin sun baked fellow lounging next to the pool. I hardly recognized Nico even though I had seen him a month earlier. He had apparently been saving money and must have been living on one gyro a day. He looked around ten to twenty pounds lighter and had a much darker complexion than just a month before. But when I heard his high pitched squeaky voice I knew it was him. He called out, "Yo!"

We waved back to him and he immediately jumped from the chair to follow us up some rock steps. The steps led us around back to the entrance of our rooms. Stefania pulled the room keys from her pocket and placed them in my hand. It was time for us to settle in.

49

MY NEW ROOMIE

Three of us entered the first room and stood staring at each other. Nico stood waiting outside near the entranceway. I looked to Kwab and Mike concerning sleeping arrangements. Without words each of them dropped their luggage next to the two beds. I originally planned to bunk up with Kwab. He was most familiar with me and had never spent much time alone with Mike. But Mike wouldn't budge. He stood there next to Kwab holding his spot. A light bulb lit up in my head. It finally occurred to me that Mike would have nothing to do with sharing a room with Nico. Their last room sharing experience did not go very well.

The three of us, Mike, Nico and I had spent a weekend in Harpers Ferry, West Virginia just two months earlier. My new vacation home in West Virginia was under construction and only one room had carpet at the time. Hence this was the only room suitable for sleeping. The three of us attempted to share the room but Mike snored in his typical bellowing volume. He was disturbing everyone; particularly Nico. Once I fell asleep I no longer subconsciously commanded Mike's snore. Nico was exhausted and irritated lying on a floor next to Mike.

In order to reduce the volume of the snore Nico decided he would punch Mike as he slept throughout the night. Amusingly this resulting in a polka dotted pattern of welts that were visible on Mike the next morning. He did not find it as funny as I did but at least he managed to get some sleep. The night ultimately resulted in Mike moving to the basement of the house. The basement was under construction. At the time there was nothing more than a concrete floor and a roll of cat soiled carpet. In Mike's tired confusion he had apparently crawled into the piss soaked rug. Again he didn't find this funny either. He blamed Nico for the resulting stench of his cat pissed clothing.

I looked back at Nico, picked up my things, and moved on to the next room. He and I situated our things upon our selected beds.

My room at the Meditteraneo had a painting of the Santorini volcano, marble tiles and stucco walls. It was a nice little room with an island feel. The small clean bathroom and blue bed spreads were similar to that of the Delfini Hotel. There were two doors which opened inward from a patio balcony. I walked out and I could see that we were just above the bar overlooking the pool. We had a spectacular view of the city of Charos. The island breezes blew the hanging blue curtains into the room. I could hear the motor of an occasional car moving up the hill and could smell food cooking in the distance. The courtyard of our pool was quiet. No one was swinging in the hammocks, drinking at the bar or lounging near the pool.

Now that my land legs had returned I requested that Nico lead us forth towards the local food of the island. He is the king of affordable food. I had no doubt that he would lead me to something I could really sink my teeth into. Nico informed me of the perfect place just around the corner. I checked back to room one and saw that Kwab and Mike were still unpacking. Before leaving I informed them of my plan. I would meet them by the pool a little later. Nico led me down a path, passed the pool, and across from the main town square. Just two shops away stood an eatery that offered the corner stable of the Greek traveler, the gyro. I hastily ordered up the chicken gyro. For some unknown reason there were no other meats available before nightfall. I sat down with a huge bottle of water and waited anxiously as the local women cooked the food. There were two ladies standing behind the counter, both were Greek.

One woman looked around fifty. She had long thick hair and long painted fingernails. She even sounded high maintenance as she bantered with the other women. The other woman was an older, shorter version; probably her mother. The tasty smells from the grill were very appealing. They lofted over the countertop as the chicken sizzled on the grill.

I handed over the best two Euros I had ever spent. It was the deal of the restaurant. They offered other Greek specialties but the Gyro was significantly less expensive. It was designed for the poor traveler. The chicken gyro was a soft, fresh, cooked slab of pita bread filled with seasoned chicken, lettuce, homemade tziki sauce and some of the freshest deep red tomatoes imaginable. The gyro was topped off with a hand full of thick french fries that were laid upon the gyro like the famous sub restaurant in Pittsburg, Pennsylvania. Before she handed it across the counter she shook a liberal amount of paprika over the fry laden sandwich and wrapped it in a paper covering. Hot sauce was also an available option.

I sat down and nearly inhaled my first real Greek gyro. It tasted far better than any other gyro I had ever consumed in an American diner. She leaned over the counter and asked me, "Did you enjoy the meal?"

I replied, "I would have if I had taken the time to taste it."

She smiled with a wave. I waved goodbye and reassured her that I would be back soon accompanied by friends. I headed back to the pool where Mike and Kwab had already settled into their lounge chairs. Mike had his shirt off and was applying globs of suntan lotion. He offered some to Kwab. Kwab declined and rolled his eyes. They had already found a beer and were relaxing with the company of the hotel owner Sal. Intentionally throwing a wrench into their relaxation I started barking out orders, "Kill the beers! It's time to invade the Austrian Camp!"

I was excited to meet up with Georg down at the Austrian base on Yialos Beach. Mike cried, "I need to feed."

I packed up the pool supplies and started for the gate. I looked back at Mike, pointed forward, and gave him a nod of confidence. I knew just the gyro shop where Mike would fall in love.

50

THE AUSTRIAN BASE

Mike and Kwab finished their beers. We walked out of the hotel gate and headed down the street with Nico as our local Sherpa. We stopped off at the gyro store and I ordered more food. Mike was disappointed that the woman only had chicken gyros available during the daytime. He was on the hunt for lamb. He also found it odd that other meats would only be available after dark. Does lamb meat ignite like a vampire in the sun? The woman behind the counter looked up upon my return. She smiled and was obviously impressed at how quickly I held true to my word. I ordered another gyro for myself and officially the gyro eating competition had begun: Mike-1, Matt-2.

We finished up and headed down an old donkey trail towards the distant Yialos beach. We carefully navigated each step of the steep path which I refer to as the "Goat Path." Moving down the path Mike and I questioned Nico about his island home. I asked about the painted outlines of each and every rock along this path, "What's the deal with the white paint?"

Each was colored with a white outline of paint. I noticed the stones back in the main city square were outlined as well. Nico sharply answered, "Why does everyone come here and ask me questions like I'm their fucking tour guide?" He continued, "I don't know why the shit is painted. I've been coming here for fifteen years and I don't know shit. I haven't even gone beyond Milopatas Beach."

Milopatas beach was less than two miles away but in Nico's case this all makes sense. Nico is a creature about the sun, the sand, and the party. He pretends to be a cultural connoisseur but is actually a party enthusiast who just happens to travel. In Nico's early years I could have asked him the island ratio of men to women on July 17th in 1994. He would have easily answered back with the exact ratio as well as the data on nationality and age brackets. He could have referred back to the notes written in his 1994 travel diary:

Man Whore log date July 17th, 1994, 3:26am -
I finally nailed the elusive letter X while accidentally attempting to shag a letter Z by the name of Xena. I was privileged to take her virginity as she demanded that I keep the lights off and only take her from behind. It can be interestingly noted that I found her deep voice and hairy mid section unusually attractive.

And so we quietly continued to follow the *(formerly)* self proclaimed man whore down the goat path while Kwab and Mike took pictures of the scene below. Nico is a fast walker, as am I. He would occasionally hold up to check back on Mike. "What? Did Myers have a fat attack?" he casually asked.

"Probably," I simply replied before we continued. We waited up once more before we crossed the main port road over to a chain of hotels that fall along Yialos Beach. I took the time to look over a posted map of the island. There were only around five roads. The path of the roads squiggled in every direction through the rough terrain shown on the map. The road was paved but there was a lot of dust lying on the pavement. I thought about the fact that all of these roads were dirt just seven years before. Modern conveniences such as asphalt had slowly spread to this distant island. Eventually Kwab and Mike had caught up and we crossed over the road. The very first hotel along the grouping was Petros Place and it was the one that the Austrians had booked. We followed Nico in through the back pool entrance. He had already been down to visit with Georg previously during their stay here on Ios.

As we entered Nico was already telling the tale of Georg's drunkenness. It had been a regular occurrence in the village of Charos on the previous nights. Goerg can be a drunken terror. He always seems to have a good time after consuming a few select beverages. We walked up along side of the pool bar where Georg and his Austrian companions were sitting. They were currently downing beers. We were greeted with cheers of welcome and I gave Georg a big hug. Introductions went around as we met with the various characters who accompanied Georg to Ios. They were all his former study mates and had a reunion every five years. They looked like an average bunch of Germans but I would never tell them as such. They wore the stereotypical black socks and sandals. Their shorts were too short and their hair too long. One had a very European looking goatee. This was the year they came to Ios for their five year friendship reunion. I imagine they didn't know what they were getting into when they decided to travel with Georg to a remote party island.

Their English was limited. It was only slightly better than the German that Mike and I attempt to use. Georg on the other hand spoke near perfect English and had learned a lot of slang from Mike and me. Other English speakers are probably confused when Georg says that the dinner they prepared was *"love."* Once the introductions were complete the Austrians pretty much went back to speaking German within their tribe. Georg was the only one left who continued to engage us in English conversation. We caught up with Georg about his family and I referred to the fact that they still call his son "Constantstink." I invented this nickname a year before during a family trip that Georg and I took together. Combining his name Constantine with his little stinker type of behavior created the fitting name Constantstink. He and my own little stinker nicknamed, Stink; were a fitting pair of companions. It's nice to see the childish debauchery passed on to new generation.

We spent the day hanging out by the Austrian pool while

Kwab and Mike had a few beers with the Austrians and the Greek bartender Yannis. Yannis was a young man who stood a thin five feet. He carried a serious but relaxed demeanor. Georg and I threw a small football around the pool while everyone continued to take in the sun and the day of fun. Some "Scandis," a term used to describe Scandinavians, floated on a raft in the pool. Kwab attempted to nearly miss them with the football in an effort to spark up conversation. It didn't work. These Scandis appeared to be a bit snobbish and wanted nothing to do with the filthy tribes of Austrians and Americans. The next night the snobbish Scandi was found vomiting onto the streets of Charos. Georg always enjoys mocking the overly intoxicated or hung over. His humor is entirely hypocritical considering how he often ends up. But he'll never pass at the chance to recommend another shot of vodka to a sick intoxicated drunk. As the hung over Scandi laid ill by the pool Georg walked over and asked, "Do you FEEEEL GOOOOOOOD?"

After some time in the pool I was anxious to take my first swim in the Aegean Sea. I tried to recruit a team to head with me to the nearby Yialos Beach but only Kwab decided to join. Kwab and I bid a temporary farewell and headed a short distance to nearby Yialos beach. The beach was mostly deserted as Nico had once foretold. Apparently the visitors of the island spend the day sleeping or by the pool. Looking down the beach I pondered about the numerous empty cabana chairs that covered the majority of the beach. I thought to myself, "Why aren't they full?"

I'm quite sure thousands of Ocean City beachgoers back in Maryland would much rather be sitting here. In Maryland everyone is crammed six inches apart from the next blanket of loud mouthed simple folk. But this was a beach traveler's heaven and it was nearly deserted. Kwab spent some time walking in the surf while I waded a short distance from the break.

According to the locals the wind was much stronger today than usual and the small waves that continued to break upon the shore were unusually large. The water looked as blue as it did from The Highspeed-3 as I looked out toward the horizon. The color of the water changed to a greenish hue as it crashed upon the coarse volcanic sand. The deserted beach was quiet. There wasn't even a cry from a seagull. The skies were deserted as well. As the sun began to retreat Kwab and I decided to walk back to Petros Place to reunite with the group. We hoped to spend more time up in city of Charos and headed back to work out our plans with Nico and Mike. The four of us decided to head back up into town. We wanted to clean up and get some dinner. After dinner we could search for the Austrians in the village square.

51

IOS GREECE – NIGHT 1

Austrian free, we trudged back up the goat path. This fifteen minute hike up the hillside is one heck of a workout. It was very reminiscent of the many inclined sections I've hiked along the Appalachian Trail near Harpers Ferry. Very little talking was done as our mouths were strictly dedicated to oxygen inhalation. Mike and Kwab stopped along the path for breathers while Nico and I trudged forth. Tortured by this path, I still found myself looking forward to it each day. There is no better workout than a steep hill for sweating old beer out of your system. Eventually we reached Point Medditeranneo and waited up for Mike and Kwab. Together we agreed to grab a few hours of sleep on the advice of our local Sherpa Nico. The island of Ios prides itself on being the island that never sleeps, at least during the night. I can vouch that this statement holds true. After a few hours we awoke as the sun had fully set. We each showered to prepare for dinner and the night in the village to come.

As I stepped onto the patio of my room I could see the evening lights of Charos illuminating the churches and various buildings among the village. The city was coming to life. The white and blue domes of the churches and buildings looked like colorful building blocks propped against the hillside. It reminded me of a mountain of dirt where I would play as a child. The mount looked like a life size version of the pile where I sculpted roads and tunnels for my toy cars. The scene was magnificent and I could hear the nightlife already beginning to liven with the sounds of echoing voices, laughter and music. The sounds carried across the village square directly to my patio. The four of us met down by the pool and the collective food selection of the night was Thai. So far we had consumed Icelandic goo subs, a variety of English pub meals, London's Indian and Italian cuisine, as well as Greek cocoons and gyros. We were ready for some spicy, flavorful Thai.

We wound out of the hotel, moved across the street, and passed the main playground of the village center. Only a glimpse of sunlight remained as the local children of Charos were out and about running around the dusk lit playground. They were chasing around soccer balls and playing tag seemingly oblivious to the foreign zombies which rose as the sun fell. It was the kind of scene you would see depicted in a high school foreign language book. Some kids were riding skateboards while others sat along a white concrete wall. Groups of little girls were sitting in circles. They were pointing at various boys in the vicinity while the boys ignored their calls. All the while the vampires of Ios rose from their sarcophagus.

Following Sherpa Nico we headed into the catacombs of Choras to a little restaurant named Ali Baba's. I had imagined Ali Baba's to be a much larger restaurant and club venue. It was a humble outdoor patio that stood before me. Mike and I were familiar with this eatery from the Ali Baba facebook page. Mike could not wait to tell the owner of the personal invite, "We received an invite from Ali Baba himself."

Of course this personal invite was through a mass facebook invitation. Mike informed the owner that we flew a quarter of the way around the world just to eat here. The owner seemed very impressed, not. *(Sorry I just had to throw in a not joke.)* The waitress brought us a bowl of local hors d'oeuvre olives with our re-hydrating drink order. I had ordered multiple bottles of water to go with my spicy Pad Thai. Mike ordered a soulvaki chicken dish while Kwab requested the red curry. Nico was in the mood for curry as well and ordered the milder green curry dish. We relaxed and chatted while we waited for our food to arrive.

The meal was relatively uneventful. The highlight of the meal was pouring the huge water bottle evenly into our four glasses. Along a ledge, above our table, a young local boy was fooling around with the foliage which draped down into the restaurant. This immediately sparked Mike's overall dislike for anyone male and under the age of eighteen. This fact alone made his past marriage to a single mom with a teenage boy a complete disaster. Mike looked up and gave his best evil eye to the young boy peering over the wall. The boy disappeared and was off to find some other form of entertainment. Kwab and I swatted at a couple of flies that had congregated on the table. The local flies were faster than lightning. Kwab and I had made a sport of chasing them away.

Our food arrived and we hungrily dug in. The owner of the restaurant, a large bald Aussie and an old friend of Nico watched over us as we ate. He was the largest man I had seen on the island and could snap Mike like a twig. He was a member of the "seasonal business owners club" that came and went to Ios yearly as did Nico. He and Nico discussed the slow tourist season and the lack of profits thus far. This seemed to be a major topic of discussion amongst the island as I had only been here a day and had overheard local merchants mention this before. I didn't mind the lack of people; I no longer enjoy the results of crowded locations. Yes, I was quite happy to be without crammed alleyways, slow food service and long bathroom lines.

Unfortunately for the Island of Ios, the summer profits were cut short as would be Nico's stay. If he didn't find work within the next two days he would be leaving with us. Considering the slow year, the resulting lack of jobs, and his new found love; Nico decided to head back to his temporary home in Switzerland. Last summer Nico came to Ios and met a traveler from Geneva. They hit it off almost immediately. Breaking the unspoken law of the island Nico fell in love. He spent the last off season with his new found love in Switzerland. Together, the two lived the sweet life of Swiss thrill seekers. They spent time in her chateau while taking time to snowboard and enjoy the winter wonderland together. In the last several months I had heard plenty about her and his time spent with her. Perhaps she was the one? Or perhaps age was finally catching up with Nico? I just hope he hadn't *"matured."*

Nico contemplated the torturous decision of leaving this paradise for another. I really didn't have much advice for him. Either decision sounded a lot better than my fateful return to a five foot square cubicle. I was going to spend the next fifty-one weeks locked up *and not abroad.* To me it seemed fairly obvious that Nico and his future life was somewhere other than Ios. Mike offered his advice but it didn't matter. Nico's new life and this new woman were pulling him away from his fourteenth season in Ios no matter what advice he received. To the surprise of many, the very next day he eagerly, yet reluctantly, purchased his ferry pass back to Athens and plane tickets to Geneva. It was his new calling. Consequently, I noticed Nico's facebook posting that appeared just two days after he arrived in Geneva. It stated, "Looking for a bartender job in Ios."

Apparently he was having trouble with his decision even after landing in Switzerland. After small talk and the meal the boys packed up their purses to head down for drinks in the village square. In the voice of a runway host I announced, "Nico looks strapping while wearing his fine denim European handbag. He surely is the most sheik debutant of the village square."

52

THE VILLAGE SQUARE

We moved down slope along the winding catacombs of Charos to an area known as the village square. Before we could get into the main open square, a fellow with an English accent pulled Kwab into his little establishment. He was another Nico type that had been coming to Ios year after year. But this year this Ios enthusiast made a big investment. He opened a bar. He was around my age and well dressed in semi-formal attire. I felt like I was in the presence of a desperate used car salesman who was playing the role of secret agent 007. The man had decided to open his own bar that was located just below the main square. He pulled us into his place and introduced us to the DJ while advertising his DJ's amazing skills. The bar owner claimed that he is the only disk jockey who plays Hip Hop on the entire square. I immediately had my doubts. I recognize a bad sales pitch when I hear it.

We ordered a round of beers and the owner also brought us a free round of shots. This was a friendly gesture that was also meant to guilt us into hanging around a little longer. Guilt only works on real Catholics like my wife. I was a convert and a poor one at that. It was apparent that he was eager to keep us spending. I could feel his sense of desperation as he stood nearby trying to spark up conversation. He found out that we came from the Washington D.C. area and he immediately filled us in about his time spent living in

Alexandria, Virginia. He continued the small talk with Kwab and Mike as I convinced the group to exit the place. I wanted to be out under the open skies of the Greek isle and not inside listening to pounding Hip Hop. The breeze was crisp and the air was sweet. I was ready for a comforting setting and not this loud adobe hut. It was no bigger than a beaver lodge and contained very little beaver. Once we finished our drinks, I thanked him personally. I gave a large tip to the bartender and we left.

We moved out and up eight steps to the heart of the village square. It was a modest open area in between a group of bars. It was somewhere midway up the side of Mount Charos. Each bar had an outdoor section of tables where you could sit and have one of the seasonal foreigners wait upon you. A large evergreen tree reached high up above the side of the nearby bars and added nicely to the natural décor of this small village square. We sat down at one of the tables and were greeted by a familiar accent. Most of the waitresses were Irish but ours was a rare Austrian employee. Mike won this game of "Guess the Accent" so fast that no one realized the game had been played.

Everyone ordered a beer except me. I went straight for a red bull, a sprite, and a couple of shots. My body clock was screwed up beyond belief considering our seven hour time differential. This was combined with the odd sleeping sched-ule that included long daytime naps. I kept watch throughout the evening. Mike and I were both disappointed not to have an Austrian presence in the village square. Still the four of us were having a great time just taking in the scene. This was a great place for people watching and I took to the spot immedi-ately. One of the first things we noticed is that many patrons were wearing t-shirts with a clown face that read, "Killin' IT!" "How fitting?" I thought to myself.

Looking around the village square many various nation-alities were mixed in conversations. While ease dropping I could hear them sharing stories of their culture. Each one had their own personal story of Ios. Ios is such an obscure place. It sits out in the middle of Aegean Sea and has a short season for tourism. It isn't exactly the tourist destination you see as a vacation package on the Wheel of Fortune game show.

This paradise setting has tons of affordable alcohol and an overall care free attitude. The stories of debauchery were all around us. One of the best stories I heard involved a nude woman riding on the back of a mule, but that story is for later. The Irish workers and tourists were very friendly and probably very drunk as well. They seemed to outnumber the rest of the nationalities at least two to one. Many of the doormen working at the entrances of the bars were Australian and had a stereotypical surfer look. I can see how Nico would fit in here and why he was often mistaken for an Aussie. Many of the Aussies reminded me of a younger Nico. I wondered how many of them would still be here with Nico fifteen years from now.

Looking around the square you could see about six to eight tables in front of each bar. In the center is a walkway which leads down the middle of the square for the patrons to pass. Mike and Kwab were making small talk with many who passed while I sat and powered up with my red bull and vodka shots. Local teens were walking around the square attempting to sell glowing wristbands. When my head was turned, one young lady attempted to lace my wrist with a florescent purple band. She was a local girl around sixteen wearing a long gown with exposed cleavage. I quickly removed the band and handed it back to the girl. I stated, "No thank you."

She replied, "But it looks so good on you."

Kwab was staring across the table into her cleavage. He commented, "Yeah, but it looks better on you."

We all received a stern look from her grandmother. She was standing nearby watching over the teenagers who were working the crowd. Grandma looked like the old lady from Steven King's "Thinner." I decided to give her one Euro as a peace offering. Instead of buying the fluorescent bracelet I bought our table an evening of peace. No more loitering from the teens and no gypsy curse from the old lady. At the price of one Euro, it was the bargain of the night. We continued to talk, laugh and tell stories pertaining to the lot of us while Kwab took pictures with ladies of various nationalities. He was attempting to take a photo with a female from each country or at least that was his opening line.

As the night moved on I still wondered what happened to our good friend Georg. I speculate that he never left the mounting collection of empty beer bottles that gathered by the Austrian pool. I looked across the square and saw what looked like one of Georg's Austrian companions. I turned to Mike. He confirmed, "That is an Austrian."

Mike waved him over to us. It was the Austrian called Rinhard, who went by the nickname Fish. In college I had a continual roommate called Fish. I had always thought of him as Fish because he appeared oily. So did the Austrian that stood before me. Mike invited Fish to sit down and join us for a beer. We immediately inquired on the whereabouts of Georg. Fish informed us, "Georg has been in the area for the past several hours."

I found it curious that we had been sitting in the center of the square for well over an hour and had not seen him. Fish continued using hand gestures and broken English to communicate. He informed us that Georg was so inebriated that he was on what Fish described as auto-pilot. Apparently Georg was walking about randomly yelling at strangers in a zombie like state. This came as no surprise. I've witnessed this behavior on many occasions. On our walk up the goat trail Nico had mentioned seeing Georg in this exact condition just two days prior. I gave Fish a nod of understanding.

Many times I've had to help carry Georg's limp body off of the bar stool that he precariously managed to unconsciously sleep upon. He possesses the sleeping balance of a horse. He can fully sleep while remaining balanced and in an upright position. Most people would have to see this to believe it. I've seen Myers and my own kid, Stink; sleep with their eyes fully open. But seeing Georg sleep on a bar stool is whole different ballgame. You may not think this is possible, but I promise you, it is. I can still remember the first time I witnessed it in a downtown Baltimore club called Orpheus. One minute he was drunk dancing with the movements of a pantomime boxer and the next he was perched asleep atop of a bar stool. To this very day I tell the story and sometimes imitate the Georg transformation from dancing boxer to unresponsive paperweight. And tonight, just like the night at the Orpheus, Georg did not ever make another conscious evening appearance.

Mike and Fish continued a conversation in broken English pertaining to the usual get to know you chit chat. I watched as Kwab attempted to have his picture taken with the various Irish women that were now monopolizing the scene. I found the Irish of the island to be an extremely likable and fun group. Their accent alone just illuminated a tone fit for ordering another beer. Smiling, jovial and expressive, they seemed to take lead of the overall communal party as they mingled from table to table. They alone were worth an evening entirely dedicated to people watching. The Irish photo models, not to be confused with Hungarian models, became more and more interesting as the night and week went on.

53

SWEET IRISH ROSE

The time had just passed four in the morning when the bar merchants of the village square started their clean up routine. They had begun to stack the chairs and push the drunken patrons out of the square. The drunks were directed down the sloping walkway away from the center of the village. Sherpa Nico led us down the walk passed several other bars including Club 69, Circus, and bars with other typical themed titles. As we pushed our way passed the groups of party goers we dodged, jumped and stumbled over those who had become beyond drunk. Many of the drunks now rested along the steps of the closed shops.

We passed the local money machine and walked along side of the area parking lot. I looked up to see my old friend, the gyro shop, who was gleaming in full illumination. At nearly five in the morning I now understood the nightlife of Ios and the reason why beef and pork gyros were only served after midnight. To the right of the daytime restaurant stood an open rolling metal door that revealed the secret hidden during the day lit hours. Within the opening stood a man serving up the real gyros from a slab of meat that must have weighed more than Myers and I combined. A tear ran down my eye as I saluted to her, the meat, not the man. Reluctantly I moved onward towards the entrance of a nearby nightclub called The Sweet Irish Rose. As Nico pulled me towards the entrance I whispered back to the rotating meat angel, "I will come back for you."

Nico had arranged our cover free entrance with Tommy, the sun baked owner of the club. Looking at the man I'd swear on the rack of gyro that Tommy was Nico's true father. I know that Nico was supposedly born from another man he calls Dad but Tommy was Nico Senior. He looked at Nico with the eyes of a proud father as they discussed work on the island. Tommy seemed like a much better fit than Nico's biological father. Tommy was more like Nico in style and in persona than any other dad I had ever heard about. From his sun baked tan to his ragged beach dress; Tommy was Baby Nico's Daddy. I didn't hesitate to question Nico. Had Mommy Joan possibly been involved on a trip to Ios? Perhaps she traveled to Ios back in the 60's? My questions were waved off with a precarious laugh.

Mike, Kwab and I followed Nico up a set of wooden stairs and into the booming sound, sights and lights of the Sweet Irish Rose. We ordered a round of drinks as Mike was eying up the dance floor. The lights and music had taken over the room. Mike quickly disappeared onto the dance floor. He was like a man possessed with the rhythm of the night. After six hours of slow paced alcohol consumption I was more interested in having a secret affair. I was ready to spend time with the meat angel that hung a mere sixty feet away. Mike and the droves of youths dancing on platforms had nothing on the Greek goddess of meats. Kwab stood nearby and looked tired from the ongoing thump of techno music.

Kwab and I had reached a more relaxed state. We sat down together in a nearby booth to take in the scene. The activities of the Sweet Irish Rose included dancing, drinking and people watching. He and I decided to partake of the latter two. Mike, the gentle giant was harmlessly out on the dance floor intensely rocking left and right to the music. He loves to dance but it's like watching the Incredible Hulk trying to knit. He was casting an eclipse over the strobe lights that were unable to reach the other patrons in his shadow. Nico had taken off his beach sandals and was now dancing near Mike. He was up on a dance platform just above Mike. I was waiting to see if Mike would drop into one of his drunken break dancing routines.

I sat patiently listening to the changing music and hoped that a familiar musical track would motivate me to move from my comfortable booth. A little moving around might be a good thing for me in my intoxicated state. But the music was failing, and so was I. I thought back to the meat angel hovering outside. The vision of her spinning glory over the hot grill would become my needed motivation. Kwab leaned over and tried to communicate but the pounding bass was too much for his voice to be heard. All sound was overtaken by the beat that poured out of the surrounding speakers. The dance floor encompassed the room which was otherwise surrounded on all sides by the bar. The bar was filled with a mass of patrons that stood around ordering drinks.

Hoping to add some spice to my evening I looked towards the dance floor to watch Mike and Nico as they danced. They were enjoying the primary purpose of this club and the two of them often enhance people watching. I could not imagine what was going on inside of their intoxicated minds. Within the moving crowd of distorted lights Mike was wearing a bright yellow shirt that shone like the sun while Nico stood high above him. Nico had climbed high upon a platform and was now four feet taller than his usual six feet, three inches of lean height. The younger dancing stars surrounded Mike and Nico in orbit as the beams of light highlighted the various sections of the dance floor.

Suddenly, the atmosphere came to a big bang as Nico reached for his foot and had apparently cut it on some broken glass. I sat bemused as Mike helped him down and he hobbled drunkenly over to the bar. Nico had his priorities straight. He was trying to keep from spilling his beer as he hopping on one foot. His unheard agony had forced him down from his celestial pedestal and onto the hopscotch path before him. On his way to purchase another beer he grabbed a handful of napkins to stop the bleeding. At this point, I had seen enough. It was late. I had already taken in an hour of people watching since entering the Sweet Irish Rose. Using drunken sign language I briefly informed Kwab that I was ready to go. A visit with the meat angel was in my near future. I walked towards the exit and puttered down the steps. I was ready to seek out my beloved.

The gyro man welcomed me with the open arms of a long lost brother. He was a hairy burly fellow who regarded his post with the utmost duty. I imagine he was the husband to the daytime chicken gyro woman and the hunk of meat before him was his nighttime mistress. No wonder she could only be seen at night. The man was on a mission to supply the vampires of Ios with late night feeding. He had noticed me earlier when I had passed by his shop. He was very protective of his meaty dance partner; and rightfully so. He quickly but gently carved out the pork gyro that would put an end to my cravings. I finally felt as though the night was complete. As I finished the carnage I noticed that the sun was ready to rise over the hills of Charos. Would my skin burn when touched by the light? I quickly headed back to the Mediterraneo and pulled out my camera for this spectacular photo opportunity. I grabbed a bottle of water and sat down on my patio. I waited for the prime moments of my first sunrise in the islands of Greece. As the sun rose I took the picture what would become my latest facebook profile. It was a fine self portrait with the sun pouring into Charos in the background. I watched the dawn for a few fading moments and then joined the vampires of Ios. I crawled into my coffin and began another day lit session of sleep.

54

MOONS OVER MY – LOPOTAS

Thursday June 25th – I awoke just a few hours later. I didn't want to miss this spectacular day on the Greek Island. I was surprised to find that Mike had already finished a gyro breakfast and was already down by the pool. Kwab was apparently still laying dormant back in his room, as was Nico. Determined to hit the most famous beach on the island, Milopotas Beach, I went up to wrangle the boys and get the day adventure into gear. Sherpa Nico awoke quickly and met Mike and I down by the pool. For an early afternoon breakfast he suggested a nice place that promised a spectacular view overlooking Milopotas Beach. Nico knew the owner of the establishment and also planned to surf the internet for his Swiss departure itinerary. Nico usually skips out on breakfast and the internet would keep him busy while we enjoyed ours. Kwab and Mike also liked the idea of having an internet break. The thought of catching up with reality was on their minds too. Mike expressed a growing concern that something terrible had happened to his girlfriend back home. She had not answered his latest email. She was probably just pissed off because he left her home for a European adventure with his friends. Kwab just needed his world news. He had spoken to his sister over the phone and knew she was fine. He was being called to his addiction to American politics.

Sherpa Nico led us up and over the top of Charos and down

a winding little road towards Milopotas Beach. As we walked
along we passed a bar that I had hoped to visit. It was called
The Scorpion. Unfortunately the local bar owner Tommy did
not have plans to open it until mid-July. He could maximize
his profits with the wave of Italians who would soon arrive
and overthrow the island. Tommy was already busy running
the club that we visited last night. Unfortunately he doesn't
run both clubs until the tourist season is in full swing. I was
a bit disappointed to miss out on the Scorpion. My astrological sign is the Scorpio and what better place to go when you're
in the land of fourth century astrology. The only place more
historically tied to astrology would be Babylonia. That is in
modern day Iraq. Needless to say I don't wish to find myself
in any Iraqi place period. We arrived at the hotel café and sat
down at a table overlooking the vast beauty of the Aegean Sea.
I could even handle Icelandic food with a view like this.

Words and pictures cannot describe the beauty of this
Milopotas scene. It must be experienced first hand to be truly
appreciated. Of course I'm talking about the combination of
a full service breakfast menu with the waves of the Aegean
Sea in the background. The deep blue waves were busy pouring themselves onto the sands of Milopotas Beach below. We
were perched high and could not hear the sound of the surf.
Mike was fixated on the menu. The waiter stopped in and
Mike ordered a soulvaki platter. Kwab and I both ordered
a traditional breakfast. Being in Greece I ordered the Greek
omelet with feta cheese and olives while Kwab requested traditional eggs, bacon and toast.

The setting of this breakfast retreat was much different
than any diner back home. The nearby pool bar played some
very familiar techno music which included artists such as DJ
Tiesto and iiO. There was a children's play area placed directly next to the bar and sound system. It was setup on the
patio near the edge of a fifty foot drop off. It looked like a nice
place for kids to play even though the baby swing swung out
near the edge of the cliff. If I watched my kids play near this
wall I would have a massive heart attack. The heights and
cliffs are an everyday feature on this island. You had better

figure out gravity early if you want to live to the ripe old age of five.

We ate our breakfast completely enthralled with the view while Nico was inside purchasing his ticket out of paradise. Nico came back to the table and informed us that he would be leaving tomorrow on the "Slow Ferry." Knowing Nico he's probably saving money by renting a dim witted homosexual or "Slow Fairy" to row him back to Switzerland. Taking the slow ferry is a ten hour ride that I could only imagine in my worst nightmare. He specifically chose to take this boat and the cheapest air cargo plane in order to save his travel nest egg. It doesn't matter to Nico if his flight happens to be carrying illegal cargo or flying over enemy airspace. He would ride on a shark and tie himself to the wheel of a plane if they took Visa. Nico has all the time in the world and his goal is to travel as long as he can. If there is money left in his account, this is what he will do. Nico has always been a thrifty fellow. Drinking pocket bottles of cheap vodka is the most disgusting vise. I will say this. He has mastered the art of stretching a penny to live well. For him the goal is not just traveling, it's traveling on the least amount of money for the longest period of time.

Once Nico finished up on the computer Kwab and Mike took turns on the internet. Mike had been searching for his missing reading glasses since this morning and continued to dig through his backpack to no avail. Even so Mike decided to use the computer by initiating the George Costanza eye squint technique. He puts his face about two inches from the screen to see and then down to the keyboard in order to type. It's very amusing to watch. It takes about two minutes for him to give up. Mike's regular crisis' concerning vision happens more frequently than Velma from Scooby Doo. He always looses his glasses or drops one contact into the pool. I can't tell you how many times I've helped Mike look for one of his contacts. The worst part is when he finds it. He shoves it into his eye using a wad of spit. Just last month he tore his cornea. This was about the seventh time he has done so. I'm not sure how many times you can do that before you go blind, but I'm pretty sure Mike will find out.

After a short period of squinting Mike was finished. I took hold of the keyboard to see what was going on in the world. Nothing special caught my attention as I scanned through my email and then logged onto facebook. I made a short status update to tell the facebook world of my breakfast with a view and then logged off. Right now nothing outside of this moment seemed more important than enjoying the view and heading down to the beach below. Before we moved on I prompted Mike and Nico to pose for a picture. They were lying out in the sun next to each other so I requested that they hold hands while I took the photo. Jokingly, they briefly held hands and I quickly snapped the shot. This picture now holds a special place at the top of my all time funny photos. It's even funnier than the shot of my *macho* brother-in-law seated on a Key West bench posing with a couple of transvestites.

55

MILOPOTAS BEACH

Walking down towards Milopotas beach we cut across the main road and down another goat path. As we climbed down our pace was slowed behind a few other visiting beach go-ers. Looking down, the beach appeared in the shape of a cres-cent. It lies deep within the outer coastline of the island. I had heard much about this beach. It is known as the main party beach near Charos. In the distance, behind the beach, I could see a group of hotels which cater directly to the beach patrons. Sitting before the hotels was a bus stop and a bath house. There were also various shops and food vendors. Beach cabanas were spread out and set up along the beach. Nico, the avid surfer and former surf instructor was looking intently at the water. We soon reached the bottom of the goat path and he immediately commented on the immense height of the waves as we started our trek along the beach, "Damn those waves are big."

Apparently in his fifteen years on Ios he had never seen waves this big, waves that could be ridden. I doubted that in his fifteen years on Ios he had ever been awake early enough to see waves this big.

We walked along the road leading to the beach as we took in the scene. I noticed a sign that advertised camping. Mike commented, "Who in the world would want to camp on this hot rock island?"

In my opinion most European hotels were only one step above the average campground facilities of the states. I agreed. I couldn't imagine camping here. Mike and Kwab decided to stop in the shops before we set up on the beach. Shopping was always their first priority. I informed them that Nico and I would be on the far end of the beach. My plan was to survey the entire strip. I wanted to see all of the real estate before choosing a spot to settle down. Nico and I walked along the beach to do just that.

I had heard many good things about this beach from Nico but especially from "Bailing Bob." Bob is my friend who actually scheduled off work for this week but decided to forgo the trip. With a tear in his eye, Bob described this beach as the closest thing to heaven that he had ever seen. Bob was particularly fond of topless woman and Greece offered plenty of that. In preparation of this trip I had questioned Bob about Milopotas. He broke into a five minute monologue about women playing beach games topless. He had actually started to well up with tears as he went into specific detail pertaining to his last days on Milopotas Beach. As we surveyed the scene, Nico expressed his daunted content. He was glad that Bob had not come along on this particular trip. He solemnly expressed that he would have been disappointed. Apparently this trip was much tamer than Bob's previous experience. The description of that vacation sounded like a teenage B-Movie from the 80's.

Bob's stories had left my imagination scarred with a topless version of "Weekend at Bernies." I pictured Bob in the role of Bernie, the corpse from the movie. Just like Bernie, Bob always had a huge rigor mortis smile. He was a perfect picture of joy with the smile etched upon his face as topless women sat upon his decomposing lap. But today was not 80's filming day at Milopotas Beach. It was just another usual day under the Greek island sun. Bob's thong adorned topless women lay still upon their chairs and without a beach volleyball in site.

In the theme of 80's cinema, there was a topless wild dog which ran down the beach hauling a stolen soccer ball in his teeth. Two young Italians attempted to chase him in what looked like a rehearsed attempt to attract attention. The dog was having the best part of the good time. The two young soccer stars unsuccessfully attempted to wrestle the ball from his mouth. They repeatedly dove at the dog but only fell into the sand empty handed. The dog easily out maneuvered the two buffoons. Eventually the entertainment factor wore off and they pulled the ball from the dog's mouth. The two men looked extremely foolish and walked away from the dog as he continued to jump for the ball. He was doing his best to convince them to play another round of "Don't you look dumb."

Mike and Kwab returned from shopping with Kwab's new towel in hand. As they arrived we spread our towels onto the sand at our current spot. We were about half way down the long beach. Nico and Kwab sat down upon the coarse sand and I headed out into the Sea. Mike decided to come join me for a bit of wading but immediately went back in due to the rough surf. I loved the feel of the surf and the salt on my skin. There appeared to be a pretty strong undertow so I stayed close to shore. I could keep my footing on the bottom of the sea floor. The bottom had areas of flat, but not slippery rock, as well as large sections of sand. Back home I was used to standing on the rocks out in the Potomac River but they were always slippery and covered with algae. Due to the high salt content of the sea the bottom was lifeless and hence algae free.

The water of Milopotas beach looked more of a greenish color when standing chest deep and it wasn't as clear as the waters of Cancun or Jamaica. Although looking down I could see fairly well into the water considering the high winds and relatively large waves. I floated around a bit and did a little swimming. I was enjoying the sun and the clear cool water. As I floated I caught something moving in the left corner of my eye and my shark alarm went off. I tried to stand but couldn't get a firm hold on the bottom so I began to swim towards the shore. In a state of panic I was unaware of the fact that sharks could not live in his much salt. I hastily started towards the safety of the beach.

As I swam inward I heard the sound of gentle smacking

upon the water and my heart began to pound. I didn't want to look back as my anxiety was growing. Once I was far enough in to get my footing I stood firm and looked back towards the sea. What looked like a mermaid was about twenty feet out and had just crested the surface in the motion of a swimmers kick. I continued to watch as a thin, deeply tan Greek woman gently glided along the top of the water. She was very graceful and swam passed my position in a matter of a few strokes. Once she was about ten feet passed she immerged onto her feet. She threw back her dark thick hair and started her ascent towards a chair which waited on the shore. She was a piece of Bob's heaven, topless and laden in thong. I looked at the other men sitting upon the beach and laughed as the heads to the right all faced west and the heads to the left all faced east. It appeared as if the men were hiding behind their sunglasses while each soaked in a long look.

After the show I decided to swim out a little further. Since the mermaid did not drown I was now more confident in my own swimming abilities. I swam out from the shore for about thirty feet. I was far enough to reach my personal goal of swimming into the Aegean Sea. I turned around and started to swim back in towards shore. I realized that the mermaid had made it look easy. There was a strong undertow and I quickly appeared to be getting nowhere. Just as a slight tinge of panic set in I remembered the old swimmers rule to swim along the beach while in an undertow. I swam along gingerly for about thirty feet and then tried coming into shore once again. It was still a bit challenging but never the less I was making progress. After some additional hard strokes I made it back into shore and sat down with my fellow travelers to catch my breath.

The wise old surfer expressed recognition of the undertow based upon the swimming pattern he had watched me take, "Bad undertow eh?"

It was good to know an experienced swimmer was keeping an eye on me while I swam from the imaginary sharks and worked my way back to shore. If Nico did actually need to rescue me, it would have been like a barracuda attempting to drag in a blue whale. After another half hour in the hot sun we decided to pack it up. We headed over to the bus stop to catch the bus back to Charos. The bus was only a little more than one Euro. The long uphill ride would be well worth every European cent.

56

THE GAMBLING GAME

We decided to ride the bus all the way down to the port of Ios and to the Austrian camp. The goal was to catch up with Georg and make plans for later tonight. We missed the zombie like antics of Georg last night and wanted to ensure his company on this evening's adventure. As we exited the bus Nico suggested a one euro wager. This was big money for a guy that can live a week off of just ten Euros. He made the bet that Georg would already be intoxicated and slightly slurring. I took the bet and was quite sure that Georg would be nowhere near slurring considering his previous night of hard drinking.

We laid down a list of ground rules for the bet and elected Kwab and Mike to be our judges. We immediately walked towards Goerg and the table by the pool that he now called home. Nico could taste victory as Georg held a beer in one hand while another bottle lay empty beside him. I asked a few general questions and not one bit of slurring poured from Georg's mouth. I inquired, "How's it going?"

George replied, "Good," as he took a sip of his beer.

"Drinking already I see," I commented.

He responded, "Yeah. I was really fucked up last night. Taking it easy today."

It was evident that he was still sober and Nico knew he was beat. Kwab and Mike concurred as I held out my hand in victory. Nico reluctantly handed over the one euro coin equal to half of a fully packed gyro.

Everyone headed over to Yannis, the pool bartender and ordered a beverage. I was sticking with water during daylight hours but everyone else started off with beer. I gave Georg a mature look and reminded him, "I hope you will be coherent in about five hours."

If he kept the same pace as yesterday he would not be going out later tonight. He nodded in agreement and we began to discuss what he remembered from last night. According to his memory, he had scoffed through the village square several times looking for us. I imagine that it was well before eleven in the evening. Time doesn't mean much to an overly intoxicated zombie. The square doesn't even pick up before eleven. By then Georg, in his daylong drunken stupor, was probably already sleeping somewhere along the goat path.

Moving forward I recommended that he take a beer break and consume some water. It's not every day that I get to spend time with my Austrian friend. I wanted to guarantee his attendance at the evening event. Georg enjoys a good mixed drink even more than repetitively guzzling beer. I informed him, "I've got a gift pack of tequila and margarita mix waiting for yooooouuuuuu. It's back at our hotel."

"Hmmmm," he replied.

I brought the margarita pack all the way from the states in anticipation of the liquor prices of England and Greece. I was also afraid it might be tough to secure some quality tequila on a remote Greek island. It turns out the liquor in England and throughout Greece was very expensive but not too bad here on Ios. Either way I knew I could finish a bottle of tequila faster than congress can give away stimulus money. Even with the "good" prices of Ios an entire bottle of good tequila would run around fifty euros or more. Georg liked the idea of joining us for Margaritas and agreed to meet us at the American camp around ten in the evening.

As Georg and I continued to catch up, Nico gulped down all of the nut and pretzel mix that was within his reach. Most bars in Greece often slide out little bowls of snacks. Nico had managed to survive solely on this source of sustenance. Squirrels don't stand a chance in the company of Nico. I even considered posting a "Please do not feed the wildlife" sign. I felt bad for Yannis. He constantly had to refill the bowl. But Yannis seemed oblivious to the nut consumption rate. He was distracted and involved in deep A&E conversation with Mike. Mike was taking in as much as he could from Yannis as he probed him about the remote sections of his island. *(This last sentence was in no way a sexual reference but if you considered it to be one then you have mastered the pursuit of immaturity.)*

Yannis was a short thin local Greek and looked more like a light skinned pigmy when standing next to Mike. Mike likes to collect pictures of him self posing with local patrons and bartenders. He has many of these photo shots from around the world. One of the best was from a trip to Quebec. It contains a Canadian posing as if he is going to shove a bottle of Jagermeister up Mike's ass. Mike stood next to Yannis, he put his arm around the tiny man, and asked Kwab, "Take a picture."

Sadly Yannis didn't grab the bottle of Jagermeister as he hopped up and sat upon the bar. It looked like Mike was a ventriloquist with his hand up the back of a wooden comedic doll.

Kwab took a picture then sat down under the shade of the bar and continued to drink his beer. Occasionally he would wrestle a nut free from Nico. This was the first time on the trip that all five of us were together and I requested that Yannis take a group picture. We all handed him our cameras and he took multiple shots. Of course sometime last night while I was in the village square I drunkenly dropped my camera onto the rock floor. My camera took blank white pictures of nothing. This fulfilled my earlier prediction and was yet again another occurrence that supports my theory on intuition. Oddly, Kwab's camera also would not produce a picture. It was as if some mystical force was not going to allow evidence of our five person pentagram of evil. Fortunately Mike's camera eventually worked. He must have been silently repeating the prayer of Saint Michael the arch angel as it had successfully warded off the supernatural camera disturbances.

As the five of us sat relatively sober we began to tell the old tales of traveling debauchery. They went deeper into an array of philosophical discussions. I interjected the deep conversation to lighten the mood with a quick synopsis of the whole scenario. I stated, "What this entire conversation boils down to is the fact that we each have our own personal passion."

They all looked at me inquisitively.

"Nico, you love to travel. Georg, you love to drink. Mike, you obviously like to eat. And Kwab, I'd say you fixate upon women."

Kwab rolled his eyes. We all had a good laugh and then Nico replied, "Well, what is your passion?"

I answered back, "Simple. I'm a people pleaser."

Everyone nodded in agreement and then each returned to their drink in hand.

Eventually the conversation turned to our airport experience through English customs and to the topic of being arrested outside of your home country. Goerg had spent a night in a New Orleans jail cell. Mike had spent a night confined in Germany. And Nico, surprisingly, had spent a night locked up here in Greece. Considering there is only one police officer and only one jail I didn't think this was possible. Yannis the bartender spoke up and noted in his Greek accent, "You *REALLY* do not want to spend a night in the island jail cell.

It turns out that Nico had actually been arrested in Athens for breaking into the Acropolis. The story was a very fitting one for Nico. He had decided to take a friend for a private tour at three in the morning. I do believe Nico had his pants on when the guard shined the flashlight on him. Amazingly this had just happened the year before. Mike on the other hand was arrested in Germany back when he was a college student. Oddly, he was detained for throwing oranges at houses while roaming around drunk on the streets of Munich. But I guess that is a fitting story for Mike as well. I wonder if he has a picture of a German bartender shoving an orange up his ass.

The lazy day continued with relaxing conversation by

the pool. After a bit of nagging from Mike and Nico, Goerg handed his phone over to the two beggars. Both Nico and Mike each had a desire to make some calls but didn't want to bother with purchasing a calling card. Apparently each had a bit of pending business that required Georg's phone and Georg's minutes in order to get the job done. Mike called back to the Delfini Hotel in Piraeus in order to track down his missing reading glasses. Nico called back to Switzerland to track down his missing girlfriend. Both of calls resulted in success. Everyone was able to relax now that their business was done. The Delfini Hotel found Mike's glasses and would hold onto them until our return. And even better, Nico's girl-friend found his testicles and agreed to hold onto them until his return as well.

As the sun hung low in the sky Nico again reminded me that a nap would come in handy before our second night in Ios. Kwab, Mike, Nico and I bid farewell to Georg and headed towards the goat path. As we crossed the road, Nico acci-dentally dropped his diary from his purse. "Hold up," Nico called out as he reached down to pick up his notebook.

Kwab looked inquisitively. I informed him, "You have to raise your game if you want to keep up with the fashionable lifestyle of Nico."

Not only did Nico have the best purse on the island but he carries the finest diary as well. With the little padlock key and attached pencil Nico can write his daily notes. I informed Kwab that he could steal it and find out who Nico *"liked."* Tired and about to face the uphill goat path, Kwab was not amused. He was showing signs that he was tired of walking and tired of my jokes. As we started up the path he opted to wait for the city bus to carry him up the hills of Charos.

The rest of us trudged onward and in about ten minutes we were back at the Hotel Medditeraneo. I was ready for a dive into the cool pool. Before heading in for an evening siesta, Nico and I dove into the clear but highly chlorinated water. Mike eventually appeared from his climb drenched in sweat. He joined me for a short swim as Nico headed off to sleep. The water felt good and the scenery of nearby Mount Charos beckoned to be conquered. Mike and I swam short laps reluctant to nap while floating in such beautiful surroundings. The soothing island sounds and breezes were heavenly and the row of topless women that lined the pool didn't hurt either. I stated, "Why aren't there more Scandinavian tourists walking around DC?"

As we reluctantly climbed out from the pool, we headed towards our rooms for a nap. Looking back we agreed that climbing Mount Charos would be a priority for tomorrow.

57

TWO-MAR-GAR-ITA-WAKE-UP

I woke from my nap to the sounds of the wind blown patio door bumping against the side of the wooden bed frame. It was approximately nine in the evening and I could not help but think of the excitement that would befall us. A night out with Georg is always a blast as long as he is coherent enough to make the waning hours of the night last. I rolled out of bed and headed into the shower to prepare myself for night two in the village square. I was also looking forward to breaking out my long awaited margaritas. As soon as I was clean and dressed I headed down to the nearby grocery. I liked the idea of fresh fruit mixed in with my drinks so I picked up some additional juice for mixing. When I returned Nico was up from his nap and he was currently washing in the shower.

Since Nico was occupying my room I thought this would be a good opportunity to wake Mike and Kwab from their slumber. I knocked on their door calling out lines from the movie Tommy Boy in the voice of a Mexican hotel maid, "HOUSE-KEEPING! YOU NEED ME FLUFF YOUR PILLOW! YOU NEED ME GET FRESH TOW-WEL. YOU NEED ME JERK YOU OFF!"

They reluctantly moaned as I opened their door. I clapped obnoxiously and reminded them that it was time to get up and drink! Kwab looked up and rolled his eyes. I announced, "Drinks are on the patio in fifteen minutes!"

I crossed through their room and out onto their section of the patio. In preparation of the margarita consuming comradery I moved all of the chairs over to my patio and arranged them neatly in good form. The four chairs now sat around our table which overlooked the night lit skyline of Charos. As Nico put on his trademark pair of flip flops, he began to load his purse for our evening on the town. I entered the room and went to the refrigerator to start mixing the drinks. I felt like Isaac from "The Love Boat" and I was ready to entertain the crew. Anyone who knows me knows that I enjoy entertaining.

I had prepared a couple of clean super sized water bottles to perform my mixing magic. I filled both bottles with fresh lime-aid, margarita mix and tequila. After a big shake I started to pour the mixture into plastic cups for me and Nico. I handed a cup to Nico for the taste test which I must have passed. Nico's eyes lit up with pure pleasure. "Thanks dude," he said.

He loves a good drink and specially one that comes free of charge. Eventually Kwab and Mike came over to join us and I poured two more margaritas. It was a nice change of pace from the beer that had been previously consumed by the collective group.

We briefly began to discuss the evening that was about to unfold as we heard the shouts of a loud mouthed Austrian. "KAA-WAAAAB, MYYYY-ERRRS, HOOOFFFF-MN, NEEEEE-KO-LAAAAS," bellowed up from below our patio.

We called back to Georg and directed him around towards the room entrance. But he had something else in mind. Instead he decided to perform a cat like leap onto the wall of our patio. He swayed back and forth as he balanced along the wall which sits directly above the poolside bar. Once he was close enough he awkwardly dropped onto our patio floor. I quickly poured him a margarita as he sat perched along the patio wall. "Mmmmm, NOT BAD!" he announced in his Austrian accent as he took the first sip.

He then took a gulp of the margarita and nodded with approval. I passed the two pre-mixed bottles around the table as we continued to drink. Both bottles of the tequila mixture were gone within a half an hour. Nearing eleven we decided to shovel down to the village square and to let the night begin.

58

THE U-HAUL STORY

Sherpa Nico led us down across the street and up into the village. We passed by some familiar faces as Nico greeted the plethora of travelers that he had become familiar with over the years. We reached the village square and sat down at the same table from the previous night. Our Austrian waitress had a short introduction with Georg and briefly bantered in German about their homeland. The rest of the group proceeded to order beers while I requested Sambuca. The sweet licorice beverage would go well considering the night had started off with hard liquor. I thought it was wise to stay with hard liquor. It was my ongoing selection of the evening. Shots of "Buca" were only one Euro. I ordered three along with a bottle of water and a separate glass of ice. The waitress brought out our order and I created my very own "Buca on the Rocks." I stuck with this drink for most of the night. It seemed to be working out quite well.

Through many rounds of drinks the more vivacious drunken tales of our youth began to surface. The tales of hood surfing and practical jokes were going around the table. Everyone was taking turns. Every possible story pertaining to each of the bodily fluids was told. They often dominate these unfathomable stories. Each of the short stories had been titled with a humorous name that alludes to the story in hand. They become even funnier when Georg narrates them in his slightly drunken Austrian accent. Myers face lit up with glee as he pantomimed the motions of various events associated with the time our friend Marlene slipped onto the urine soaked floor of a U-Haul moving truck.

The U-Haul story was one of the group favorites and pertains to one of my brighter ideas. A windfall of amusing incidents occurred when I attempted to haul beer and around twenty drunks to the local Baltimore bar district called Fells Point. This was my version of mass transit and did not turn out so well for some. It started as a *Going Away* Party for Mike and turned into so much more. Mike was leaving for Eastern Europe and the Peace Corps and I decided to throw a party with every rapscallion ever known to tangle with Mike. In order to transport an excessive number of drunks from my house to the downtown bar district I needed more than the average limo. I was in my early twenties and even the smallest of limousines did not fit into my budget.

U-Haul night started with a clean empty moving van, one full keg, and around thirty ideal participants. Everyone was an astute member of the immature generation. Needless to say we started the evening by drinking half the beer from a full keg. It wasn't long before Mike was performing challenges that included mixing food into a long beer bong tube. I'm pretty sure he was the first person to ever consume a baked bean beer bong. He managed to swallow the beer along with one cup of baked beans that were floating inside. It looked like a long skinny lava lamp with small chunks of brown lava. Mike was prepared for the evening to come. He opened up his parting gifts before loading into the moving truck. A friend Desiree gave him the best gift of the night, a rubber vagina named Sandy. She figured it would come in *handy* once he's alone in a foreign country. *Dishwasher Safe* was noted on the back of the package. But before he had time to give Sandy a test run I directed everyone to load into the truck.

I lifted what was left of the keg into the truck and handed the keys to our designated driver, Jerry. That was the only smart idea of the evening. Eighteen persons climbed into the back of the U-Haul and got comfortable. There were seventeen males and one brave female, Marlene. She prided herself on her ability to keep up with the stupidity of men. We closed the gate and had our first revelation; it would be pitch-black. To solve this problem we decided to leave the gate open. Our plan was to drive down a highway in an open U-Haul hauling eighteen drunks and one keg. Jerry and my old roommate Joe climbed into the cab and started up the truck. We pulled passed the police station and onto the main road leading towards the highway. As the truck began to move up the first hill we had our second revelation; the floor of a moving truck is like an ice rink and there is NOTHING to hold onto!

The group began to frantically look for something to cling to other than each other as the truck was picking up speed. We were all sliding downhill towards the open gate. We would all soon be dead or wounded. My roommate Tarsia was on board and he spent a lot of time on the outside of vehicles. He was the primary hood surfer of the group. I grabbed his arm and directed him to swing his body out for Jerry or Joe to see. Perhaps he could somehow signal to them in the side view mirror. As my sneakers gripped precariously to the edge of the truck I lost my grip. Tarsia and his skin tight jeans went tumbling out into the road. Filled with alcohol and adrenaline he immediately rose and began chasing the U-Haul in a full sprint. Our sober cabin crew soon recognized the problem. Jerry pulled the truck to the side of the road as Tarsia continued to sprint towards the moving truck. Joe jumped out from the cab and surveyed the scene. Tarsia and his bloody knees jumped back into the truck. I instructed Joe to lock us in. We were more likely to survive the trip locked in the dark.

We all stood in the back of the truck and decided to celebrate our survival with none other than mouthfuls of keg tap beer. Blind in the solid darkness we swayed to and fro. We were gripping to the walls and to each other as we took turns drinking from the tap of the keg. It was about thirty minutes to the downtown bar district and we decided to pass the time drinking and laughing. I heard the sound of running liquid and will never be sure which person urinated first. Others joined in and released their piss onto the floor of the U-Haul. We had the third revelation of the night; wet moving trucks are VERY SLIPPERY!

I don't who was first to piss but I do know who was first to fall; Marlene. Once we hit the curvy turns of Interstate 83 South; it was inevitable. I'll never forget the sound of her cry as she fell and called out, "Help me up! I'm rolling around in someone's PISS!"

Mike and I carefully helped her to her feet. We didn't want to get pulled down onto the piss covered floor with her. Marlene was a good sport considering the roar of laughter that drowned out the sound of the road. Five more minutes and we had arrived in the neighborhood of Fells Point. We climbed from the back of the parked truck and assessed the situation. Marlene's shirt had taken the brunt of the fall and Mike had an extra shirt tied around his waist. We gave her some privacy and she changed shirts. The keg of beer was almost gone and Marlene had the honor of finishing it off.

Even though the night was not over for Marlene it was almost over for Mike. He wasn't looking good after consuming a quarter of a keg along with a number of baked beans. I led him to 723, a nearby dance club. It was one of the larger Fells Point venues that had a dance floor just inside of the entranceway. It was a good place for my mission to sober Mike up. I could extend his evening by sending him onto the dance floor armed with a glass of water. This technique had worked on several other occasions. Unfortunately tonight he was having trouble standing. He was still vomit free and appeared fairly lucid as he swayed out onto the dance floor. I walked to the bar to acquire some water as he went the other direction. Quickly Mike scuttled up behind a petite girl that was dancing in front of him. He placed his arms upon her shoulders and fell forward pancaking the hundred pound ballerina onto the floor. Before I could react a team of bouncers had hauled him up and threw him out the front door. I followed the ruckus to the entrance and found Mike outside clinging to a small tree.

Sperka and Desiree appeared in a small pickup truck at

the perfect moment. I loaded Mike into the back of their truck and waved as they pulled away. Later that night I went back to check on Mike. I found him a few blocks away still sleeping in the back of the truck. Apparently the passing drunks had some fun with him. He was covered in empty beer cans and fast food trash. This made a great picture. Once the night had ended and the bars had closed five of the original twenty people returned for the ride home in the moving truck. I climbed into the cab with Joe and Mike. Mike's brother John and his college roommate Gamble climbed into the back. As we drove the U-Haul home we could hear three thuds in the rear of the truck; one loud bang and two following thumps. At each highway curve; the empty keg, then John and Gamble were crashing back and forth against the walls of the truck. The U-Haul cleaning fee was seventy five dollars. The cost of opening the back of a urine-soaked, sun-baked truck: *priceless.*

59

MORE DRINKS AND MORE TALES

As the drinks poured on so did the stories until the inevitable arrival of the Irish. I imagine if any group could top our own tales of debauchery it would be the Irish. They were a wild bunch of travelers and their numbers currently dominated the island. Most of them were young ladies in their twenties and full of Irish spirit or "spirits." As they poured in they would come over, sit down on our laps and boisterous throw out accusations. Their comments usually pertained to nothing more than motivational drinking phrases. I would love to have a pack of wild Irish running around at every bar district in the states. Their vivaciousness was endless and they were illuminated with celebration and life. Mike would go into various A&E inquiries pertaining to Ireland and the locations of various townships. None of the Irish lassies new of these townships or cared what happened there. Mike was famous for his random history lessons aimed at attractive young ladies who frankly did not give a shit. Although over the years his drunken ramblings have occasionally worked out for him.

Kwab was working his camera like a five year old girl at Disney World trying to get pictures with each of the Disney princesses. Nico, always the hunter, surveyed the scene and continued to maintain small talk with one or two of the Irish within his vicinity. As all this was going on I looked over at Georg. He sat quietly with a wry snicker. As he pulled up

Kwab's camera from beneath the table I became astutely aware that Georg had been sitting at our table with his drawers pulled down to his ankles. Apparently he had been working on his under table photography techniques. With six cameras to work with he had plenty of camera battery for the flashes that went off under the tablecloth. Pornographic Under-Table Photography *or PUTP* has been Georg's hobby since the days of his youth. Several cameras were laid about the table in front of him and who knew how many had fallen victim. His smile stretched like the Grinch when he recognized that I had discovered his little prank. He looked up and proclaimed with his accent, "They will LIKE IT!"

Georg was famous for taking advantage of the prudish way Americans shy away from general nudity. The fact that Europeans are generally much more comfortable with nudity was obvious here on Ios. Being an American I could not help but notice the mere topless factor on the beaches. Even some of the most *so called* liberal Americans would gasp at the practices here on the island of Ios. I recalled a time back in college when I was relaxing in my hot tub. Accompanied by some American college friends we were enjoying winter beers within the jets of the tub. As we sat in our full American swim trunks we turned to see Georg and European friend Marco strolling out from my house in a couple of bathroom towels. I assumed they were wearing their usual European banana hammocks. As the Europeans walked in, they casually dropped their towels on the table nearby and proceeded to climb naked into the hot tub. My two American friends jumped from the hot tub as if someone had just shit into the water. The lesson learned is that naked male hot tub sessions are not something that the average American twenty-two year old is accustomed. But wearing a bathing suit in a hot tub is simply bizarre to the average European. It took several weeks to convince my American friends that they had not been accosted by a pair of deranged homosexuals.

How things have changed. Now I find myself sitting in a Greek courtyard with a half naked Austrian taking pictures of his uncircumcised "Pig in a Blanket." To the average homophobe this would quickly be defined as gay but it simply means that Georg has an odd habit of exposing himself in public. I as well as many, many others can testify to this. On my bachelor party at Fantasy Fest which is Key West's version of Mardi Gras, Georg was renting out a peek of his sausage to anyone who wanted a pay. I guess this officially somewhat makes him a whore. Among his customers was the local homosexual who was taking a three second peek in exchange for the free drinks. The man had obviously mistaken Georg for a member of the club. Georg was only wearing a banana hammock and a cape that read, "COUNT DRUNKULA."

The man asked to see what was hiding under the skin tight bathing suit and Georg replied in a drunken slur, "I will show you but you must BUY ME A DRINK!"   Considering the amount of alcohol in the frozen eight dollar drink, this was not a bad exchange. Fortunately for Georg, this type of transaction is actually fairly normal at Fantasy Fest.

The photo shoot was over and I convinced Georg to reach under our courtyard table and restore his shorts to their rightful position. Coincidentally just moments later a couple of homosexual youths shuffled over to say a quick hello. Apparently they had flocked to Georg and the Austrians sometime previously during their trip. I gave Georg an inquiring look. He explained his story from three nights ago, "I was pretending to be Bruno last week. And theeeeeeyyyy LIKED IT!"

He has adopted a habit of overly expressing the last part of every sentence. He learned this from Mike.

Georg had been acting out the new Austrian persona that is being circulated by Sasha Baron Cohen in the movie "Bruno." Bruno is a comedic character created by Cohen and just happens to be a flamboyant gay Austrian fashion designer from Vienna. I wonder who does a better Bruno, Cohen or Georg. Coincidentally, in German the name Georg is pronounced, "Gay-Org."

But back in the heterosexual world, a young drunken Irish girl had sat down upon Kwab's lap and was pinching his cheeks and calling to him "My little chocolate bear."

She went on hugging and pinching him. In a boisterous Irish

accent she kept exclaiming, "OH HOW I LOVE MY LITTLE CHOCOLATE BEAR!"

Kwab rolled his eyes. I personally was laughing so hard I nearly pissed my shorts. Have you ever seen a black man blush? I have. I think Kwab enjoyed being referred to a chocolate bear about as much as he enjoyed Mike offering him gobs of sun tan lotion each day by the pool. She kept calling out to her little chocolate bear while smothering Kwab with hugs and kisses. Apparently this ample attention from an attractive Irish woman was enough for Kwab to endure. At least he put up with it for now. And so the night progressed. At one point I heard Kwab mutter, "I'll show you a *little* chocolate bear."

As the drinks continued to pour and the conversation loosened up the topics at the male table turned to the usual three. These three are none other than feces, sex and food. None of these topics offend me. As a father of many I've faced every single ass wiping, food cooking, sex stopping challenge on Earth. Hell, I even once wiped five different asses, not including my own, in one single day. I'll tell you one thing, there will never be another parent free birthday party organized by this Daddy. I have newfound respect for anyone working in a nursing home.

The conversation at our table started with the old drunken tales including the time we spent partying in the states. These stories sometimes include rest room misfires or several tales of desperation explosions. One particular loss of bowel control occurred while surrounded by a heard of buffalo. Georg became particular enthused as the stories were told. Referring to the buffalo story he proclaimed in his Austrian accent, "When in wild, DOOOO like the wildlife."

I'll proudly admit to joining in the defecation stories which often involve Mike's dysfunctional bowel system. There was even a story from this past fall that involved Mike and an innocent toilet located at Pittsburg's Heinz Field. In revenge for the 2005 defeat of his beloved Seattle Seahawks Mike opted out of flushing the toilet of the stadium restroom. The next Pittsburg fan that entered the stall would smell his wrath.

Mike's anger was often misdirected. This time the innocent victim would be a janitor or a local fan rather than the poor officiating of the 2005 Super Bowl. In his own way Mike had shit on them.

One of Mike's most comical misfires occurred on a tubing trip down the Potomac River. This particular story occurred the summer after Mike's college graduation. At the time there was a gimmick alcoholic beverage that had recently become popular. I'm not talking about Goldschlager or Jagermeister. I'm talking about "Tattoo." Tattoo was a flavored schnapps beverage that came in a multitude of fluorescent colors. If a person took a shot of Tattoo, the person's mouth would become soaked in the corresponding food coloring. Then the person can walk around the bar or party with a bright red, blue, or green mouth. The tongue and teeth would be stained as well. Like wearing a real tattoo the point was to draw attention or *"express one's self."* Blue was the select color of the night as Mike was, and still is, a huge Seattle Seahawks fan. Mike's blue teeth added color to the evening of festivities.

On the next particular morning Mike had awoken after drinking the entire bottle of Blue Tattoo. Be warned, stomach problems can be a side affect to the consumption of an entire bottle of cheap alcohol mixed with food coloring. Also, washing it down at three in the morning with a cheese steak is not a good idea either. But even so, morning came, and it was a beautiful summer day. The plan was to rent tubes for a trip down the Potomac River. Many church groups, scout troops and colleges plan organized tube runs on the busy summer weekends. And on this weekend Mike and I had joined them. We were about fifteen minutes into the middle of a wide river when Mike felt sick and had a little accident under the water. I paddled backwards to make some distance between myself and his mysterious blue turd that had surfaced. Is this what the Beatles meant by a yellow submarine? It picked up speed, floated downstream, and joined an innocent group of boy scouts floating on the river. The troop soon spotted the enigma and called in the scout masters for investigation. One scout pointed and hollered, "Mr. Brantley, what is that thing in the water?"

How can I put this nicely? The Boy Scout armada got more out of their tube ride than expected. The Scout Masters had never before, and will never again, scientifically investigate a blue Baby Ruth Bar.

Back at our village table the blue fecal tale managed to mutate into stories that involve every other imaginable body fluid. Eventually the topic of sex is inevitably reached. Sorry but I cannot share any of these stories with you. As it turns out one of the members of our party claimed to have written and published a book pertaining to sex. Everyone at the table appeared shocked. He was the sex expert of the group? Each man at the table probably thought to themselves, "Hell if he can do it, I should write a book!" I know I did. I've searched for this mysterious sex book since returning home but haven't found it yet. The bizarre sex stories went around the table one by one and eventually turned into the topic of food. This was very stereotypical of men. Things always seem to go from the crapper, to the bedroom, and then finally into the kitchen.

Mike and the tale of the elusive lipstick sub was always a group favorite. Mike was usually jobless in his college days and had often eaten the leftovers of each man sitting at this very table. One time he took this money saving technique a step further when he attempted to secretly consume the lipstick stained remnants of a cheese steak sub. The sub had been abandoned at a nearby table. I recognized his secret mission after he had darted off to the nearby restroom. I also realized that the lip stick sub had mysterious disappeared as well, yet the plate remained. I followed Mike back into the restroom. I walked in, kicked open the stall door, and apprehended a twisted version of the Hamburgular. Mike sat guilty on the toilet seat with a mouth full of lipstick sub. This story often leads into the infamous underwear sub. That particular story involved a friend named Rhode and a pair of soiled panties that were used as a food topping while dining in a Subway restaurant. I don't remember seeing edible underwear next to the lettuce or tomato. The conversation soon came to an end after one last story. It included Mike, some fries, garlic-toast and pancake syrup. He has a way of gathering the leftovers from any group to create an authentic recipe. The syrup covered, French-fry garlic bread sandwich looked disgusting. The stories of food would eventually lead Mike and this evening to the infamous Ios Special.

60

THE IOS SPECIAL

My mind started to become a little hazy as I continued ordering rounds of one Euro shots. I made sure *not* to order any Tattoo. At this point I was ordering shots for everyone in the group including the Irish lassies. I was energized from the tales of debauchery and ready to move from our planted table. I wanted to investigate the inside of the surrounding bars. Drawn by the beat of a pounding rhythm I squeezed myself and our motley crew into a bar that was right across the square. It had the familiar smell of old beer and a hint of vomit. It was the same smell that filled just about every Fells Point bar back in Baltimore. Girls were moving around on the dance floor and along the walls. They were also dancing up on the bar. The scene in this bar was what I expected to find in Ios and I needed evidence to take back home. My camera had miraculously come back to life so I decided to take a few pictures for Bailing Bob and the other men who did not make the trip. Once the camera shots were taken I drunkenly moved to join the others in the middle of the dance floor.

After a song or two I eventually noticed that Mike had disappeared from his spot. I leaned out of the front door to search the village square. Out of the corner of my eye I saw him darting out of sight and into a nearby doorway. Either he had found a Hungarian model or he was on one of his super secret missions into the nearest food establishment. I've seen

him like this before. Once back in Baltimore he and I went
on a *"Myers-style gyro-adventure."* We had left a dance club to
seek out gyro. It was two in the morning when we arrived at
a nearby restaurant that had been left unattended. Hungry
and free of any inhibitions I catapulted myself over the countertop and reached for the twelve inch serrated knife. I had
always wanted to do this. It was like I had finally reached
gyro fantasy camp. I sliced through the spinning wheel of
meat and cut thick slabs of gyro as I handed them off to Mike.
As soon as his nubs were full he ran from the restaurant and
left me at the scene of the crime. I was holding the bloody
knife and searching for an exit route. Before I could escape a
bouncer stopped in to check on the shop. I was caught meat
in hand. Already tired of dealing with drunks he let me go. I
thanked him and went back to the original club to find Mike.
As I walked in I could see that a circle of patrons had formed
in the center of the dance floor. In the middle was Mike. He
was flamboyantly dancing around the floor while biting and
waving the slabs of meat.

Looking back I saw that Kwab, Georg and Nico had disappeared as well. I headed out into the village square to find
out what Mike had discovered. I looked up from the square
and could see a handwritten sign that said, "The Ios Special."
As I turned the corner into the doorway I came upon a young
blond haired man who was working pancake dough across a
hot skittle. Standing in front of him was Mike. He was anxiously waiting with his Euros in hand. Drooling like a dog, he
looked over at me and said in a mesmerized voice, "I - ordered
- the - Ios - Special."

Apparently this item was similar to a gyro except that it
was rolled up inside of a giant crepe instead of pita bread.

The garlic ridden Ios Special was Mike's definition of
heaven. I handed over a napkin to keep the drool from dropping down onto the protective glass. Mike was busy playing
guess the accent with the young man. Mike had improved at
his guessing game as the trip progressed. With no trouble at
all he determined that the young man was from Latvia. The
chef handed the stuffed crepe over to Mike and he immedi-

ately dug in. "Youf got to get one of 'ese," he said from his muffled mouth that was full of crepe.

As he chewed his eyes rolled into the back of his head like a shark. I was tempted to order one for myself but I didn't want to fill up on garlic ridden meat and tziki sauce. Unable to deny myself food in the midst of Mike's food orgasm I ordered the cheese crepe. It had the same pancake dough with three kinds of delicious cheeses but wasn't soaked in garlic like the Ios Special.

We sat down in the back of the eatery with our food in hand and continued to eat. Moments later Nico appeared out of thin air and looked on hungrily. "Why don't you get one?" Mike asked.

Nico answered, "Let me try a bite of yours," as he immediately reached over and snatched the bone from Mike's paws.

Nico took one giant bite and Mike displayed an expression of pure horror. Quickly retrieving his food Mike continued to devour what was left of his "Ios Special." Nico had enjoyed his supplemental meal of the night. Mike finished up, looked to me, and noted, "The Ios Special counts as number three in the gyro competition."

I gave it some thought. Even though this gyro was wrapped in a pancake, I agreed, "The Ios Special meets the regulated guidelines set forth by the (ICGS) or International Committee of Gyro Standards and henceforth officially counts towards gyro number three."

61

THE CONFRONTATION

Feeling full from the combination of cheese, pancake and random hard liquors I moved back out into the square. I looked over and saw the Irish drunken chocolate bear girl who was now being accosted by a young Italian man. Nico looked on and immediately informed us of an Ios phenomena which occurs around the beginning of every July. Hordes of aggressive Italian boys and men flock to the island and begin to accost every woman, living or dead. He went into detail pertaining to the known rapes and gang rapes by these particular groups of Italians. Drunk and infuriated, I had heard enough and I walked over to see if there was a problem.

The young man waved me off as I questioned him but the Irish girl grabbed a hold of my arm and whispered in a soft Irish accent, "Get this guy away from me."

I had planned a subtle approach and wanted to reason with the young man but Nico had another plan. He walked up and physically pulled the young man aside. Speaking in slow clear English Nico told the boy, "Go back to your home. We don't want you here. Do you understand? Go home. Go back. Leave!"

The young man gave a puzzled look as Nico continued the same phrase in a louder tone. The Italian knew what Nico was saying but decided to play dumb. I could hardly believe my eyes. I watched the shrewd stalking tactics of this young Italian boy even as Nico laid into him. I have heard stories of aggressive Italian behavior before as well as pick pocket stories about them. But this was my first encounter with the Italian phenomena. Nico kept the young man busy as I walked the Irish lassie away. I looked back and watched the Italian boy following her every move. It was as if he was hunting his prey. The Irish girl was in no state to defend her self so I found another Irish group willing to watch over her.

As Nico continued drilling the Italian I walked back to confront the young man and ask for his side of the story. He claimed, "She is now my girlfriend and I am not responsible for my actions."

He informed me that his actions were now totally controlled by the fact that he was in love. Inquiring further I found out that he had just met the girl last night and had thrown himself upon her. Now he claimed her as his own. I imagine that these skewed interpretations of reality might be the result of a strict catholic upbringing. Considering the country from which he stems, it's probably pretty tough to get laid while the Virgin Mary is the local hero.

As I spoke to him I noticed that he had two other Italian friends watching from across the court. They appeared ready to lend assistance to their love struck friend. I looked at them with a glare that simply delivered the message, "Don't even think about it."

They looked like the two boys who had chased the dog on Milopotas Beach. I walked the boy further away from the Irish Bear and continued to calmly explain that women have the right to choose the men that stalk them. It reminded me of the Sasha Baron Cohen line from the movie Borat. When he was told of a women's right to choose a partner Borat replied, "That's not so good for me."

This statement fits the current situation of this young stalker. The young man would not give up his argument so I put it very firmly that he was going to stay away. He was going to stay clear of the Irish Bear and I planned to watch him all night if necessary. I gave another stern look at his two Italian friends who continued to talk amongst themselves.

Just as I was about to let him go Nico walked down the steps from the village rest room. He started hugging, grabbing and making kissing gestures towards the young man. The boy tried to block Nico's advance. Nico kept grabbing and hugging as the Italian attempted to thwart his relentless approach. Then Nico at a near yell repeated his phrase from earlier. Nico's point had been made. I calmed Nico down and told him that everything was now settled.

As Nico stomped off he passed Mike and pointed him in my direction. It was now Mike's turn to put in his two cents. He started yelling into the boy's face with drill-sergeant spit-laden screams. As I stated earlier, Mike is not particularly fond of younger males, especially one such as this. Mike laid into him for about thirty seconds. Once he was out of breath and red in the face I asked him to go check on Nico. I assured him that everything was now settled. Then I released the young Italian back into the wild. To my utter amazement the boy immediately walked over to the Irish Bear. He proceeded to beg for her love. I walked up and wedged myself between the Italian badger and the Irish bear. I asked her group where they would be going next.

The Irish group decided to go into a nearby bar. I escorted them up to the front door and became the volunteer bouncer of the bar. Policing the world seemed like a very American thing to do. I was doing it because nobody else would. As the Italians walked towards the bar I put out my arm and told them to piss off. They cautiously informed me that I could not keep them from going into a public bar. I stepped towards them and told them that I could. They stood outside of the bar for about ten minutes while Mike, Nico, and Kwab passed by. My travel companions wondered why I appeared to be the new bouncer. "Did the bar give you a job?" Nico asked.

I just waved them on. It was no trouble for me. I simply asked Mike, "Bring me a beer," and I was happy.

I didn't care if I spent the rest of the night standing in this spot. Eventually the Italians gave up and moved down the sidewalk in search of their next victim. Hopefully the new target of their attack would be less drunk and better equipped to repel their relentless approach.

The night progressed as the bars of the village began to close. This was the moment that the word of Michael Jackson's death spread amongst the party goers. I found it odd that these young kids, who would have likely been potential molestation targets, were so upset over the passing of an 80's American pop star. Some of these kids were in tears. And even one bouncer donned a single glove in remembrance of his falling pop hero. Don't get me wrong, I don't wish Michael any ill will. I even think that the molestation claims were likely false. But come on, the guy had a few top forty hits back when I was twelve. Later that night the word had spread that poisoning was suspected. Homicide was a possibility. Everyone knows you should never put ten year old nuts in your mouth. None of these kids had a clue of who he really was. They idolized him based on the bizarre media coverage he received. They could only name the songs Beat It, Thriller and Man *"with"* a Mirror. The Michael Jackson phenomena will always be an odd social topic and one that I will never understand.

As the Jackson stories were shared amongst the group, I shared mine. One time, my old college roommate Joe and I were on a spring break in Myrtle Beach, South Carolina. We entered the only venue, The Gator, that would allow persons under the age of twenty-one. The big show of the night was La Toya Jackson. She was lip synching the songs of siblings Janet and Michael. As cheesy as it was, it was a fun experience that Joe and I will never forget. He and I were dancing below the stage when we were pulled up into the spotlight to dance with La Toya herself. Looking back we were the logical choice. We were the only ones in the crowd *not* waving the La Toya Jackson issue of Playboy.

Back in the Ios square we joined our fellow square inhabitants near the outlying clubs. These remain open until seven. Georg looked exhausted and decided to take his pig in a blanket back down to the Austrian camp. We bid him farewell and walked under the meat angel hanging for all to see. With my competition standing behind me I ordered two gyros. This would bring my gyro count to five. Mike followed suit and ordered two as well. Twenty minutes later my gyros were gone. Mike was astonished as he could only finish one. What he didn't realize is that all I had previously eaten in the last twelve hours was one cheese crepe. At this particular moment I had the competitive edge. As the sun began to rise, he wrapped up his final gyro, number five. He joined me as we walked back to our rooms. Once in bed I quickly fell asleep. Mike stayed up later to catch some photos of his first sunrise over Charos.

62

THE DECISION

Friday June 26th – I awoke a few hours later. I didn't want to waste my last spectacular day on a Greek Island. I got dressed and headed to the pool. I found Mike lying in a chair and informed him of my intention to walk down to the Austrian camp. He acknowledged his desire to go but planned to go later. He first wanted to spend some time alone in the village square with another Ios Special. The consumption of the Ios Special had become a religious experience for Mike. Apparently he had finished gyro number five last night and was now intent on another Ios special before nightfall. Mike had his plans and Kwab did not appear to be out of bed. I decided to relax for a bit and wait for Kwab to appear. Perhaps he would like to accompany me on my journey to visit the Austrians. I sat down in the hotel hammock and spent a little time swinging in the island breeze.

Nico arrived by the pool. He was packed and prepared to leave Ios. I decided to give up on Kwab and walk down the goat path by myself. I went back to the rooms and quietly informed Kwab that I was heading down to the Austrian base. I planned to see both Mike and Kwab later in the day. Nico had plans to catch his ferry back to the mainland and then fly to Switzerland. We said our goodbye as I escorted him to the nearby bus station. The bus arrived. I held the bus while he loaded his case into the storage compartment under the bus.

He boarded his final 2009 shuttle ride from the hills of Charos. Nico waved goodbye from the bus window. He disappeared around the corner and out of sight. He was gone as quickly as he had first appeared. I had seen Nico do this so many times before. His entrance and exit was a trademark occurrence. He was like Zorro. I checked my stomach for a slashed "N." As I started my walk onto the street I waved good morning to the gyro woman. I continued down the goat path towards the Austrians and Yialos Beach.

Walking alone I was free from Mike's informative banter and Kwab's rolling eyes. I was able to take in the peace and natural surroundings along the path. Cuckoo birds were hollowing out their coos as I gazed out over the port of Ios. The homes along the path were adorned with roses and other attractive flora. As I passed the little homes and entrance ways I could hear families cooking and the sounds of children playing within the small adobe structures. After the five minutes of downhill walking I reached the bottom and crossed over towards the Austrian stronghold. I found the group of Austrians already awake and drinking beers by the pool bar. Georg was not to be seen. Fish informed me that he was still sleeping in his bed.

Goerg never missed an opportunity to wake me up so I thought I would return the favor with retaliatory immaturity. Quietly, I snuck into his room where he laid face down in his bed. I entered through the patio door and crept into his bathroom as he slept. Before waking him I decided to leave what this Austrian likes to call "A Geshenke." In English this would be defined as a present, gift, or bestowment. In the case of a very impressive Geshenke it would be a "Geschenk des Himmels" or Godsend. Afterwards I came back into the bedroom and gave him a stiff elbow drop awakening. Confused from his drunken slumber he lumbered out of bed and into the bathroom to release last night's intake of beer. "OH, WHAT A WONDERFUL GIFT!" he exclaimed from the bathroom. He continued in his Austrian accent, "Perhaps I should leave it here for my Austrian friends. They would like to join in a game of Toilet Jenga!"

Just then I heard the sound of a flush as he ultimately decided to end the game. I wouldn't recommend trying this game on a newfound Austrian host. It is tradition held today by a very select few that live within the city of Vienna. This prank would not go over well in the castle at Salzburg.

Georg freshened up and fumbled into his European banana hammock and then stumbled out to join me by the pool. The Austrians had already determined a very organized German plan for the day. Today they would seek out a remote beach somewhere on the other side of the island. One of them had rented a car that could carry the lot of us and they asked me to tag along. Hesitantly I agreed. I felt guilty leaving Kwab and Mike behind when such an interesting adventure presented itself. But who knew how long Kwab and Mike would be lounging by the pool. Shopping alone could take hours so I agreed to join the Austrians on their journey.

We hopped into the car and were moving up the hillside of Charos heading into town. We planned to stop in Charos as Fish needed some medical supplies. He had taken a drunken tumble some time last night. The actual island medical center was right next to the Austrian base and this made logical sense. It was at the lowest point outside of town. If one was to tumble drunkenly in Charos, then gravity would pull your body to this spot. If you had to be hauled then you could easily be dragged down the goat path. As we drove upward nearing the top of the path I saw Mike and Kwab walking with their towels in hand. They were lumbering down hill towards Yialos beach. We pulled over and informed them of our intentions to travel across the island. Mike yelled out, "OK, catch you later."

But Kwab gave a look of either annoyance or disappointment. They waved and I waved back as the car slowly moved up the hill.

The Austrian-mobile stopped for Fish to get his medication. This gave me time to think more about this adventure. As Georg and the Austrian driver argued and fumbled over the accompanying island map I was having second thoughts. The island only has around five roads. But the way in which the

Austrians were pointing gave me a bad feeling. I was starting to sense that I was about to experience the biggest goose chase of my life. I couldn't understand the German bickering but I watched as they pointed across the map. I could see that the route they were about to take was going to be a rough winding two hour ride. As I waited in the back seat of the hot car I started to weigh the option of abandoning ship. Mixed with my intuitional warnings I felt a little guilty for leaving Mike and Kwab. My intuition was now tapping on my forehead. It was warning me of some impending doom more than it had at any other point of the trip.

At thirty seven I had enough insight to know that I should listen to my intuition more often than not. The wisdom of recognizing one's intuition is the ninth step in male evolution. It can be reached only after surpassing step eight, or coming to peace with one's groin. If you can first learn to stop listening to the little voice below, you can start listening to the little one in the back of your head. I've heard that most men reach the eighth step by around age thirty and then revert back to step seven in their mid-forties. Immature as I may be I did manage to progress all the way to step ten at only thirty-seven. I am still working on the tenth step in male evolution, or the ability to realize what is important in life. I thought more about heading back to my two abandoned friends. It would be a nice surprise if I strolled out onto Yialos Beach and donned them with my glorious appearance. But in the end, the number one primal male urge was the deciding factor. The aroma of chicken gyros were drifting through the air and from my backseat car window I could see them being joyfully consumed by other food coinsures.

With a new mission ahead of me I climbed out of the car and bid Georg farewell with a stern, "Good luck!"

Immediately I ordered gyro number six and headed back down the goat path. I was more confident on my decision to forego the Great Austrian Adventure. I crossed the bottom road over to Yialos Beach and I could see Mike walking the sand in the distance. As usual Kwab was relaxing under a cabana and appeared to be reading. As I approached, Mike was inquisitive to my arrival and I filled them in on my reasons for changing direction. This included taking first place in the gyro competition. They reassured me of their independence but now that the three scorpions were reunited, I felt that I had made the right choice.

63

MOUNT CHAROS

Mike and I headed into the still waters of Yialos Beach. There was no wind today and the Aegean Sea looked more like a soft rippling lake. The water was very clear and the ground under the surf had some soft spots and flora that looked like sea urchins along the bottom of an aquarium. The gentle water was very warm and calm. We spent about twenty minutes relaxing in the salty sea while people watching.

There were only a few beach goers that were actually using the beach. A family of Greeks had set up under a nearby tree. They were laying out their towels and putting on lotion. I sensed my internal culture shock that was a product of the topless island women. It was still affecting both Mike and I. It seemed so odd for a middle aged woman and her twenty-some year old daughter to be lying about topless in public. I guess it takes some time to get used to the many cultural differences. You can free America from the English but you can't free the English culture from the Americans. It's funny to think that just thirty years ago American movies with boob shots were rated R.

We dried off and met up with Kwab who was still sitting under his cabana. He was people watching as well. He expressed that he still wanted to get some shopping done before tonight. Mike and I still wanted to tackle Mount Charos so we decided to head back up into town while the sun was still high. "Ready to continue the gyro competition?" I asked.

Mike nodded then informed me of the private time he spent with yet another Ios Special. Apparently it occurred just before he and Kwab headed down to Yialos Beach. I made a note of his achievement. He tied the gyro count at number six. As we headed towards the goat path I volunteered to treat us to a ride on the bus. I didn't feel like taking the uphill path before Mike and I would attempt to reach the highest peak in Charos. Our bus arrived in less than a minute and it carried us to the plaza in front of our hotel. We freshened up and changed out of our wet bathing suits.

With separate missions, the original three amigos headed into the village. Kwab stopped off at the first set of shops and Mike and I moved up the steps of the village square. We continually wound upward and found the bar called Circus that supplied the "Killin' It!" t-shirts. Unfortunately, they were closed during the afternoon hours and I decided I would make an effort to buy some shirts when they opened later tonight. Oddly, as with the gyro stand, everything would open up and come to life near the hour of midnight, long after the setting of the sun. For now the village was a ghost town. It was quiet and only held an eerie silence.

Mike and I continued winding up through a maze of staircases and underpasses. They were reminiscent of the intertwined stairways in the 1953 drawing by M.C. Escher. His drawing entitled Relativity was a perfect reflection of the confusing scene. Staircases, entrances and dead ends decorated the side of Mount Charos. The rays of the sun would peak into the openings along the alleyway. It highlighted various sections of the rock. Other areas within the halls and stairways were completely covered in shade. As we looked down into the village we could see a few trees that jetted out of the many courtyard areas. The large pine which sat inside the main village square no longer appeared to be so tall.

At this moment Mike and I heard nothing. Only silence rose from the town below. I imagined how much noise rises up and fills these homes at night. The mixed sounds of loud music and voices carry for miles. No wonder Ios is known as the island that never sleeps. That much noise must keep the kids up all night. They also sleep during the day. But right now things were relatively quiet. The high perched homes of Charos were silently abandoned. As we continued upward we could hear families within the houses below. Kids were playing, pots and pans were clanging, and every sound of a family echoed inside the acoustic homes. I turned the corner and came face to face with two dogs that were behind a fenced entranceway. They barked viciously and nearly gave me a heart attack. As I moved on their barking began to fade into the distance and all I could hear was the sound of my companion following behind. Soon the noise had vanished and completely transformed back into silence with nothing more than the sound of Mike's panting.

A few more turns and we reached a small Greek Orthodox Church perched upon the peak of the mount. This was once the lookout for the island. It was easy to see why. You could see for miles in every direction. Our hotel and town looked more like an arrangement you would see in a toy train garden. From this vantage we took turns taking pictures of one another in front of the surrounding panorama. In each direction we could see the rocky hillsides and partitioned walls of Ios or the deep blue shimmer of the Aegean Sea. The white painted building tops looked more like they belonged to families of smurfs than their actual Greek inhabitants.

The sun was hot as Mike wiped the sweat from his eyes. At this point both of our shirts had become drenched with perspiration. It was humid but felt more like a desert on top of the sun baked rock. Other than the church there was nothing more at the peak than scattered pieces of trash. The trash was probably left by late night drunks who climbed up for the late night view. Surprisingly there was no random stray dog of Greece waiting at the top of Mount Charos. Thus far each Greek significant point of interest had been carefully guarded by Cerberus the three headed dog of Greek mythology. If not Cerberus himself there was at least one of his single headed counterparts filling in. It only took a few more moments in the hot sun before Mike and I decided that Mount Charos had been conquered. We sat for another minute as the island sun beat down upon us and then decided to begin our descent. Before we headed down I took one more picture of Mike which soon became the picture on his facebook profile.

Along our descent we passed through the similar sounds, scenes, hallways, underpasses and stairs until we arrived back in the village square. Mike saluted to his Ios Special restaurant as we passed the bars and headed further into the village. After the hike, hunger was once again knocking at the door. Last night during the bustle of drinking and conversation I had overheard someone mention a restaurant called "The Nest." It served authentic Greek dishes. We wanted to find some authentic moussaka for lunch. Our search to find the village Nest had begun.

Mike and I stumbled upon The Nest with little difficulty and took a seat at the first available table. The Greek chef and waitress greeted us with enthusiasm. They both appeared genuinely excited at the arrival of two burly Americans with healthy appetites. We ordered up tziki and bread, salad, and two orders of moussaka. As we ate quietly in the silence of zombie free Charos we agreed that the meal was delicious. It was a little different than expected. The moussaka was more of a potato mixture in a slight cheese bake and very different than the tomato based moussaka of American Greek standards. Mike thanked our waitress a hundred times over and we headed back to the Mediterraneo to enjoy some pool time before our regrettable but inevitable departure from Ios.

64

THE LEAD SCOUT

After showering I headed to the pool bar and found Kwab playing shot glass checkers with our host Sal. Kwab was quite the checker pro and poor Sal didn't stand a chance even playing with the home advantage. Mike eventually came down to join us and we discussed our plans for our last dinner in Ios. As we pondered our evening Georg appeared in the entrance of the hotel. He looked solemn and worn. His eyes were swollen and his posture slouched. He came with sad news. There was only one night left on the island but he would not be joining us for dinner or drinks. As he flopped down on the nearby chair it was obvious that he had fully done himself in for the night. He felt sick and it showed. Apparently too much time in the car, too much time in the sun, and several days worth of beer had finally caught up with him. It was probably for the best. I pictured our last night to be too laid back for Georg. Before boarding the long boat ride to Athens we would not be partaking of Georg type events. I hoped that tonight would be a more relaxed evening, free of streaking and projectile vomiting. Georg congratulated me on my choice to forgo the beach road trip. The distant beach was hell to reach. As it turns out the secluded beach was no better than Milopotas which was only one mile away. We said our goodbyes to Georg and felt comforted in the fact that we would see him in the states before the end of the year.

We continued talking with Sal and another traveler named Simon who both recommended a village restaurant that was popular with the locals. It was famous for the Greek goddess Aphrodite who worked as the sole waitress. The name of the restaurant was only displayed in Greek. I could never remember it but I recognized the place when I found it. We knew it was the right establishment when we were greeted by the well known six foot prodigy of Greek beauty. Aphrodite showed us to our table and sat down next to Kwab as she took our order. We eventually decided on a few authentic dishes. They had Greek names that I did not recognize. We drank our water and waited to find out exactly what we had ordered. Fortunately this was not Iceland. We were comfortable with our random selection. We felt confident that we were not going to consume testicles or other unfavorable animal parts. I ordered a standard tabouli salad. I was still full from the earlier dish of moussaka. We all enjoyed a variety of flavorful Greek dishes which included beef, lamb and rice in a savory sauce. Eventually Aphrodite delivered the bill that comes with every goddess and we bade her farewell.

We worked our way through the crowded tables of local Greeks and down the pathway to the village square. It was relatively still empty. We grabbed a table to enjoy some drinks as the village came alive. Some familiar faces had appeared in the square as various Michael Jackson songs played in the background. The three of us knew that tonight would be different. Our brief encounter with Nico, Georg and the Austrians had ended. Some of the Irish showed sober faces. It was only eleven in the evening and the night was still young. The Irish Bear looked a bit solemn and hung over as she stood outside of a nearby doorway. She glanced over and I could feel a sense of shame as her eye contact dropped to the floor. As the courtyard filled and the crowd picked up the usual drunken atmosphere had begun to arise. But tonight we were in a different mood and chose to seek out a new atmosphere. With the mellow attitude of the group we decided to head down from the main village square and find someplace quiet.

We discovered a small courtyard where the mainland Greeks accumulated and dined. This was the atmosphere that we sought for this particular evening. There were groups of tables set up under a tree. This square was much more open and larger than the one in the main village. The patrons sat and listened to a local musician that was acoustically playing a local instrument similar to a guitar. He was singing Greek ballads while his audience offered their applause. This area appeared to be a bit more age appropriate for our trio. The main village square has a greater concentration of partying twenty-somethings. We decided to stay in this new square as Kwab and I grabbed a nearby table in the back of the courtyard. Mike walked over to a cash machine to add to his diminishing spending money.

He withdrew some Euros and was approached by two young ladies. They were a couple of the good old Irish women that do so much to bring additional energy to Ios. Mr. Smalltalk began to chit chat with the two ladies who were obviously somewhere caught in deep intoxication. They were impressed with Mike's international travels and wanted to get his email address for future excursions. Kwab was paying attention and quickly dug out a pen from his purse. He instructed Mike, "Grab one of the money receipts."

They were lying about around the money machine. Kwab couldn't help but comment on the extremely short dress worn by the second Irish lassie. She came over and stood next to me speaking with Kwab as I began to write down Mike's email address. Kwab was sitting across from me and had a bug-eyed blank stare as I slowly repeated each letter and number of Mike's email address. The young lady was standing at my side. Once I had finished I handed the paper with Mike's information over to her and she walked back towards Mike.

Kwab had some news he wanted to share. He had just finished scouting the courtyard and our new Irish friends. It's a well known fact that men make a sport of scouting and pointing out attractive women to one another. It's almost like a game in which the man who scouts the most attractive or most scantily dressed women earns the highest points. Throughout this trip Kwab had easily taken the lead in points and little did I know that he had just received a triple word score.   In a serious tone Kwab looked me in the eye and said, "Did you just see that?"

"See what?" I asked.

"Bush," he replied.

"The president," I questioned. Confused, I spoke again, "What ARE you talking about?"

He answered, "While you were so precarious writing and reading back Mike's email she scratched her leg and hauled her dress up for me and for the whole courtyard."

Imagining that I just missed the Sharon Stone shot from the movie Basic Instinct I replied, "Damn, I always miss the good shit!"

Kwab burst into laughter. The young lady finished speaking with Mike and came back to join us at the table. She walked over and hiked up her dress as she slipped the phone number somewhere up under her dress. She pulled out a chair and took a full-monty seat in between Kwab and myself. I went completely blank. I might have been prepared for such a sight had I been at a bachelor party or sitting in a strip bar but this scene took me by surprise. I'm quite used to the occasional conversation with a drunken half naked European but this was an entirely different situation. This was no European friend who just decided to relax with his pants down. I had not yet developed the etiquette skills for this particular scenario. My mother had given me an etiquette book as a teenager and I was pretty sure I missed this chapter.

Kwab and I sat speechless for what seemed like moments while the young lady began to talk about Ireland. She was referring to some traveling scenario that I was unable to focus upon. I really couldn't be sure what she was saying. I don't think I comprehended a single word. Neither of us held eye contact with her. With all the skill of Billy D. Williams, Kwab gently reached across the table. With both hands he assisted the young lady as he pulled her dress down. He had ever so cautiously leaned over, pulled down the dress and softly commented, "Here, let me help you out with that."

In shock I bumbled out, "Yeah. *(pause)* Good idea. *(pause)* People are tying to eat dinner and shit."

I shook the cobwebs from my brain as Monty and his two friends were now safely snug under their canopy covering. My subconscious mutterings revealed that my state of shock had transformed into concern for the nearby patrons. I didn't want to offend the young lady and I'm sure her comfortable attire was appreciated by some. But I don't think that the lower lip drapes fall under the category of accessories for a dinner gown. After a little awkward small talk, she and her Irish friend were off to seek out an Italian raping somewhere in the village square.

This was supposed to be our relaxing evening and we were ready to order another round of drinks surrounded by some normal patrons. We took some time to sit and discuss what had just occurred. Apparently Mike was the only one who missed out "on the good shit" and Kwab had pretty much sealed his victory as lead scout of the vacation. As we sat at our table, two thirty-something Greek women had looked over in our direction. They were seated at the next table and began speaking with Kwab. I immediately thought they were going to comment on the show they had just received. But after a little conversation it turns out that they were unaware of "the good shit."

Our two new friends were a beautician and a hairdresser who travel to Ios yearly in order to escape the mainland of Greece. The beautician looked as though she enjoyed being around make up as she was fully done up. The hairdresser also appeared to enjoy her work; perhaps a little too much. They like to take their yearly holiday here in the islands. Their English was quite good and Mike enjoyed absorbing as much culture from them as possible. They had not yet been to America but expressed their love for the show "Sex in the City" and stated their intention to travel to New York. I informed them that they should be OK as long as they avoid driving to and from JFK airport. The rest of the evening was relaxing and pleasant until the inevitable time when the staff began to clear the tables of the village square. As the drunken patrons rolled down the sidewalk I stopped for one final gyro. I consumed lucky number seven and headed back to my room. For the first time since arriving in Greece I managed to get into bed before the rising sun. I was glad *not* to see morning rays for a fourth day in a row.

65

THE ROAD TO OUR LAST
NIGHT IN GREECE

Saturday June 27th – I awoke and headed down to the pool
where I found Mike already taking in his last batch of afternoon sunshine. Kwab was once again over by the bar playing
checkers with our hotel owner and bartender Sal. I sat down
at the bar and ordered some toast and juice for breakfast.
Kwab headed to his room to finish packing. I sat and listened
to Sal and some other tourists talking while I ate. Mike finished lounging by the pool and also headed up to join Kwab.
He still needed to prepare for the long boat ride towards home.
After I finished eating and ease dropping I walked to the local grocery store and purchased items to take home. Rather
than cliché t-shirts and toys I purchased Greek nuts, olives
and candy to bring home as gifts. I brought my simple bag of
offerings back to the hotel and loaded my luggage. Ten minutes later I met with Mike and Kwab as we waited by the pool.
They talked with Sal while waiting for Stefania to give us the
order to load up the truck. As I sat in the poolside chair I took
in one long last look at the village of Charos. Together, we listened to some Ios stories from Sal.

The most interesting story pertained to a night when
Stefania woke him because there was a donkey in the pool.
He ran out to the pool area to find the donkey not actually
in the pool but strolling around the outside of the pool. It

walked in circles while carrying a woman dressed only in a crown of ivy. Apparently she was intoxicated, naked and pretending to be the goddess Athena. The stories of Ios all had similar topics that often revolved around persons having sex in the hotel bushes. As well as these stories they also involved destruction to Sal's hotel property.

Stefania came out and we loaded up the truck. We handed her the keys to our rooms and for the last time we took the winding and frightening ride down to the port. We unloaded the truck and said our goodbye to our lovely hostess Stefania. As we stood in the sunny dock, we waited patiently for the distant ferry Highspeed-3 to arrive. The temperature was extremely humid and it reminded me of home. I took off my shirt to take in the last few drops of sun. I was no longer too shy to walk around topless. If the women could do it; so could I. In the last few moments before the ferry had docked Mike grabbed his final gyro. He had successfully tied the gyro competition at seven. Kwab had set his own record. He managed to consume seven hamburgers since departing from Maryland.

Mike finished his gyro and headed over to converse with a group of young Americans that were also preparing to board the Highspeed-3. Mike had overheard a conversation about American football. It had been initiated by a group of travelers from New England. Mike was more than happy to squeeze in his plug about his beloved Seattle Seahawks. Then he squeezed in some facts about the West Virginia Mountaineers. Then he squeezed in the fact that he was a high school football coach. *Then* he squeezed in some more. It was better to listen to Mike and his anti-Pittsburg banter than listen to what the New England group had to say. They never stop talking about their precious Tom Brady and his band of Patriots. As we stepped onto Highspeed-3 I could not imagine a better American topic than good old fashioned football. It reminded me of home. I was always ready for some Redskin and Raven time. I refer to it as my weekend of R&R.

The ride back to Athens was much more comfortable than the ride to Ios. The Aegean Sea was as smooth as glass with hardly a wind blown cap. The boat moved swiftly across the flat water as we started up a new conversation. Today's topic of deep thought was our general opinion on the validity to astrological signs. We discovered that all three of us are water signs. I am a Scorpio, while Mike and Kwab are both Aquarius. Perhaps there is something to the astrological signs, considering the fact that we had managed to peacefully travel together in close quarters for nine straight days. There is much to be said for this and for the simple fact that no one had mentally snapped.

We each reviewed our current and past relationships which revealed an interesting fact. The majority of the persons we previously dated also had similar signs. We also discovered that we all disliked persons of the same zodiac sign as well. Reviewing through lists of persons and zodiac signs was a great way to pass the long boat ride. After completing our review of Greek Astrology 101 we agreed that even though astrology is primarily just for fun, there might actually be something to the pseudo-science.

The boat had pulled up to the dock and we had returned to the town of Piraeus. It took the boat a little over four hours. We headed back to the Delfini Hotel to retrieve the pair of glasses that Mike had left. It was our first mission of the day. We ducked in, grabbed the glasses, and quickly headed for bus number X98. It waited across the street in a long line of buses that were headed throughout Athens. This bus was our ride back to the airport and subsequently on to the Holiday Inn hotel. I imagined that a bus ride couldn't be any worse than the metro we took to get here. I squeezed into the first available seat and piled my luggage on top of my lap. Kwab sat down in the row across from me and Mike grabbed the row behind.

This time Mike, rather than Kwab, would have the best ride across Athens. The other riders loaded onto the bus. Kwab and I were cornered in by a young traveling couple while Mike was joined by a pleasant Norwegian. She looked all of six feet tall with pure Norwegian blond hair. Mike had the ogled look of a man in tall blond heaven. This female version of Odin was Mike's dream girl. Upon introduction he never stopped talking. I'm surprised he didn't pass out from a lack of oxygen.

I was sitting directly behind him stacked under a pile of luggage listening to his jabber. It continued for the entire fifty minute bus ride. Day nine and I was about to lose it. Mike had officially gotten under my skin. His incestuous ramblings to strangers with long winded ass kiss sessions had become more than I could handle. If I heard one more ingratiating comment about some foreign country I was going to puke. Fifty minutes later and not a moment too soon, we exited the bus. He immediately started rambling about the need to go hiking in the countryside of Norway. He went on and on as I tried to tune him out. I weighed the option of pushing him into oncoming traffic.

We dragged our luggage into the airport and down the escalator to catch our Holiday Inn shuttle. It would take us to the nearby hotel. This ride was much more enjoyable. It was better ventilated, spacious and the fifty pounds of luggage was not crushing my lap. Mike kept rambling to Kwab. I knew it was time for me to completely tune him out before I snapped. Ten minutes later we arrived at the Holiday Inn and rolled our luggage up to the counter. Mike and I stood silent as Kwab began to check in and ask the attendant about our accommodations.

The young man behind the reception desk explained that the room had two twin beds. They did not have an available rollaway. The man continued to explain that the room was booked for one person. If three persons were staying at the hotel then another room would be required. I was quietly paying attention and quickly volunteered some new information, "Kwab, don't worry about it, I have plans to stay in the city tonight."

Since I would not be staying there, there was no need to charge us for an extra room.

As often was the case, Mike had not been paying attention. He immediately started to question why I was staying somewhere else. I threw him a stern look to shut his mouth. I could only imagine how much it would cost to get another room. The price would certainly be high. We were standing in a premiere hotel chain that also happened to be parked right next to the airport. Fortunately Mike accidentally diverted the conversation. He began to ask Kwab and the hotel worker about the internet availability here at the hotel. Kwab looked back and rolled his eyes.

We were so close to the end of the trip. Both Kwab and I were starting to lose patience with Mike. I could see that the internet topic was beginning to annoy Kwab. I tried to usher Mike away from the counter has he called back over his shoulder to ask about internet access once again. As Mike and I walked away I could hear the man reconfirm that only two persons could stay in the room. Kwab waved a gesture of understanding to the young man. Moving Mike away from the counter appeared to have helped the situation. If I wasn't standing in the middle of a hotel lobby I would have swung around and grabbed him by the throat.

I felt like Steve Martin in a scene from the movie "Planes, Trains, and Automobiles." I was loosing it! Mike had gone into full "John Candy - Chatty Cathy" mode. I was ready to snap and start pulling Mike's invisible Chatty Cathy strings from the air. I continued to walk out the door as Mike headed back towards Kwab and to the nearby elevator. Once the man working at the lobby desk was involved with the next customer I scuttled up behind Mike and Kwab. We stood waiting for the elevator. My patience had officially run out. I could not take one more clueless comment from Mike and this elevator had better hurry up!

66

ATHENS ANYONE?

I was ready for some solitude but Athens waits for no man and I did not want to travel alone. With an Athens Map in hand we rolled up to the room and set up. I split one of the twin beds by separating the mattress and the box spring. This can make two separate comfortable beds out of one. I looked out as Mike fuddled with the window. It would be dark soon. I freshened up and quickly posed the big question of the day, "Who's going to Athens with me?"

I was hoping that both companions would accompany me, but Kwab's ability to tolerate the comical team of Hoffman and Myers had run out. He quickly volunteered to stay at the hotel. He wanted to relax and watch some television. After our original taste of Athens on the downtown metro I could hardly blame him. I had my own doubts about Athens and could have used some time to myself as well. If I had the room to myself; I might have chosen to stay behind. I'd probably never come back to Athens and didn't want to go into a foreign town alone. So I asked again, "Who's with me?"

It was only a ten mile bus ride to the capital of the Greek Empire and the Acropolis. Reminding myself of this I found enough motivation to get my butt in gear. I knew Mike wasn't going to miss this chance either. I walked out the door and Mike followed behind. I took a deep breath as he and I headed down to the nearby bus stop. It was time for me to find my inner sunny disposition. Bus ninety-five goes from the airport to downtown Athens for just a few Euros. It would drop us less then a quarter mile from the Acropolis. The bus arrived a few minutes later and we boarded our ride into the center city of Athens. When the bus stopped downtown I immediately noticed that we were in a much better looking part of town. We were in the section of Athens that had been cleaned up for the 2004 Olympics. Surrounded with westernized hotels and food chains like TGIFridays we took a mental note of this location. Americanized food was beginning to sound very appealing. There were clean buildings, clean streets and clean vehicles all around us. It looked like a section of northwest Washington D.C.

We exited the bus and found that the locals of Athens are unfortunately much less friendly than the locals of London. As we walked along we asked several people to point us in the direction of the Acropolis or Parthenon. All of the locals claimed that they had no idea where it was located. I'm pretty sure if I lived or even worked in Athens I would be able to point in the direction of the BIGGEST AND MOST FAMOUS STRUCTURE in the entire city. The rude locals were living on a butt yet they claimed to be unable to point us towards the hole. We eventually followed some random tourists. They led us to the foreign embassies and to the front of the Athens war museum. Mike posed for a few pictures with some outdated jets. They were parked outside. They looked like older F-16 fighter planes.

We saddled along side of the city parliament building and weaved our way through a blocked off road. Standing in the middle of the road was a full unit of security forces. They were wearing full riot gear. They looked as if they were expecting some sort of trouble. I couldn't see any trouble in the near vicinity but it looked like they were ready for the attack of Godzilla. This area of the city was very clean and attractive but the riot equipment took away from the beauty. As we turned the corner, we were standing in front of parliament and could see a group of Christian protestors holding signs. The banners had slogans like "Jesus Saves." I'm not sure why billy-clubs, mace and shields were needed for such a non-threatening group, but I wasn't sticking around to ask questions.

We turned left into the central city park. It was very clean and filled with various Greek statues. The paths and streets were lined with mimosa trees. The mimosas smelled of a blooming perfume aroma and looked beautiful with their flowering soft pink buds. It is one of my favorite trees. I had recently planted a mimosa in my front yard. I always enjoyed the smell of their bloom since I was a child. My mother would open my window in the summer and the breeze would carry the smell of fresh mimosa into my room. But as far as the tree is concerned, many people consider them to be a giant weed. I was happy to see them here. They lined the streets with dignity like the palms of L.A. or the weeping willows of the south.

Moving through the park we came across our first ancient Greek structure, the temple of Zeus. When we first stumbled upon it I thought it was the Acropolis. At first glance I thought we were standing at a different angle from pictures I had seen. We looked up at a distant structure perched to our right. I thought it was the temple of Poseidon. Ever since I took a trip to Mount Rushmore in South Dakota I always imagine famous structures are going to be smaller than expected.

Mike and I took in the sight of the ancient structure that was the Temple of Zeus. The remaining pillars were ancient and majestic. They stood as a reminder of the fall of a once great empire. It was first built in 520 BC. Only a few pieces of the structure remained after several centuries of the destruction and rebuilding. It reminded me of a pile of tinker toys that were left lying around. It looked as though it had been built and then torn down over and over. Zeus must get pissed off every time he steps on his kid's toys. We took photos and moved along following the flow of tourists towards the setting sun. Mike asked a local hotel worker for directions. We were now confident that we were walking the right way.

It became obvious that the Acropolis was something more than the pillars of Zeus. We walked along another path for about a quarter of a mile until we reached a promenade. It was the path that leads to the Acropolis. This promenade is the tourist area near the entrance to the ancient site. Here visitors can stop, relax and eat items like gyros, hot dogs or club sandwiches. It is very reminiscent of the tourist areas around Washington D.C. Along the way I stopped at a vendor for an ear of roasted corn. It was a nice snack as we trudged on along the path. Hot and humid we stopped again. This time at a vendor that sold frozen ice. Mike and I enjoyed the tasty frozen beverages that were similar to an American slurpy. We took more photos and took our time as we reveled at the marvel that was standing before us.

With our heads tilted back we looked up at the ancient structure high above our line of sight. The Acropolis is a flat topped rock which is almost five hundred feet above sea level. It protrudes from the surrounding city of Athens. Below the northwest base lies the old town village of Plaka. To the southwest lies a huge rock where people like to sit and look out over the city below. We walked over to the rock and climbed up to see the view. At the top of the rock we were surrounded by hoards of tourists and locals alike. They had all come to watch the sun set over Athens and Plaka below.

The view over looking Athens was breathtaking. We could see far beyond the ancient structures and mesas. Each structure looked like a majestic trophy standing upon a base-like mesa. Spotlights had lit each beautiful building and each shrine to exemplify the magnificence. The mantled buildings looked like the inspiration for today's man made skyscrapers. These skyscrapers were made by God himself. The outlying city was nestled in a pocket between the mountain of the Acropolis, the rising mesas, and the distant mountain range in the west. Couples sat holding one another looking into the distant sunset and picture flashes erupted around our vicinity. Those who sat gazing into the distance sat in silence. Only the muffled murmur of voices rose from the city below. Everything rests deep below the Acropolis.

Mike and I decided that we were ready to do what we do best. Seek out a meal. TGIFriday's still sat in the back of our minds. If it was high a top a mesa we would climb there. As we bid farewell to the sunset on the rock we were on a mission to find some food. But before our stomachs had taken full control we found another path that led to the base of the Acropolis. We climbed around the rocky lookout and walked over to the front platform that rests before the mesa. Surrounded by the familiar dogs of Athens we stopped for another magnificent photo opportunity. The kings who sat within the Acropolis must have truly felt like the king of kings. We had found a new vantage that was worth postponing any feast.

To own this incredible piece of real estate would be reason enough to proclaim oneself as God. The property overlooks the never ending sea of Athens humanity. It explains why some of the residents have proclaimed themselves to be the incarnation of a God. But as I stood along side the dogs of Athens I came to grip with reality. Like those lying around me I was another dog of Athens. Collared and beaten but still allowed to roam the streets. We continued along the base of the Acropolis attempting to circle around to the protective Cliffside. The straight rise towards the Acropolis looks like a challenge that Arnold Schwarzenegger would face as the character Conan. How could any warring invader breach the natural protection of this fortress? Compared to the Acropolis the London Tower should have been a piece of cake to conquer. Yet London has held strong while Athens has fallen time and time again.

We continued on our search for dinner and came to a point where we could walk no more. The path had ended at a construction fence. It kept tourists away from the base of the cliff that lies below the Acropolis. As we backtracked the sun had completely set. Now the area was dark and filled with sketchy characters. They were sitting about the low walls. Fortunately the few ruff onlookers did not appear to be very threatening. Mike and I have a combined weight of over five hundred pounds. I don't think they even considered approaching us. We doubled back a short way from the dead end and headed down a set of rock stairs. They led toward the muffled sound of voices below. We needed to get to them and used their sound as our directional guide.

As Mike and I worked our way to the distant voices we discussed our final grandiose meal that was to come. Other than Mike's seventh gyro and my ear of corn neither of us had eaten a meal. Fairly worn on the local food we planned to have a taste of America. We were intent to walk back to the TGIFridays that we passed when first arriving downtown. As we continued to wind down we reached the bottom and unknowingly entered the old city Athens. This area is known as Plaka. The fate of our next meal was not to be our own. We walked along a stone street when a tourist train popped out of nowhere. It was the type of thing you'd see in a child's amusement park. It slowly chugged up the hill towards us. A tour guide was speaking over a loudspeaker in multiple languages. Key West, Florida has a similar train. This one seemed so out of place in the middle of the ancient streets. As the train approached it swung left down a narrow street. The voice of the tour guide disappeared within the walls of the alleyway. I looked towards Mike and suggested that we follow the train. I wanted to see what it had to offer. He agreed.

We walked down the alleyway and were quickly immersed within Plaka. The street opened into a vibrant live courtyard. Strings of lights were hanging from restaurant to restaurant. There was no TGIFridays here. There was a plethora of outdoor restaurant seating. The local shops and fruit markets surrounded us. They were mixed into the streets with courtyard fountains. There was a large tent that offered covered seating in the center of the square. People were everywhere. The atmosphere was comforting and lively. Tourists from all over the world had sat down together. It appeared as if they were all seated at one table having a huge communal meal together. Even though the seating was spread between a hundred restaurants they all flowed as one. The waiters bustled from one table to the next. Confused and lightheaded we were starving. We stood along the walkway until our restaurant chose us.

The nearest Greek restaurant owner came over and began speaking in German. Mike replied and the man recognized us as Americans. We were his easiest sale of the night. He began a speech about the way in which he created the restaurant recipes himself. Then told us of the awards he received for his food. We were swept over to a table faster than Mike could order up the Tziki and bread appetizer. Finally relaxed we sat and waited for our drinks and appetizer to arrive. We watched the restaurant owner continue his work.

Our entrepreneur was by far the most aggressive recruiter in the area. I saw a look of despise in the eye of another restaurant owner that was working nearby. Our barker approached every passing group, every couple, and every street dog. He wanted to have them spend their euros on his food. With great skill the man spoke to the patrons using at least a dozen languages. Mike tested the man at his first opportunity. The man spoke, English, German, Spanish, Italian, Chinese, Japanese, Slovak, Czech, Hungarian, Norwegian, Russian, and many others. Of course he spoke Greek as well. He kept the patrons coming in and placed them into seats. He personally assisted the waiters with taking orders for the foreign patrons. A Japanese couple was seated next to us and the man had no difficulty assisting them in Japanese. Linguistically, this man had Mike and his foreign language skills beat. Mike admitted this was true.

The food presented to us would be a welcome surprise. Our waiter returned with the drinks, bread and tziki sauce. Then he took our order. We ordered a cooked vegetable dish, a lamb dish, a beef dish, and an egg dish. The food came out one item at a time and it was beyond delicious. The egg dish was a type of eggs-over-easy creation. It had the village sausage baked into a special sauce. It was phenomenal. I will find it again if I am ever back in Athens. The rest of the food was just as good. Mike joked with the waiter. He said that it was so tasty that he wanted to eat the leftover bones. As our meal came to an end, we both agreed that the fates had taken us down the proper road. We had ended up with a final meal that highlighted the end of our journey.

It was late and Mike was running low on cash so we decided to head straight back to the hotel. We needed to get some rest for our big day of traveling home. Mike only had enough euros to cover our Sunday breakfast so I took care of the check. We got back on our feet and walked across the old cobblestone streets. Moving on, we continued down through Old Towne Plaka until we exited into the main city of Athens. Our sour taste of Athens had been rinsed free. We had been overtaken by the charm and beauty of the city of the Gods. Hailing the first cab sitting outside of Plaka we negotiated our ride back to the Holiday Inn. The discovery portion of our adventure had officially ended. We stepped into the taxi and sat down with a sense of accomplishment and satisfaction. London, Athens and the Greek Islands had been conquered. We had fulfilled every one of our expectations. We had "Killed It!" As midnight passed it was officially day ten of the trip and the work of traveling home was about to begin.

67

ONE DIRECTION FROM HERE — HOME

We were officially heading home. No more side trips down stone alleyways, no more overlooking blue laden beaches, and no more secret downtown discoveries. From here on out it would be cab, hotel, shuttle, plane, shuttle, and car. To look on the bright side, there was no boat ride mixed into our list of conveyance.

I tried to focus on the excitement from the last ten days as Mike started up with his usual small talk with the cabbie. Immediately the cab driver informed Mike that he did not speak ANY English, but the renowned linguist doesn't always agree with that statement. Mike started to go on in slow worded English. He continued to inform the man of how beautiful the city of Athens was. How wonderful the food was. How attractive the women are and so on. My ears began to itch with irritation. I was waiting for Mike to exclaim his love of the Athenian toilet water. It must be a gift from Poseidon himself. As the man continued to shrug and throw up gestures of confusion I snapped, "Mike, he doesn't speak English! If they guy keeps shrugging and looking back he's going to plow into oncoming traffic; so SHUT UP!"

Mike became irritated and quietly muttered his disagreement; but finally kept his mouth shut.

As we continued towards the hotel Mike instructed me.

"We should only inform Kwab that we took some nice pictures," Mike suggested.

"Do not to tell him of how impressed we were with Athens," he continued.

Mike did not want to unnecessarily hurt Kwab's feelings. Since childhood Mike has always had a bad habit of lying to avoid any form of conflict. He uses this technique to avoid even the most trivial confrontations in relationships. I brushed him off with an agreeing motion. There was no point arguing about this odd request. I gave up reasoning with Mike a long time ago.

As we arrived back at the Holiday Inn we crept up to the room and found Kwab surfing the local television channels. Kwab inquired upon our investigation of Athens and to Mike's dismay I was honest. "It was AWESOME!" I exclaimed.

He didn't roll his eyes. I informed him of the pure enchanting qualities hidden in Plaka. They were far from the metro line that gave us our prior poor opinion. Kwab had enjoyed his time alone. He didn't have any hurt feelings pertaining to Athens. With the new information on Plaka he agreed that he had more reasons to return to Athens. His next trip to the Greek Islands would also include a stop in Plaka. Kwab had a nice break free from Mike and me. He admitted that his time alone was well worth missing Athens. I cleaned up in the shower to prepare myself for the cleanliness of the states. Clean and ready for home I laid down on my box spring and effortlessly fell to sleep.

68

TAKING OFF FOR HOME

Sunday June 28th – We all awoke eager to get back to our lives, our friends, and our families. We had all communicated to our loves ones and gave them confirmation of our Sunday evening arrival. We headed down to the lobby and hopped onto the Holiday Inn shuttle. It was ready to depart. Ten minutes later we arrived at the Athens Airport with two and a half hours to spare. Our designated time to board was before noon. We picked up our tickets and enjoyed an uneventful entrance through airport security. It was going to be a long ten hour flight. We stopped along the way for some breakfast sandwiches before moving on to our gate. I managed to squeeze ten euros out of Mike. He considered this much money for breakfast to be outrageous. He decided not to eat merely on principle. It is a high price but every one knows that's how it goes when eating at the airport. It's funny that he didn't have any principles last night when I paid for dinner and the cab. Mike's principles are very selective. That tab ran eighty plus euros. Anyhow, I sat before Mike flamboyantly enjoying my ten euro meal. I even treated myself to dessert and offered him a bite. We finished up and headed down to gate thirteen. It was still about an hour before our departure.

Being a little superstitious I wasn't looking forward to spending a lot of time on gate thirteen. We arrived and found some separated seats and individually sat down. This was one of the most opportune times for reading since I left the states so I got right back into my book. As I read, my mind began to wander. My daunting anxiety towards the upcoming ten hour flight heightened. It was nearly boarding time when a voice came over the load speaker informing us that our plane had mechanical problems and would be delayed another hour.

The flight was now a noon departure. Everyone listening to the announcement let out a sigh of disappointment. I continued to read. I was approaching chapter ten in my book and I took my time reading about the adventures of back street America. "It could be worse," I thought to myself.

Time ticked away and the loudspeaker came on to announce bad news once again. "This could not be good," I thought to myself.

They had not resolved the mechanical issue with the plane. Now the plane would be boarding at 1pm. I sat there looking at my air stub which showed gate thirteen and noticed that our row was also thirteen. It was really not a good sign for the superstitious.

Travel exhaustion and a bit of vertigo were wearing on me. I started to become increasingly paranoid. I imagined the Greek crew assembling the plane that I was about to board. "Holy crap," I thought to myself.

We were now boarding at 1pm as well. That's military time for THIRTEEN HUNDRED HOURS! I was feeling less confident about my upcoming ten hour flight across the Atlantic. At least it wasn't a thirteen hour flight or I would surely be doomed. I had another hour to pull myself together. Seeking a distraction, I went back to reading my book. I turned the page of my book to start the next chapter. To my utter dismay I had just started chapter thirteen. Damn! That makes four thirteen's in a row. Superstition was beginning to warp my travel worn mind. "This is bad," I thought.

But perhaps I had destiny in my hands. Maybe I could break the spell of unlucky number thirteen.

There were thirteen more minutes until I potentially boarded this death machine. I can get myself to chapter fourteen and be free of the curse. I needed to release myself from the evil numeric forewarning cosmically delivered to me. I read with haste as Mike and Kwab briefly distracted me. They wondered why I was looking so peaked. I replied, "BECAUSE I'm HOT! THAT's WHY!"

Reading like a man on fire I scanned each line of words and worked my way through each page. I attempted to stay focused on the book. I did not want to drift into the memories of our last Greek airplane. On that flight I sat in my seat literally clenching onto a broken piece of the plane, the window frame that had fallen into my lap.

Time was running out. Furiously I read page after page, each riddled with a small town that the author had critiqued. "Tell me something reassuring!" I mentally screamed to the author.

I could hear the fuzz of the loudspeaker click. I knew the inevitable time had arrived. The woman on the loudspeaker announced the boarding of rows twenty-five through fifty. I was in row thirteen. "Yes!" I thought, "That gives me more time."

I pushed forth and looked ahead to chapter fourteen. I tried to rationalize, "Just two more pages until I reach chapter fourteen and the curse of thirteen shall be broken!" I read each word carefully but quickly. I knew that if I was to cheat I would surely go down in a fiery ball of jet fuel! "YES!" I proclaimed.

I had finished the chapter. All would be safe in the world. The loudspeaker called out for all other rows and I felt somewhat relieved. The magical forces in control of my world had been vanquished. Everyone was ready to safely head for New York. The boarding passengers hastily pushed their way onto the old Greek DC10. I thought to myself, "Didn't they retire all of these planes?"

As I walked down the isle I looked out of the plane window. I saw the same rusty old marked up wing that was on the last Greek flight and I immediately went into prayer. Mike, Kwab and I got seated in our row and made ourselves as comfortable as possible. I continued to pray. Pathetically I mainly

call on the higher being whenever I'm in pain or fearing for
my life. I imagine the job title "Supreme Being" would probably pertain to a pretty crappy list of duties. The requests that
one receives in that position likely pertain to the begging and
whining of trillions. No wonder they call him father, begging
and whining are what my kids do to me all day long.

I silently recited a few "Our Fathers" and even tried to mus-
ter up a "Hail Mary." Being a converted catholic my prayer re-
citals were not that good. I really didn't pay much attention
during the Hail Mary chapter and it came out more like the
lyrics to Madonna's "La Isla Bonita." I recited, "Mother Mary
full of grace, blessed are you, La Isla Bonita."

Even with the several months of rigorous conversion classes
I didn't retain much more than a few jokes from Father Vick.
Perhaps the almighty would like to hear one of those?

Thoughts of my first confession with Father Vick ran
through my mind. "I wasn't totally honest with him," I
thought.

I hope that doesn't factor in when it comes time for my judg-
ment. What are you supposed to say when a priest you hardly
know is asking about your sex life? Perhaps if we had downed
a bottle of communion wine, I'd be a little more forthcoming.
Thoughts of Father Vick and a description of his battle against
the evils of the godless world ran through my brain. There is
nothing like an old Italian priest being forthcoming about his
hot Italian lust for women. But in that moment I was just glad
he said women. As I sat waiting for my coming doom, my
mind reverted to a story he told from his youth.

One time I engaged Father Vick in a philosophical conversation. He told me a story that explained the religious and
political views from his days as an Italian boy. In those times
it was a greater sin to get divorced than it was to murder your
wife. Henceforth there were a lot of couples going hiking
along the nearby cliffs. Considering his Italian lust, I guess he
chose to be a priest to avoid Italian divorce. I had my doubts
to his story but not after meeting the stalking Italians of Ios.
I am now a believer. Amen. After some reflection I managed to clear my mind and revert back to the good old fash-

ioned "Our Father" prayer. Reaching deep into my protestant roots I offered up the protestant version of confession. This is better known as the "Direct Man to God confessional beg for mercy." I swore that all the childhood games of doctor had been strictly for medical research.

As the plane taxied down the runway I listened with superhuman power to the sounds of each and every mechanical device on this flying tin can. A cold clammy sweat had overtaken me. "This take off had better sound exactly the same as every other," I thought to myself.

We barreled down the runway and into the air. Things went surprising smooth and I thanked God for that. I took a deep sigh of relief. I don't think I could have handled one unscheduled dip or drop in cabin pressure. As we began to level out I thought to myself, "These blood pressure pills had better be working."

Kwab was flipping through the pictures on his digital camera and came across one particularly odd shot. He handed me the camera and asked, "What the hell is that?"

I casually answered back, "Oh, that's Georg's dick. He said you would like it."

69

ALMOST HOME

Other than a brief disagreement with Kwab and some grape leaf cocoons, the majority of the Greek flight was fairly uneventful. Kwab argued that the flight was around seven hours. I noted that the flight time listed on the ticket stub spoke for itself. The flight was indeed ten plus hours. His hopeful optimism had misguided his brain. He was becoming as screwed up as I. Fortunately the flight had movies running continuously and this helped pass the time. Alvin and Chipmunks debuted. Suddenly the fiery ball I once prayed against didn't sound so bad. The next movie portrayed a German Tom Cruise and his attempt to thwart Hitler. The story was actually quite good but I agree with the negative critics. Bad accents and poor actor selection prevailed. Finally, I sat through the latest Leonardo Di Caprio flick titled, "Revolutionary Road."

The story of the film Revolutionary Road was very relevant to our trip. The underlying theme of the film was to live life and avoid the overwhelming norms of society that determine fate. The three of us had done just that, at least we had done it for the past ten days. The characters in the film ultimately failed. They fall victim to the expectations thrust upon them by an American male working society. This is better known to me as the American Cycle. We were all victims of an updated version that also promotes keeping women in the cubicle too. The moral is that most Americans never live life, but only live. Eventually we fail to overcome the merciless pressure of every day routine and societal norms. To live within their designated guidelines is to become a slave to the unrealized ruling force. In the last ten days me and my companions lived free of them or at least free of any pertaining to the United States.

Ironically, Mike and Kwab couldn't wait to get back to another fifty one weeks of societal norms, routine and pressure. Although Mike's routine pertains to college, beer and football. So I took Kwab's cocoon and pretended as if I was going to shove it into Mike's snoring open mouth. Kwab and I laughed as I pulled back the cocoon and pointed at Mike's Greek twin. He was a stout man with a mustache who was snoring directly behind Mike. The two of them were competing in a loud snore-off competition that disrupted everyone in the nearby vicinity. I grabbed a second cocoon and motioned to the snoring Greek as well. With these two on board, no one would enjoy any sleep including Kwab and myself.

Soon I began to feel the sweet joy of descent. The clogging of my ears and gentle change in pressure were welcome sensations. I knew we were dropping closer to New York. I could see the city below as we gently eased towards our airport destination. We landed, exited the plane and headed right for customs. After half an hour waiting for our luggage we loaded up and headed for our shuttle. The shuttle driver was a sight for sore eyes. His broken English was music to my ears. He drove us to our car and we saddled in for the ride home. We fit into my Acura with relative ease and headed on the road. The digital Lorelei led us forth. Two hours of painstaking New York traffic and we finally reached the New Jersey Turnpike. We were on a straight line for the old line state.

Starving after disposing the Greek grape leafs on the plane we stopped along the turnpike. A travel stop of New Jersey had become our new oasis. We headed right to Roy Rogers and each gulped down… you guessed it… good old fashioned hamburgers. Nothing could have tasted better than the corner stable of the American diet. Roy had the Fixin Bar set up just for us. It was filled with all the classic toppings he had become famous for. It looked like a three way food race between Kwab, Mike and I. None of us spoke except for the gargled sound of agreement as we consumed our food. Of course we washed them down with a side of French fries and Mountain Dew. Dew products tend to be hard to find in Europe. I knew that in less than one week I would be sick of every form of American fast food but at this moment it was perfect. Apparently abstinence makes the stomach grow fonder.

We finished up by "Killin" a few napkins and walked back to the car for the final stretch. Kwab took over behind the wheel and we were again on the road. Upbeat 90's dance tracks pumped needed adrenaline into our lifeless traveled bodies. Not much was said. There wasn't much left to say. We hoped to be home by ten in the evening but the inevitable mess, Interstate 95, brought us to a screeching halt. In an effort to get around the constipated highway we took the first exit for Old Route 40. We moved at a faster pace along the old route driving passed highlights such as the bars we visited back in the 90's. Attitudes 2000 was long gone. It was now replaced by some other bar with a title that was more fitting for the year 2009.

Continuing on we made it around the I-95 backup and reached White Marsh Boulevard. It is just north of Baltimore, Maryland. This is the office location of the former employer to both Mike and I. Reminded of our enslavement to society, we gave them a big middle finger salute as we passed by the old office. Soon we were on the Baltimore beltway. We zipped around until we passed Woodlawn. This is the home of my current employer. It is where Kwab and I now spend the majority of our daily conscience hours. Kwab works for a nearby company and I work within the confines of my government cube. My current employer was spared the middle finger. It now employs me. After all it did help me pay for the ten day escape from the mundane. I felt I owed it some respect. I find it interesting that I still feel indebted to the one who enslaves me. It reminds me of the sign posted over Nazi concentration camps, "Arbeit Macht Frei" or "Work Will Set You Free."

Riding down Interstate 70 to Route 29, I looked forward to my quiet arrival at home. I imagined a direct path to my bed. Both Kwab and I had to wake up in about five hours for Monday morning back in the office. Mike on the other hand did not have to report for anything until sometime in August. I somewhat loathed him for this and his overly free lifestyle. I guess that is the reward he receives for what he refers to as *"Going out for milk."* This was a code phrase for living responsibility free. He was living as close to freedom as any average American could. Things were not the same for me. Until my next trip, I new that freedom would only be a story told over a few beers.

Like the old saying goes, the things that you own, ultimately own you. I had chosen my path. It was filled with family, children, and material things. I have far more things in life than Mike, Kwab or Nico. Each of those things required a donation of my freedom. That was the tradeoff. I have a loving wife, children, cars and homes but I also had a million duties running through my head. I knew these duties would have to be addressed as soon as possible. As we pulled into my neighborhood I kept thinking about them and how many would be waiting for me. We turned onto my street and pulled into my drive. Kwab shut down my car, the last moving conveyance on our journey home. We were here. I quietly but quickly pulled the luggage out of the car. I laid it on the driveway for Kwab and Mike to retrieve. I pulled my second car out of the driveway. It was blocking Mike and Kwab. I parked it along the front of the yard. Simply with the word "Later" I waved goodbye to both of my travel companions and entered my porch. I never looked back.

As I lumbered onto the screened porch I heard Mike telling Kwab to call him when he got home. Apparently Mike wanted to make sure that the thirty eight year old Kwab would get home safely. Amusingly, we had just traveled a quarter of the way around the world and Kwab managed to survive. I think he'll make it for the final twenty minute drive down Route

32. I let out a low tired laugh at the prospect of Kwab actually calling Mike and then headed into my kitchen door. I stopped off at the hall bathroom on my way to bed. I found out that purchasing toilet paper would be one of the first items on my long list of duties. I thought to myself, "How were these people wiping their ass? Were they dragging their butts across the foot high lawn?"

With a smirk I walked up to my bedroom. I shed my clothes and dropped into bed. Without a yawn I quickly nodded off to sleep. I dreamt of life, liberty and the happiness that is buried deep beneath a blue sea of immaturity.

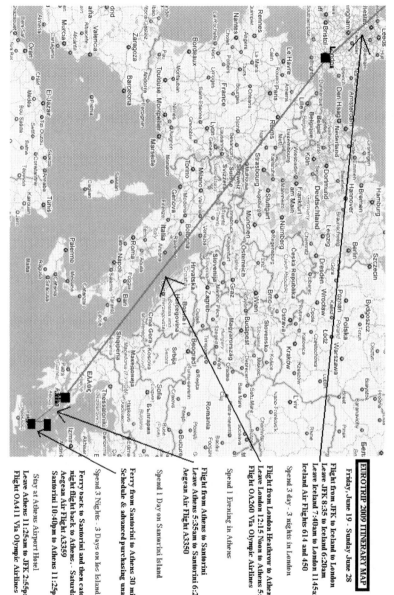

EUROTRIP 2009 ITINERARY MAP

Friday, June 19 - Sunday June 28

Flight from JFK to Iceland to London
Leave JFK 8:35 to Iceland 6:20am
Leave Iceland 7:40am to London 1145am
Iceland Air Flights 614 and 450

Spend 3 day - 3 nights in London

Flight from London Heathrow to Athens
Leave London 12:15 Noon to Athens 5:50pm
Flight OA260 Via Olympic Airlines

Spend 1 Evening in Athens

Flight from Athens to Santorini
Leave Athens 5:35am to Santorini 6:20am
Aegean Air Flight A3350

Spend 1 Day on Santorini Island

Ferry from Santorini to Athens 30 minutes
Schedule & advanced purchasing unavailable

Spend 3 Nights - 3 Days on Ios Island

Ferry back to Santorini and then catch
night flight back to Athens.- Saturday
Aegean Air Flight A3359
Santorini 10:40pm to Athens 11:25pm.

Stay at Athens Airport Hotel
Leave Athens 11:25am to JFK 2:55pm
Flight OA411 Via Olympic Airlines

EUROTRIP 2009 ITINERARY	DATE/TIME		DETAIL
1 - Acura car ride to long term parking outside of JFK	6/19	Noon	**NEW YORK**
2 - Shuttle to airport from the long term parking	6/19	4pm	AP-Airpark
3 - Icelandic flight to Iceland capital	6/19	8:35p	IA Flight 614
4 - Transfer to flight from Iceland to London	6/20	7:40a	IA Flight 450
5 - Tube (Metro/Subway) blue line to South Kensington stop	6/20	Noon	Tube Blue
6 - Transfer to Tube yellow line to Bayswater stop	6/20	12:30p	Tube Yellow
7 - Walk a few blocks to Hotel 63 on Princes Court	6/20	1pm	Hostel 63
8 - Spend 3 days touring and partying in London	6/20 – 6/23		**LONDON**
9 - Tube Yellow to South Kensington stop	6/23	8am	Tube Yellow
10 - Transfer to Tube Blue back to Heathrow Airport	6/23	8:30am	Tube Blue
11 - Fly via Olympic Air from London to Greece	6/23	12:15p	Flight OA260
12 - Take Athens Cab down to port town of Pireaus	6/23	6pm	**ATHENS**
13 - Go to Delfini Hotel, go to Hellenic Seaways dock for tix	6/23	7pm	PIREAUS
14 - Check Pireaus/Athens then boat ride from Pireaus to Ios	6/24	7am	Hellenic HS3
15 - Arrive in Ios, walk by Yialos Beach (Austrians)	6/24	12:30pm	
16 - Continue on to Charos and the Mediterraneo Hotel	6/24	1pm	
17 - Spend 3 nights in Ios partying, beach, etc	6/24 – 6/27		**IOS/Santorini**
18 - Get back on Highspeed3 from Ios to Pireaus	6/27	12:30pm	Hellenic HS3
19 - Cab to Athens and check in Holiday Inn Airport	6/27	4pm	
20 - Check out Athens one more time	6/27		**ATHENS**
21 - Board Olympic Air flight direct to JFK	6/28	11am	Flight OA411
22 - Shuttle from JFK to long term parking	6/28	3pm	AP-Airpark
23 - Drive the Acura back to Maryland	6/28	7pm	**MARYLAND**

EUROTRIP09 Packing List

1 – Medium to small sized suitcase with wheels for Check-in. Easy carry or roll.
1 – Backpack for carrying items while touring, beach, and plane.

ITEMS for Suitcase for Check-in

1 – Pair of black slacks for the bar/club scene in London
1 – Pair of jeans for bars/ and in case it gets chilly at any point
3 – Pairs of pocked khaki style shorts for rotation
1 – Pair of running shorts, just in case as a bathing suit backup
1 – Bathing suit, American, not banana hammock
1 – Polo shirt for clubs bars etc
1 – Club shirt, black/grey color combo
9 – Regular T-shirts, one for each day
9 – Pairs of white socks
9 – Pairs of boxer shorts
3 – Pairs of black socks for bars/clubs
1 – Pair of tennis/running/walking shoes on person
1 – Pair of black shoes for clubs/bars
1 – Pair of flip-flops for the beach
1 – Black belt for bars/clubs
1 – Towel for beach or shower
1 – Toothbrush
1 – Tube of Toothpaste
1 – Brush for head
1 – Bottle of Gel
1 – Bottle of Shampoo
1 – Bar of Soap
1 – Can of shaving cream
1 – Razor
1 – Pair of tweezers
1 – Bottle of Sunscreen
1 – Small folding umbrella
1 – Bottle of liquor of choice, thinking Sambuca

1 – Shot glass
1 – Mixed pills: including… Blood pressure, Triphala,
     Enchinea, Omega3, Multivitamin, Advil, & Benedryl
1 - Photocopy of passport, healthcard, license and travel docs

ITEMS for carry-on Backpack
1 – Watch
1 – Windbreaker jacket w/hood
1 – Small pillow
1 – Small blanket
1 – 2 Books
1 – Pair of Sunglasses
1 – Candy/Food
1 – Motion Sickness pills, just in case
1 – Pen for custom forms
1 – Itinerary list
1 – Set of Maps
1 – Documentation including passport, healthcard, license &
     travel docs

THREE POLICE STORIES

Predator Re-enactment:
In the days of my pre-alcohol youth I occasionally enjoyed a good open fire deep in the woods of Columbia, MD. This was always a trouble-free good time in 1987 as the Howard County Police Department did not venture too far from major roads and helicopters were not yet in the budget... or so we thought. I was spending the evening in cave male fashion, hanging around a modest campfire when we began to hear a loud rumbling overhead. Suddenly a bright spot light was centered on us. We threw sand onto the fire and instinctually scattered like kangaroos in the bush. Since I recently viewed the movie "Predator" I bolted right for the muddy riverbank, slid down and hid under a fallen tree which crossed the river. It worked for Arnold Schwarzenegger against the predator and it worked for me against the HCPD. My two hunter friends also did well hiding in the brush but managed to stay a bit more clean. I continued to enjoy wooded campfires and even today want to jump and run when I hear distant chopper blades.

Trigger's Big Night:
In the early UMBC college days I would throw a lot of parties in my small Westland Garden row home. Freshman pledges worked the door and monitored the groups of students that would pour into the party. One night a local straggler de-

cided to slide in with a group of students and my freshman security force didn't question a thing. Barely past midnight I heard a ruckus coming from the basement and was notified by carrier-pledge that someone is unconscious on the dance floor. Usually this would not be a big surprise, but this time the scene was different. The partygoer, whom I later found out was named "Trigger" was lying in a pool of vomit and mouth foam. Being the experienced EMT that I am not, ordered the pledges to carry him up and lay him on the front lawn. Fortunately, two of the pledges were training to be EMTs and recognized that he did not have a pulse and was technically dead. One EMT trainee dialed 911 as people either cleared out the back door or hid behind the closed front door. Baltimore County Police arrived with an ambulance. They loaded trigger up and questioned me. Fortunately, they only cited me for a fire code violation as they recognized "Trigger the local crack head." Later the fire code citation was dropped by the court. About one week later I heard a pounding on the door, opened it, and there stood "Trigger." And I quote, "That party jammed, when you throwin' the next one?" I informed him that I would be sure to post the time and date of the next party and that he would be top of the guest list.

One Nut Job for a Dollar:
Throughout my twenties I spent a lot of time in Fells Point. The regular routine was a lot of bars, a lot of beers, and perhaps a late night gyro... but not on this night. Things were sliding downhill in Fells Point. This bar zone often housed the average homeless chap wearing signs like, "Will Work for Beer." By 1998 droves of patrons were often met not only by the homeless, but by entrepreneurs, aka dealers and hookers. This was my first such encounter within my home town of Baltimore. I was shocked when a strikingly foul young lady asked me if I had twenty-five dollars for (let's say) a good time. In my intoxicated state I refrained and decided to compete with her. I began to boisterously offer my services with the pitch, "One Nut Job for a Dollar." I figured that I could easily beat her twenty-five dollar offers with a simplified version

of her services at a much lower cost. Eventually, the police officers standing twenty feet away decided to inquire upon my offered services. It was difficult to explain in my current condition that I was only joking. After some assistance from some friends, the kind officers decided not to book me for prostitution charges. Later on the walk back to the car, I held out five dollars to the local homeless man and only used the repetitive phrase, "Where's my GAR Parked?" Yes, GAR is not a typo. Anyhow to finish this long story, the "homeless" man dropped HIS homeless "bit" as a stumbling drunk and he turned into a perfectly sober con-man who was truly afraid that I might be driving home when I found my "GAR." I then countered dropped the "Gar Parked" bit told him that I was not the designated driver. :) Finally, thanks to all the Fells Point Officers who did not arrest me for the Halloween refrigerator costume with the front door meat locker as well as for the night I jumped the counter and ran away with the spinning hunk of Gyro.

THE AUTHOR

THE DEFINITION OF HOFFMAN

1. **Definition of Hoffman: From Hoofdman, a captain, a director, head or chief man. Hofman, from Hof, a court- -the man of the court.** variant of <u>Hoffmann</u> 'steward'. or occupational name for a farm laborer or a gardener, someone who worked at the *hof*, the manor farm.

25 REAL THINGS ABOUT ME

Starting in life order, (sort of a mini autobiography):

1. My father had a vasectomy 8 years before I was born... henceforth the name Matthew (<u>Gift of God</u>)... and yes... I'm quite sure he is my father... no one's disputing it. Therefore I am a living vestige of all that is right with both Pro-Life and Pro-Choice.

2. <u>As a baby</u> I had a big plastic rabbit that I enjoyed playing with (probably filled with toxic gas), later I grew attached to Teddy and Rufus... Teddy still stuffed and missing a nose, oddly became my daughters' first love. Rufus was left out in the rain one night and his pull-sting voice box became satanic and was therefore destroyed.

3. About <u>age four,</u> I ran and fell into the lower fireplace mantle of our family home (which I now live in once again) and have a scar above my eye... now I yell at my kids every time they run in the living room and tell I them this story.

4. I had my <u>first crush</u> at age five in Kindergarten. Before afternoon class, I would type love letters to Amy Easter on an old typewriter. My older sisters would shamelessly jeer me. I took my crushes very seriously while my three older sisters did not.

5. At <u>Atholton Elementary</u> I received impeccable marks and only two memorable detentions. One for erasing a bra from a newspaper underwear model. I used a pencil to draw a much better creation to share with the class. I always enjoyed current events in class. The other was the 5th grade smelly sticker scandal of 1981... I plead the 5th on that one.

6. I attended <u>Hammond Middle</u> school for three awkward years, It was divided into peer groups: the preps, the grits, and the nerds. I was an astute member of the nerds and to this day I boast that Huzi; (now a PHD Oncologist) used to copy off of me.

7. I attended OMHS, where I did not consume one drop of alcohol and perhaps therefore did not completely fit in. I hung out with St. Vincent Pallotti High folk and <u>dated the same catholic girl</u> (from Hammond Middle) for about eight years on/off. I even went dry to Senior Week. I'm now married to the newest version of the "<u>catholic school girl</u>" that I've dated for the last twenty five years.

8. Summer of '89 I <u>discovered fuzzy navels</u>. It was all down hill from there. I later became quite the <u>beer consumer</u> and found a purpose driven life. This led to ten Spring Breaks, two Mardi Gras, two Euro-trips, one US Cross County, one Oktoberfest and countless searches for the best party on Earth.

9. I <u>attended UMBC</u> but spent the first year hanging out with college park folks as my current girlfriend went there with many former high school classmates. I hung out with OMHS persons more after High School then during.

10. I joined <u>the fraternity ATO</u> after a good rush speech by Steve Lloyd (a great no-pressure salesman) and had a blast pledging and partying at UMBC.

11. I worked ten years for the slave establishment known as <u>Giant Food</u> from high school through college. I was able to pay for college and my first home in Owings Mills with the income.

12. I loved to <u>party with the girls</u> of Tri-Sig, DPhiE, ASA, and PhiMu; both at UMBC, Towson and UofM. I organized many socials and parties. I have always enjoyed having many friends in many places.

13. I spent many weekends and still do in <u>Morgantown, WV.</u> <u>WVU</u> is my adopted college. Great parties, great football and an overall fun town. My nephews and nieces still attend school in good ol' West Virginia. My next home may be WV.

14. <u>I lived in</u> Westland Gardens for three years, Towson Woods for one year and then in Owings Mills for eight. Just partying , working and eventually marrying... notice I didn't say settling down.

15. I <u>married Krista</u> Lewandowski in 1999 via introduction by Andy Eckstein. She was the Chesapeake RA at UMBC that would tear down my "Do you swallow?" ATO Goldfish bash fliers. I never knew her in college... that was a good thing.

16. I became a <u>therapeutic foster parent</u> (eventually adoptive parent) to kids from Baltimore City. My first, Elo used to sell bad things and now servers our country in the US Army. Levi used to do bad things and now lives and helps entertain other adults with special needs. Darrien will be going to OMHS next year 2010 and will always be known to me as Skids (see 2002 underwear.) Stink will hopefully stop peeing the bed, that's the only expectation I have for him right now.

17. I first became a <u>birth Dad</u> in 2003 when my daughter Boo was born. I don't plan to have any more kids the old fashioned way... but future adoptees are lined up.

18. I moved back to my childhood home in Columbia, Maryland and have the pleasure of reliving my youth as well as watching my kids relive it. I still cycle in the woods, make trails, swing ropes, build forts, and party by the fire pit.

19. I work in IT for federal agency... I do it well... but focus more on life outside of the prison walls. I've worked in IT for over ten plus years.

20. I volunteer as a community organizer and hold holiday events such as an Easter Egg Hunt, a 4th of July Parade and a Santa Night.

21. I have three persons I consider my role models: Dennis Bennett, Charles Myers, and John Scarzello. I have always admired the good natures, humor, leadership, and personal success of each person.

22. My favorite thing to do is travel and I do so ten plus times a year. When I'm not traveling I have my house set up like a resort with woods, hot tub, and all the comforts.

23. My second favorite thing is to socialize. I've been told in a derogatory way, that I am the most extraverted person anyone has ever met. Party, party, party.

24. My third favorite thing is animals. I love dogs, cats, horses, and wildlife. I prefer many animals over many people. Too bad they can't drink and speak.

25. My fourth favorite this is nature. I love the outdoors, woods, beach, mountains, and scenery. In my perfect world I would hang out in some remote natural land laughing with partying with various speaking animals.

25 FAKE THINGS YOU NEVER REALLY WANTED TO KNOW ABOUT ME

1. I was born Luke Mydekishmall; and changed my name for obvious reasons.

2. I work for Nokia enslaving the entire world using imbedded chip technology.

3. This is my fourth celestial visit to Earth, I originally arrived just before the Jomon period and bought my first seaside home on the Atlantis southern coastline.

4. I like to keep free roaming pet spiders due to my fear of flies.

5. At a young age I realized that I could read minds, but gave up this power after the 99th time my dog wanted to hump my leg.

6. Originally born in Ireland, I was banished for attempting to capture short people and demand their gold.

7. My parents were from a distant country known only as Oz and were eventually incarcerated for attacking scarecrows.

8. I often wonder why Kennedy never pardoned a single fish during lent.

9. I like to pee in my kid's apple juice so that they will be prepared once they become astronauts.

10. In order to pay mounting adult video rental fees I started business marketing gopher milk.

11. My role models are Paris Hilton and Dom Deluise; I hope to one day meet them both and assist Dom with stuffing her dogs into jelly doughnuts for his consumption.

12. Fresh out of college I moved in with Larry from Three's Company but moved out when I found out that he really didn't have a hot tub.

13. At age 28 I married into the Hutt family, but soon divorced once I realized that Maryanne is not a female name in the Hutt's native language.

14. I once ran a smuggling operation in Tibet but it was foiled by some meddling kids who ripped off my Snow Ghost mask.

15. I first became a father in 1992 when I accidentally hatched a sea turtle egg while on spring break in Cancun.

16. I actually still live in Westland Gardens in Catonsville, MD and technically it is my parent's house.

17. I am in the Guinness book or world records for eating an entire Volkswagen Beetle; I had a lot of trouble with the tailpipe.

18. I lost my virginity in the first grade and still have a deep fear of petting zoos and any goat that goes by the name Patches.

19. One time, at band camp, I got my finger caught in the wrong end of a clarinet.

20. I patented the bird diaper, to keep all beachgoers poopie free.

21. I was one of the eleven people who showed up to hear Joe the Plumber speak about his new book.

22. I like to worship in the nude, but they only allow me at the 4am Mass.

23. If I won the Superbowl, I would go to the Neverland Ranch to see Thriller Live.

24. I mugged the tooth fairy the night I lost my last baby tooth.

25. When I die, I want to be buried in shallow grave within a loose hinged coffin, so when I wake up, I can bust out!